John W. Roberts

Looking Within

John W. Roberts

Looking Within

ISBN/EAN: 9783337407148

Printed in Europe, USA, Canada, Australia, Japan

Cover: Foto ©Andreas Hilbeck / pixelio.de

More available books at **www.hansebooks.com**

THE MISLEADING TENDENCIES OF
"LOOKING BACKWARD"
MADE MANIFEST.

.

BY

J. W. ROBERTS,

AUTHOR OF

Laws of Mind, The Immigrants,
Miracles Scientifically Considered, Etc.

NEW-YORK:

A. S. BARNES & COMPANY.

1893.

PREFACE.

RENEWED AMERICA, January 1, 2027.

INHALING the inspiring breath of the new life which invigorates the nation so lately struggling in the toils of a lingering death, and cheered by the resurrection of all industries from the grave in which they were being utterly buried, we hail the dawn of a new era of progress with unspeakable gladness.

How it was possible for a people once so full of energy to become willing slaves, selling their royal birthright for a mess of pottage, is a mystery as yet unexplained. That such a people could endure bondage of mind and body for three generations is still more astonishing and inexplicable.

The object of this work is to throw light upon this enigmatical problem, warn fellow-citizens of the danger that threatens them from the alluring delusion which, like an *ignis fatuus*, is leading them along the slippery path of ruin, and prevent any such catastrophe ever overtaking our beloved country in the future.

Let the stern and hard facts speak for themselves as they are uttered by those who relate their own sad experiences in these pages. Let the truth cut its onward way, and all delusions and sophistries perish at its touch.

"The righteous shall understand," but the "wicked shall pass on and be punished."

iii

PRELIMINARY CHAPTER.

I HAD the distinguished honor of being born a citizen of the United States of America—that land of great boasters, grandiloquent orators, financial quacks, and phenomenal progress. But as I had no part nor lot in the antecedents of this to me important event, I am entitled to no credit whatever in connection therewith. It was one of those accidents or incidents of being for which the individual most concerned is entitled to neither condemnation nor approval. As far as subsequent developments have thrown light upon the subject, it may be regarded as an unexplained mystery why I came into the world at all.

I have heard my respected and revered parents, who were responsible for my advent upon "time's mundane sphere," declare that I was subject to the ordinary ailments and contingencies incident to infantile and childhood life; that many a night they were deprived of needed rest because of my innate disposition to be restless, which manifested itself in needlessly loud and prolonged demands for attention and relief, accompanied by kicks and cries for redress, which neither paregoric nor catnip tea was always efficacious to suppress or ameliorate. Then followed chicken-pox, measles, mumps, whooping-cough, and other post-teething ailments to which humanity has been subjected since

1

some period in the misty past to which the memory or
knowledge of man runneth not.

Having run the gauntlet of all these juvenile experiences, some of which came late enough to leave a
vivid impression upon my own memory, I at length
merged into the second state of an uneventful career,
and became one of that ubiquitous class of the *genus
homo* known as "Young America."

As a tribute of respect to my immediate progenitors
I gratefully record the fact that in consequence of
their careful training and vigilant watchfulness, I did
not fall into many of the excesses of that class of restless aspirants for fame or notoriety, which accounts
for the fact that I have never been arrested for crimes
or misdemeanors, have committed neither murder nor
suicide, nor seen the inside of a prison except as visitor
or spectator. Nor have I sought distinction by becoming a bandit or a cowboy *à la dime novel*. Escaping all these contingencies of becoming a "hero" may
account for the uneventful character of an inconspicu-
ous life.

Being a citizen of this great American republic, I
have been somewhat of a cosmopolitan. My acquaintance and observation have taken in city and rural life.
I have mingled with unsophisticated youth of the
country and with fashionable devotees of metropolitan
society. I have sympathized with the timid and bashful maiden on the farm as she made her modest and
unostentatious entrance into the realm of womanhood.
I have witnessed the glitter and glare of the costly
début of the young lady of wealth into the arena of the
"first circle" of the *élite*. I have conversed with the
man of millions and with the daily toiler who "eats
his bread in the sweat of his face." I have seen much

of that class whose happy condition is described as the "golden mean" of "neither riches nor poverty." Nor have I failed to interview even the tramp who by preference or necessity becomes a wandering vagabond or an unfortunate outcast.

Having thus personally familiarized myself with the various phases of the "social compact," I perhaps foolishly considered myself competent to form a fair and impartial opinion of the condition and environments of humanity in this lauded "land of the free and home of the brave." At any rate, I felt quite sure I knew as much on the subjects and questions of exciting discussion concerning these matters as any one who did not know more than I knew.

That something was radically wrong and out of harmony with the best interests of the race seemed apparent on the face of things. Whether these evils were inherent in man himself, and hence in a measure ineradicable; or whether they were the result of defects in the laws of society and the rule of government, and therefore remedial; or whether they were the outgrowth of both these causes, and for that reason partly open to redress and partly not—were questions of profound depth and interest, demanding the calmest deliberation and most profound consideration of the best minds possessed of the widest information. And yet men without knowledge, with the merest smattering of intelligence, rushed upon the scene with panaceas for all the evils of the world and quack nostrums to cure all the "ills that flesh is heir to."

Being thus in touch with humanity on all sides, from infancy to manhood, I venture to place before the great public the following pages, which contain a more ample and enlarged view of the great arena upon which the momentous problems of human destiny are being wrought, and ask for the same a candid consideration and such verdict as may be justly rendered, tempered with that mercy we may all fairly claim by reason of our own imperfections and the character of our complicated environments.

CHAPTER I.

I WAS born on a farm adjoining one of the large inland manufacturing cities of the United States. My parents at the date of my birth were in moderate circumstances. They owned the premises upon which they resided, which was a good-sized farm, well stocked and improved. But they felt the need of close application and untiring labor in order to tide over the crisis of existing conditions. My father had made some investments about the time of my advent into the family from which he hoped much in the future, but which might turn out unfortunate, or be slow to appreciate if fortunate in the end. These outlays had exhausted all the money he had accumulated in the past by years of toil and prudent economy. In view of any possible contingencies he realized the prudence and necessity of making as much as possible out of present time, strength, and opportunities, lest the evil day might come and find him unprepared to meet its urgent calls. The farm was the only possession he could now occupy and employ for present needs and future possible contingencies.

Accordingly, when only eight years old I was required to do light work about the house and in the garden to avoid the expense of hiring an extra hand. From ten to fifteen years of age I was put through the more advanced stages of labor on the farm, like other boys brought up in like manner. I was not particu-

5

larly fascinated with this experience, but under the wise instruction of my parents I tried to do my part well and faithfully. My first graduation, therefore, was in the school of labor. My father, who was well qualified to judge in such matters, said I need not be ashamed of my diploma, which was some compensation for the rather tiresome hours of toil.

This experience in the arena of labor was of value to me in after-years, notwithstanding the immaturity of judgment at that time of life.

During this period of existence I attended the city schools, which were ably conducted, during the time I could be spared from the farm, which was from four to six months every year. I was ambitious to excel in my studies; but as my associates in school had from two to four months more time in the schoolroom than fell to my lot, it was difficult for me to "keep up with the procession," as the phrase went. Indeed, the burning desire of my heart to be at the head of my classes never could have been realized but for the aid of my mother, who was finely educated, and she fully entered into sympathy with me in my aspirations to excel.

She instructed me at home, assisted me in practice and drill, conducted me through examinations in advance, and so kindled me with enthusiasm that I felt I could do anything with her help. Her words of encouragement quickened my pulses, stimulated my powers, made me feel at times as if I were invincible.

Oh, to that mother, now sainted in heaven, whose memory is more precious to me than rubies, I owe everything that is worthy or valuable in me.

My father was a college graduate and a man of broad culture and much experience, and greatly assisted in my training. He possessed a good library of well-selected books on a wide range of subjects, with the latest cyclopedias, so that I had many advantages and tried to improve them.

My second graduation was from the city schools, with full grade and honorable mention by the superintendent.

While thus attending school, I became acquainted with a girl student two years my junior in age, whose father was a manufacturer in the city. His residence at that time was out toward my father's farm, so that we children traveled the same street to and from school each day, and were frequently thrown together. This gave me many opportunities of rendering her little services, for which she always thanked me pleasantly. Judged by my standard, she was the handsomest girl in school, and I was naturally attracted to her. But she was shy and I was bashful, so that our friendship was at arm's length, so to speak, and did not progress to close relationship very rapidly. Without being able to account for the fact, I could be more free with any other girl in school than with this one, whom I esteemed more highly than any other. This may have been "boyish love," but I did not stop to analyze the feeling while I felt the attraction. She was an excellent student, uniformly kind to all her associates, and a general favorite. But she was simple and unaffected in manner, and a real lady, young as she was, in deportment. I instinctively knew she had a good mother.

Her presence always inspired me to do my best, whether in school or on the playground. I cared more for her approval than for the approbation of all the rest of the school combined. Her name was Effie, and somehow the name and its possessor became associated and blended in my mind until I thought the two admirably adapted to each other—a mere fancy, of course.

About this time my father's investments began to realize handsomely, even beyond his most sanguine anticipations. I was released from work on the farm, and in accordance with my earnest desire for a scholastic education, I commenced preparations to enter college.

When these were nearly completed, I felt a mastering desire to see Effie and bid her adieu before leaving home. Since school-days I had not seen her very frequently, but her image had become a fixture in the gallery of mind and memory. Why did I wish to see her so greatly and yet be so careless about any and all others? I did not know, and made no attempt to answer the question. I only knew the fact.

As before remarked, I was timid. This timidity prevented me from calling upon her in a regular and formal manner. I should have confided in my mother, who could have relieved the situation by her tact and love; but for the first time in my life I had an experience I was keeping from her.

I made several unnecessary errands into town, and as many necessary ones as possible, hoping to meet Effie on the street, or in front of her home. Many disappointments made me restless. Mother was quick to notice this, but the prospect of leaving home furnished ample explanation, and my secret remained undiscovered.

At length my last day at home arrived. On the morrow I was to leave for school. I went into the city with a trembling hope. It was my last opportunity. Would I meet her? I went the usual round with the usual result, and set out on my return weary and disappointed. Suddenly from a side street she stepped out before me, not a half-block distant, and was going toward home.

My heart beat quick. With much trepidation I approached and opened conversation with her. After brief preliminaries I came to the matter uppermost in my thoughts, and said:

"I leave for college in the morning."

I fancied she was a little startled, but she looked up into my face earnestly, and replied:

"So soon? I had learned you were expecting to go, but did not think it was time yet."

"Yes, the session commences next week."

"I am sorry you are going away."

"Are you indeed? Will you miss me at all?"

"Of course we shall miss you."

"We? But will *you* miss me?"

"Certainly I shall. And yet I am glad you are going to perfect your education."

"I hope you will not entirely forget me while I am away."

"I shall not. I shall remember you every time I pass along the street we have walked together so frequently."

"And I shall think of you every day when not too busy with my studies."

These remarks were not very rapturous nor complimentary on either side, perhaps, but they had the merit of truth and honesty. She replied:

"I hope you will do honor to yourself, your teachers and friends here by your studious course while absent."

"I certainly will try to. I hope no friend at home will be ashamed of me."

"Whatever else you do, be true, manly, and noble."

"I trust I shall never do anything to cause any one regret or shame for my conduct. I could not bear to have my friends think ill of me because I had merited disapproval."

"I do not believe you will forfeit the good opinion of those who esteem you," she said, with a look of confidence and encouragement, which was inspiring and never faded from my memory.

As we neared the gate to her home I proffered my hand. She placed hers confidingly in mine. The pressure I gave was somewhat ardent, as I spoke the parting words.

"Good-by."

I think she returned the pressure, though I was excited and may have fancied more than was real. But there was something in the tone of her voice as she said "Good-by" which I never forgot. And thus we parted. No demonstration, no professions of love, if any love existed. We were little more than children, but I think our mutual esteem was a source of real benefit.

I have dwelt upon this little episode in my uneventful life in youth because of its influence upon all my after-career. As this event may not be called up again in this narrative, I will take leave of it by saying that during the dark days at college and in the university, when disposed to become discouraged, the words of my little friend came to me time and again as a benediction: "I hope you will do honor to yourself and your friends here by your studious course." With those words ringing freshly in my ears, I conquered difficulties and mastered hard problems. And when tempted to go astray, as all young men are in like circum-

stances, those other words, "Whatever else you do, be
true, manly, and noble," came as a shield and a warning and kept me from stumbling. So these parting
words, and the sweet face of her who spoke them in
earnest simplicity, became a talisman which threw over
and about me its protecting ægis in many an hour of
sore trial.

CHAPTER II.

WHILE in college questions of public interest were discussed among the students and debated in the lyceum. Among these that of capital and labor held a prominent place. Theories on this topic were handled very sagely by the young men, many of whom regarded themselves as wiser than the philosophers and statesmen of ancient or modern times.

All new treatises on the subject were secured and perused. This was a part of the recreation of a few students who did not engage in the dissipation so generally prevalent.

One author attracted considerable attention because of the unique simile under which he represented the human race. They were all said to be connected with a huge coach, some as passengers in and upon it, others as toilers in the traces. The former were the rich, possessing all things, the latter the poor, having nothing. The wretched condition of the begrimed masses in the dirt and mud, tugging for dear life to drag the coach along the rugged way, was graphically described. The picture was a sad one to contemplate. The wretchedness of the miserable beings whose brawn and muscle slowly pulled the heavy load was portrayed in doleful language and placed in the most repulsive light and shade. Reading the delineation one would be led to think the writer had dipped his pen in a mixture of ink composed of tears, blood, and mire. What he failed to depict as forlorn and detestable was ap-

12

parently from lack of ability or words to say more, and not from want of disposition.

Of those riding on the coach scarcely a good word could be said. They were so far above and removed from the toiling herd in sentiment and sympathy as to have no fellowship *with* them, and what little feeling was had *for* them manifested itself in small contributions from the pocket, with no tenderness of pity, and no feeling of common humanity or brotherhood, and these pittances from enormous wealth were grudgingly bestowed to alleviate extreme cases of hardship and suffering.

This terrible condition of things was not relieved of its odiousness because of the fact that daily some of the toilers and the passengers exchanged places and positions, some tumbling off the coach and others climbing upon it; for these new recruits in each case became a part of the new surroundings with all the adjuncts. All the relief to the situation was in the fact that the conditions were not permanent and could not be crystallized into *castes*. The nabob of to-day, arrayed in his fine toggery, might to-morrow be in the traces, exchanging his fine apparel for the rags of a servant, while the servant donned his robes or put on better ones. And so the panorama moved along like a dismal phantasmagoria.

This representation of the population of the country, though striking, and as to the extremes of population not entirely delusive, is yet very defective, from this fact among others, that it utterly ignores the great middle class of the people, constituting a majority of all, who belong to neither of the other classes described. They neither ride on the coach nor pull in its traces. They labor, but it is for themselves, for their own comfort and advancement. They set their own tasks, work their own hours, and rest at their own dictation. They are the dispensers of their own time, strength, and means. Most of them have their own homes, live in comfort, and enjoy more real happiness than the lordly rich ones riding on the coach, while they are strangers to the sufferings, want, and privations of the very poor.

I was one of this class when as a boy I worked on the farm, and speak from personal experience as well as wide observation. We discussed the various phases of this subject in college, and there was quite a divergence of opinions expressed thereon.

During vacation I had numerous conversations with my parents on this theme. My mother said there seemed to her to be a lack of appreciation of the true character and dignity of labor on the part of large numbers of citizens. Many regarded it as a hardship or even a curse, with slight mitigation, others esteemed it a disgrace, to labor with the hands. While no one delighted in toil for toil's sake alone, and there is nothing in hard work of itself to render it desirable, yet in the great law of compensation there is a cheerful view of the situation. Things are not so unequal as is generally conceded even by advanced thinkers.

"In my own case," she explained, "I enjoyed the work I did for husband and son exquisitely. There was no pleasanter or more highly prized experience of my life than that of *doing* something for those I loved. If with my own hands I could make an article or perform some handiwork, or add some touches that would enhance the comfort of those dear ones, there was a sweetness about it that did not come when I hired the work done. There was real comfort in feeling that my hands had performed this labor, and that my hands should place it where it belonged. So when your father did the like for me, or my son either, the reception of such tokens of love and care for me on their part added tenfold to the joy I felt in receiving the same. Like gifts from others were never so dear nor so highly prized, because not prompted by the same motive. When husband or son brought to me their evidences of thoughtful affection I always felt like taking them to my heart in a warm embrace with a kiss of love upon the lips; and though I did not always do this, yet I felt the solid happiness these delightful experiences produced in my innermost being. It is thus that love sanctifies and glorifies labor, and renders it one of the crowning blessings of the human race."

"I know that is true," I replied. "I well remember when I secured for you the first flowers of spring or the first ripe fruit of the season, though the effort often cost no little toil and effort, how I anticipated all the while and then was so richly repaid a thousandfold by the kiss you gave me and the light of joy in your eye. The remembrance of those occasions is rich and fragrant to-day—a sweet legacy that is above price, and that nothing can destroy. We do not always see the results of our efforts as in these cases where cause and effect are so near together, but after all the mutual labors of a family united in love have the same tendency always and bring the same rich harvest of reward."

"You are right, my son. The dearest enjoyments come to us through these channels. I can now furnish to my dear ones more expensive gifts than I used to bestow, but there is a lack of the true joy of giving. It is only the purchase of money. The bright glory that

coronated the gift with its halo before is not present
now—at least not to the same extent; the brightness
is dimmed, and hence the present loses a part of its
value to both the giver and the recipient. The more
heart there is in the gift or the service rendered, the
more valuable it is to both the bestower and the receiver. That is it. Out of the abundance of the heart
is the joy of life. And this brings out another phase of
experience. The poor in purse are apt to envy the rich,
and think hard of fate, as they term it, because their lot
is one of poverty and privation. Yet which of these
dissatisfied and complaining ones would exchange
everything, including personality and loved ones, with
the richest man on earth? Who would go out of himself, out of his home, leaving wife and children, to become another person, with that other's personality,
home, and kindred? No human being who appreciates
himself or his loved ones would entertain the thought
for a moment if the other was possessed of millions
upon millions. Things are not so unequal as we think.
The law of compensation largely prevails."

"That is a new feature of the situation I had not before considered. But its application is apparent," was
my comment.

CHAPTER III.

It may be well now to pass from these circumscribed limits to a wider field of observation.

The contest between capital and labor, or the agitation of the subject, kept growing more prominent. Labor organizations became the order of the day. In the legitimate sphere of their operations these were excellent and praiseworthy. But they were power concentrated; and power is good or bad according to the manner of its exercise. If it is badly directed, the greater the power the more serious the harm in its administration. Capital is power. Organized labor is power. The one or the other may be abused and become a scourge instead of a blessing. A conversation between two laboring men which occurred in my presence will present one aspect of this perplexing problem in a tolerably clear and impressive manner.

The two men were discussing the merits of a strike of workmen that was then agitating the country. One of them was in hearty sympathy with the strikers and very bitter against their employers. He was unsparing of rebuke on the one side, and profuse in panegyric on the other. He finally appealed to his companion, who had listened in silence to most of his remarks, for his views. With calmness and deliberation he responded, growing eloquent and earnest as he proceeded.

"I cannot agree with all you say. I know the world is indebted to labor for all material development.

17

Labor carries forward all industrial enterprises, and leads all progress along the lines of productive skill. Honest labor should be fostered and protected.

"Labor organizations are valuable as aids to workmen in the exercise of proper functions; but when wrongly handled are a great curse to those who trust in them. I am a member of two of these organizations and know of what I speak.

"I do not believe forcible strikes are ever justifiable in this country. In the Old World it may be different, because the whole framework of society and usage differs from ours, so that a laboring man there has a poor show to secure more than a mere competence. But here, where the field is wide and all avenues are open, where every man has a naturally equal chance with others, and where four fifths of our wealthy men commenced their careers as daily laborers, and by their own efforts have reached their present positions of affluence, there is no excuse for the exercise of force in compelling men to quit work or to do work.

"And yet every labor organization is based on this idea of *force*—an idea born in foreign lands and not indigenous to our soil. They are so constituted that one man, or a committee of head men, can give orders which the men are compelled to obey, whether they wish to or not. Members are received only on condition of taking a solemn oath or obligation to do this very thing along with others. When a man thus binds himself he is no longer free. He is a slave to all intents and purposes. He puts himself under masters, and has no more liberty than a machine. He gets no compensation that is a fair equivalent for this loss of independence and self-control. There is no greater despotism on God's footstool than are these labor or-

ganizations as now conducted. The Czar of Russia is
not a whit more despotic than the head of one of these.

"The 'walking delegate' is actually paid usually one
dollar per day extra during a strike or other trouble to
look after matters; and this is practically a bribe for
him to foment difficulties that he may ply his vocation.
There never was a system devised by designing demagogues that more effectually enthrones tyrants and
fetters men than these same combinations. I have
been there, as I said, and know the truth of what I say.
So do you, if, as I presume, you are a member of one
of these labor leagues. You fully understand that
every member is bound to obey orders, right or wrong.

"As previously stated, forcible strikes are un-Ameri-
can. They are always evidence of the exercise of arbitrary power. I never knew one to occur where there
were not members opposed to such action. But the
iron hand was upon them, and they could do no other
than submit. This is no fancy sketch. In the discussion of modes of procedure while the strike is on, you
well know that it is proposed and debated just to what
length the work of force shall proceed. It is invariably
a part of the plan and purpose of a strike to prevent
other men from taking the places of the strikers. It is
also either settled or left with those who manage the
strike to determine how much violence shall be done
and what amount of property may be destroyed. Crime
is thus deliberately planned in the lodge, and carried
out on the theater of the strike.

"It is the right of every free man to quit working
for any man, firm, or corporation at pleasure, when not
bound by contract. But his right ends with the disposition of himself. If he tries to prevent another
workman from taking the place he has vacated, he is

a tyrant. And yet this is the very essence of the spirit of labor combines. Labor never can be and never ought to be free so long as it imposes shackles upon others. Until it can 'do unto others as it would have others do to it,' it is not in a position to ask for help or sympathy. 'Whatsoever a man' or an organization 'sows, that shall he' or it 'also reap.' This is the eternal law of justice and righteous retribution.

"Capital has the same right to dismiss one workman and take another, where no contract exists, as labor has to quit work."

"I am not sure about that," said the other. "The workmen have made the business and wealth of their employers, and have some rights which they are bound to respect."

"What rights? None whatever but those of contract or agreement. If you sell me your labor at so much a day for any length of time, when I have paid as agreed my obligation ceases. So does yours. I would have as much right to demand additional labor from you without further remuneration as you to ask me for any favor for past services rendered. Perfect justice and perfect equality is the true law that should govern. If a farmer sells his crop of wheat to the miller and gets the price agreed upon, the transaction ends with the payment and acceptance of the money according to stipulation. What would be thought of the farmer if he should then take possession of the mill and refuse to let the owner occupy and run it unless he would agree to pay the price he, the farmer, should demand for the next crop of wheat he should raise? Yet that is exactly what striking laborers do!

"When a lodge or other form of organized labor resolves to take life, or does take life, to carry its ends, it is a murderer; when it resolves to take possession of property not its own, and does so, it is a thief or robber; when it destroys property in conducting its operations on a strike, it is an incendiary: and in each case should be dealt with as such. These crimes, among the worst known, labor organizations are this day guilty of in the strikes now pending. How can laborers expect the people to take sides with them when they are perpetrating such deeds as these?

"I tell you, my dear sir, the worst enemies labor has to-day are found in its own ranks. They are the violent members of its own organizations, and generally leaders of the same.

"When did capital ever beat and maim or kill a laborer to compel him to do or not to do any work? It may turn men off from employment, and thus cause suffering and distress in the workman's home. This is harsh and cruel if avoidable. But you laborers smite and maim a fellow-laborer, not only causing the same privation and suffering in his home as in the other case, but a doctor's bill and great distress besides. With such a record how can labor have the face to ask for favors?

"You kill or maim a 'scab.' Who is a scab? A workman, frequently a better one than many of those who persecute him. Look at the folly of the thing. To-day the man is a scab. To-night he enters a lodge and becomes a member of the union. To-morrow he is all right, must be protected and compelled to persecute his brother scab of yesterday. He is not a whit better in any respect either as man or workman. Yet he was to be beaten or killed yesterday, while to-day he is enrolled among the beaters and killers. Can anything be more ridiculous or indefensible? Labor will never be crowned queen and reign while her subjects and adherents are guilty of such injustice and cruelty. Because I am a friend of labor and have all my interests there, I protest against these iniquities perpetrated in her name. She must come with clean hands and be purged from blood, robbery, and arson before she can be enthroned in the hearts of the people, or have dominion in her proper realm."

"You are pretty rough on labor."

"No, sir, not on labor, but on the false labor leaders, who are unworthy to take her sacred name on their profane lips. You know full well that what I have said is true. Will you sign a declaration of personal independence?"

"Have you done so?"

"I have."

"I will think about it. You have suggested a new train of thought, and I must have time to consider before acting."

This conversation was a revelation to me. No new facts were stated, but existing ones were placed in such a striking pose as to command attention. The silent assent of the other man was as impressive as the words of the speaker.

This scene from actual life is given to the reader just as it transpired, "without note or comment."

CHAPTER IV.

A LITTLE out of chronological order, but in harmony with the thread of the narrative, the views of some farmers are now given, bearing upon the theme under consideration. The events here narrated transpired in the winter of 1891, during the session of the legislature of the State of Kansas. A member of the House of Representatives, who was also chairman of an important committee and one of the prominent leaders in that body, was on his way from Leavenworth to Topeka traveling by rail, and occupied a seat just before me in the car. In conversation the gentleman by his side spoke of the law of supply and demand. He caught at the words and replied with scornful emphasis:

"Supply and demand! Fudge! That has no more to do with governing prices than I have with causing cold and ice at the North Pole. I used to be deluded by that old-fogy notion; but I have got bravely over it and advanced away along beyond it out of sight. I am ashamed of my former folly and delusion, and will not be caught with such chaff again. No intelligent man believes at this time that supply and demand have anything to do in fixing prices. The great combines, packing-houses, and grain gamblers fix the prices of all commodities, and pay for each article just what they please and sell it in the same manner.

"We farmers are as helplessly in their power as an infant just born and in the arms of its nurse. We can take their prices or let our grain rot or our other products go to the dogs. I am astonished that a man of your intelligence should be so far behind the procession as not to know these facts, and that the old notion of supply and demand ruling in these affairs has been exploded and its dust relegated to the owls and bats or scattered to the four winds of heaven long ago!"

Much more was said in the same strain on this and other topics introduced. The legislator was a loud and profuse talker, and monopolized nearly all the time and conversation. But at length the other gentleman found an opportunity and propounded this question:

"Suppose you had five hundred good horses and an agent of the government or some corporation should come along empowered and directed to buy five hundred horses without delay. The purchase must be made at once. Your horses were exactly the kind he wanted and must have, and there were no other horses to be had anywhere in reach. Who would fix the price for those horses?"

The legislator had cut loose from his first declaration by intervening converse, and did not see the drift of the inquiry. He replied without hesitation:

"I would, of course."

"But suppose you had five or ten neighbors each of whom had five hundred horses as good as yours, and anxious to sell. Who then would fix the price?"

"The purchaser, most certainly."

"Very well. Does not the law of supply and demand govern prices then?"

"In that case, yes. But that is an exception and a supposition not found in real life. It does not meet the case at all."

"Why not? To my mind the illustration is apt and fits the case to a dot."

The legislator would not admit the other's conclusion ; but the case was so plain all others saw it, and he was glad to shift the conversation into other channels.

Another member of the same legislature on a different occasion, but similar in all respects, opened up on the money question, and advocated the unlimited issue of irredeemable treasury notes directly to the people. After he had expatiated on his hobby for quite a time, rehearsing all the sophistries in vogue relative to fiat money, an elderly gentleman suggested as follows :

"I think I can furnish a substitute for all the prevailing theories in reference to the issue of paper currency. My plan is very simple, easily understood, and places the whole matter in the hands of the people, where it properly belongs. We the people are the government in fact. Officials of all grades are only our servants. You say the simple declaration by the government that a piece of printed paper is a dollar makes it a dollar. But your machinery for getting this money in circulation is clumsy and circuitous. Let the government make the plates for printing the money, and then furnish every head of a family with one or more of these plates, with full certified authority to print and circulate as much of the money as he needs or desires. The government, having full and unlimited authority in the premises, can as readily delegate this privilege to the head of each family as to a bank or banknote engraving company, or any other citizen or officer. No one is supposed to know as well as the individual himself how much money he needs, and by this simple process every one can have enough. The more money in circulation the better the times. Do you not see at a glance the simplicity of this method, and its complete adaptation to the wants of every household in the land? No more financial distress. All suffering from this cause banished forever!"

This was clearly presented as a bluff, as could be seen by the twinkle in the gentleman's eye; but to his surprise the legislator replied:

"By the holy spoons, that is a bully idea! It is the best scheme yet suggested. You must be one of our leaders in the background. You can go to the head of the heap. By the way, why have you not published your financial plan? It beats Peffer's 'Way Out' all hollow. Publish it by all means. It's the very thing."

"Oh, I am too bashful to do that," said the old gentleman, evidently astonished at the reception by the other of his fantastical theory.

Another farmer opened the vials of his wrath and poured out their contents upon capitalists, combines, trusts, plutocrats, and pretty much all things under heaven, except himself and his associates. He declared they were going to have the most radical changes, a complete revolution in the existing order of things. They had been downtrodden too long already and now would have their rights—"by ballots if they could, by bullets if they must."

"What are your rights?" inquired a quiet gentleman who had been listening to his bitter tirade.

"Why, sir, we farmers produce nearly all the wealth of the country, and yet we are ground to the earth. Our lands are mortgaged. We get next to nothing for our crops and stock, and are growing poorer every year with all our hard work, while the rich combines and plutocrats that plunder us are growing richer all the time. They accumulate vast fortunes, are getting hold of all the wealth of the land, and using it to crush out all that opposes them. They will soon own everything and all the people will be their slaves. The only hope we have is in revolution."

"What sort of a revolution do you propose to carry out?"

"One that will equalize things, especially the wealth of the country."

"I see. You say you are plundered. Who robs you?"

"Middlemen and combines."

"Who are middlemen?"

"The men who simply handle our produce, charge enormously for doing it, but never produce an atom of anything."

"If I understand you, the middlemen are the ones who come between you and your consumers."

"That's it exactly."

"There must be quite a number of these. Let us look after them a moment. We will say you have a hundred acres of wheat. You cultivate and produce the wheat. When it is ripe production ceases and conversion begins. The crop ripe in the field is the raw material, and you are now to get it in shape for your customers. The first thing to be done is to harvest the grain. Here comes in the first set of middlemen, and there is quite a number of them. The next are the threshers, and there are numbers of them also, all middlemen. Then there are the machines, which add to the expense; they are the same as middlemen. Then you must hire men to haul the grain to the railroad or elevator; these, too, are middlemen. Then the railway transports the grain to market, and the train hands are another lot of middlemen. Last of all you come to the commission man or other purchaser, and he is the final middleman, and, as I gather from your talk, the only one of whom you complain. But the reapers, the threshers, the haulers, and the trainmen are at least twenty while the last is one by himself. Why do you get angry at him and not at the others?"

"The others are laborers."

"So may he be a laborer. If he is not industrious he will speedily come to want. But not one of these middlemen, from the harvest field to the final market, is a producer; they are simply transmitters or manufacturers. You pay the first three classes out of your own pocket direct. The trainmen are paid by the railway company, but their wages for the work is charged up to your wheat in price of transportation. Are you going to blot out all these middlemen and let your wheat rot in the field?"

"Why, no, of course not."

"In your revolution what is to be done with the middlemen?"

"I had not thought of the matter as you present it."

"I presume not. I used to talk just as you do; but when I came to analyze the matter I learned my mistake. Middlemen are as essential to our success on a farm as the labor that produces the crop. I have found other things to be true which I did not take into account formerly. Suppose all the middlemen who assist in getting my crop to market do nothing but this kind of work—are strictly day laborers. Then good prices for me means high or expensive living for them. There are twenty of them and one of me. Their families and mine may make an offset. My selfishness prompts me to wish the highest possible price for my grain at the expense of these twenty men. Would not a philanthropic and brotherly feeling wish well to these men, so manifold more in number than myself, and cause me to be willing to receive less that they might get more? We do not think and act in that manner. We are all for self. You are going to revolutionize society and the world to secure profit to yourself, and care nothing for the twenty you cause to suffer. Are you not desperately selfish?"

"If I am desperately selfish I know I am greatly in need and want relief; and I must have it."

"That cry comes up from all classes. The burden you would throw off must fall upon all your consumers. If they were all rich it would be well; but as there are ten thousand poor ones to one that is rich, your advantage is the misfortune of these thousands. Society is so interwoven in its intricate relations, part with part, it cannot be separated. Every farmer is a capitalist, and also a laborer. The same is true of mechanics who employ hands. High wages to workmen is comfort to millions; but the consumers of the products of their toil pay these wages. You pay the wages of the men who construct the machinery you use on the farm. They in turn pay for your grain and produce, including the wages you pay all the middlemen. In your revolution are you going to blot out the wages of manufacturing laborers and give all to farmers? Are farmers to be the plutocrats in the new order of things? How are you going to reconcile the antagonistic interests of farmers and laborers in other departments of enterprise? The revolution you need is more customers as near to your farm as you can get them. If your market was by the side of your farm, what an amount of expense you would save and add to the profit of your crop. As you pay for getting your produce to its destination, every mile of distance saved is clear gain. Does your revolution contemplate bringing you and your customers nearer together and increasing their number?"

"To be candid, I had not thought of that. But if the government would own and operate the railroads, freights would be reduced."

"That is doubtful. Government usually pays more for work than private persons or firms. This is a well-known fact. Running railroads would not be likely to prove an exception to the rule."

The foregoing is given without note or comment just as the conversations took place. It shows the want of consideration on the part of those who cry loudest for reform or change.

CHAPTER V.

SHORTLY after this I met a very intelligent gentleman, whose broad views and wide range of information drew my attention. Being deeply interested in the subject, I requested his opinion of a labor strike then in progress. After he had given his views upon that particular strike and strikes in general, which were not favorable, he remarked:

"I do not see how it is possible for any Christian to be a member of the labor unions as now constituted."

To this I expressed my utter astonishment and said:

"I thought every organization expressly guaranteed to each candidate that membership therein will in no manner interfere with his religious or political views or principles, be these what they may."

"That is true. Such assurance is given. I speak from experience. It is carried out so far as belonging to any particular branch of the church is concerned. Perfect liberty is fully accorded and recognized in this matter, and no one is questioned in reference to his church relations. He can attend all the services without the slightest hindrance or molestation. His political rights are also respected. He is not required to vote for this party or that. Sometimes, however, a strong pressure is brought to bear upon members to induce them to vote this way or that; but it always stops with pressure and never extends to compulsion. The evil lies deeper than the surface. It strikes at the root of the matter.

31

"The obligation that follows this assurance of liberty, which every person is required to take when initiated into the order, compels him *to obey the orders of those in authority.* All executive authority is vested in the heads of the lodges and of the order. When these issue the command every member is bound by his oath to obey, whether he thinks obedience right or wrong. He has deprived himself of the right of choice, and is a bondslave to the order. We are frequently required to do things that I know to be wrong, such as the taking possession of property which does not belong to us; sometimes to destroy this property or greatly damage it. This to me is theft or robbery. Yet I am tied hand and foot, and cannot help myself. I am aware that men try to disguise the real facts and cover the crime by the sophism that the property is the product of labor, and therefore of right belongs to the laborers, at least in part, and that they are only taking possession of and using what in equity they are entitled to as their own. If that be true, my neighbor's house which I helped to build is partly or wholly mine. I have the right to dispossess him and occupy the place myself. The man who made his carriage has the right to take and use it at pleasure. Indeed, there is no end to the right of labor to seize upon and possess all things under the sun constructed by human hands. This is only another name for anarchy and communism.

"I sell my labor for the best price I can obtain for it. When I have performed my work and received the pay according to contract, it is the final end of that transaction on the side of both parties to it, the same as the purchase and sale of any other commodity.

"I conscientiously regard all forcible occupation, misuse or abuse or destruction of the property of another by me, even if that other be my employer and my labor has contributed to enhance the value of his possessions, to be utterly wrong and criminal, and without excuse or defense. All the sophistry about my equitable right in that property is too thin to make a shadow. I have already received the equivalent for my labor according to my own terms. Yet I am ordered to do these very acts, which, when brought to the bar of my own reason, judgment, and conscience, I am compelled to adjudge indefensibly wrong. Then comes thundering down upon my defenseless soul the command of God: 'Thou shalt not steal! Thou shalt do no wrong to thy neighbor!'

"Again, I am ordered to abuse a 'scab'; to treat him as an enemy; to drive him from work; to beat and maim him; if necessary, to banish him. That scab may be my brother, my own mother's son. He may also be a brother in Christ, a member of the same church with myself. We may sit in the same pew, kneel at the same altar, and partake of the Holy Communion together on the Sabbath. On Monday morning I must drive that brother from the work he needs to feed and clothe his family. I know this to be the fact. I know, too, that he is a skillful workman, fully equal to myself in all respects, painstaking and conscientious in all he does. But he is a scab, and must be persecuted; and I am commanded to make war upon him and prevent him from maintaining his family, who will by my act be brought to privation and suffering. This is man's side of the transaction as demanded of me by the organization of which I am a member.

"Then from the Godward side of my responsibility comes these words: 'Whatsoever ye would that men should do unto you, do ye even so unto them; for this is the law and the prophets.' 'Love thy neighbor as thyself.' 'Do good unto all men.' Here are the two commands, one from the head of the order, the other from the Head of the universe. Which must I obey?

"When a man is thus brought face to face with duty he dare not hesitate. I did not. You must know this is no fancy picture or idle tale. It is an absolutely truthful sketch from real life. That scab was my brother, my mother's son. He was my spiritual brother also, and every word I have spoken tells of actual events. No language can express the emotions which I experienced. I felt as never before the wonderful force of the words of the Master: 'No man can serve two masters: for either he will hate the one, and love the other; or else he will hold to the one, and despise the other. Ye cannot serve God and mammon.' I chose to serve God. I could do no other. Are you surprised any longer at the statement I made at the outset?"

"No, not at the statement, but more than I can express at the history you have unfolded."

"I will say more. I have never heard as much profanity and blasphemy anywhere as among labor-union men when excited. Many of them are foreign born, the lower strata of society from Europe. They have little education, and no religious training worthy the name. Hence there is little restraint. When they get angry, excited, maddened by liquor, no utterance is too vile or too profane for them to use. A refined Christian man is constantly shocked and outraged in feeling by these associations and what he is compelled to hear."

"All this is bewildering to me. If what you say of these labor organizations is true, from that side of view they are terrible things."

"Some men may look at them differently. I presume they do. It is possible that persons constituted differently from me can be Christians and retain membership in them. I cannot. Nor do I see how any one can. Yet I am not judge of my brother nor keeper of his conscience. To his own Master he stands or falls.

"At times, when commotion was high, when passion ruled the hour, when riot and murder were freely discussed by hundreds of frenzied men, I have felt as if the foundations were slipping from under me and only a slip of solid ground were left between me and chaos, and that were shaking as if a volcano were beneath ready to burst forth and rend it. At such times I have trembled for a moment at the prospect of the possible contingencies that spread like the pall of death before me. But I remembered that One was looking on who could still the tempest, even of men's passions; that not a sparrow falls without Him; and there I could rest.

"There is a peculiarity about the mode of checking the brutal element in the order, always ready for lawlessness, which I could but notice. It is this: the cool heads try to curb the radicals and hold them in check, knowing that excesses will do harm and damage their cause. But they always appeal to the heads on the ground of *policy*, never as a matter of *principle*. They do not say to those riotously disposed, 'That is wrong and criminal,' but always, 'That will not do; it will hurt us, and make us enemies.' Whether this method of appeal is the only one that can influence the men, or whether the leaders themselves have no higher conception of right and wrong, and no loftier measure of action than that of policy, I am unable to say. I state the fact as I find it. My experience and observation lead me to conclude that with some of the leaders and a large proportion of the men this is the only gauge by which conduct is measured."

"Have not good reasons been given for some strikes?"

"Read carefully the history of every one in this country. If you find one that can be justified in all its demands, or in the lengths to which it has been carried, I shall be greatly pleased to have you call my attention to it. I have never yet been able to find a single one that could be justified from first to last in all it asked or all it did. For most of them there is no justification whatever. They are often criminal and cruel."

"Then you think these labor unions will not succeed as now constituted and directed?"

"If such methods succeed it will be the success of disaster. Their oppression, crime, and inhumanity cannot meet the approbation of either God or good men. Without such approval no cause can righteously prevail. And there is a side in which the cause of labor is right and just and should triumph over all opposition."

CHAPTER VI.

Having been favored by hearing from farmers and laborers, I determined to visit a capitalist and learn his views of the situation. I sought an interview with the head of a large manufacturing establishment and stated to him my desire for information. He replied:

"I do not feel competent to give any one much light on this vexed question. It is one simple enough in itself, but it has been so distorted and overwhelmed with extraneous matter that it is now a tangled web which the wisest seem unable to unravel. The fundamental principles of political economy are few and simple, but when complicated with a thousand considerations of policy they become intricate and give rise to a multitude of divergent opinions.

"If demagogues, politicians, and agitators were banished from the arena on which this labor problem is being worked out, there would be no difficulty between employers and employees. No employer wishes to part with the workmen who understand all the details of his business better than new hands possibly could, even if equally skillful, and for this reason can do him better and more satisfactory service. I never part with one of my men except with regret. I prefer always to keep the men I know and who know me, and are familiar with the methods of our business. The loss of a good hand is always a misfortune, and is never desired on the part of the employer."

37

"I know that is a fact from my own experience," I said. "I employ laborers and never part with one except for cause, and then with regret."

"That is the experience of all employers. If our men have a grievance I am always glad to hear and remedy it if I can. With a few exceptions the labor organizations are controlled by a single head man, or an executive committee, and these, with the walking delegates, constitute the executive force and control the action of local unions and on a wider scale of the whole order. It is these head men who cause nine tenths of all the trouble between capital and labor. When laborers become more intelligent and thoroughly Americanized they will no longer submit to this worse than kingly rule, and will adopt the 'majority-shall-rule' policy, with reserved rights of conscience and independent manhood for the minority. One or two organizations have adopted this idea already in part, and it is to be hoped all others will follow the example thus set speedily, and more perfectly carry out the principle involved. The leaders will doubtless make a desperate effort to maintain and retain power, but certainly manhood and freedom will conquer in the end.

"You hear the agitators constantly contending that the employers ought to divide their immense profits with employees. There is probably no subject upon which there is more ignorance and misapprehension than this one of the vast profits of manufacturers. It is a myth, a complete fiction, a cry of demagogues to create sympathy on the one hand and prejudice on the other. There are workmen in our employ, and in every other establishment of any considerable magnitude, whose profits on investments are fivefold greater than those of their employers. Their capital is their skill. It has cost them something to become skillful workmen, but they have earned good wages all the way from journeymen to the higher places, and so the expense of acquiring present attainments has been of the minimum order. Our best men get eighteen dollars a day. Allowing thirteen days for holidays, etc., they receive for the remaining three hundred working days five thousand four hundred dollars per year— more than the best farmer can make clear on the best half section of land; more than a majority of professional men, lawyers, teachers, etc., make, and more than the salary of a member of Congress. This is made without a cent of money invested, without anxiety or care, and is clear cash. The lowest price we pay inferior workmen is two dollars a day, or six hundred dollars per year of three hundred days.

"Now if it is right for the employer to divide his earnings with the workmen, is it not equally as just and right for these men who get over five thousand dollars a year to divide with their less fortunate brethren, who get but six hundred a year? Is there not as much reason, humanity, and righteousness in the one proposition as in the other? But who ever heard of these princely wage-earners dividing with the small earners their immense increase? That is a horse of another color. The fortunate laborer can put his money out at six to ten per cent. interest, or invest it in mortgage securities, and not a word is said. But let his employer do the same thing and he is set upon by the whole pack of agitators as a pack of dogs after the quarry. We find so much more profitable use for our money in making improvements in our plant that not a dollar is loaned out on security at interest. Our employees have thousands at interest. I presume the same is true of every other manufacturing institution. It is the well-to-do laboring men and not the capitalists as a rule who loan money at interest. These facts are either not known or are ignored by agitators and the people at large.

"The facts show that capital invested in manufacturing does not yield a net return of over six per cent. per annum. It is a little less than that in Massachusetts. In Connecticut it is a trifle over, not counting the time of owners; counting all expenses, not more. Samuel M. Hotchkiss, State commissioner of labor for Connecticut, in his report recently made gives the statistics of eighty-five establishments with an aggregate capital of $49,112,149.58. The net profits for the year were $3,297,861.99. They employed 27,094 laborers and 1446 superintendents. Laborers were paid for the year $12,032,412.95, superintendents $1,191,255.54; or a total of $13,223,685.43, which is more than four times the amount of profits earned. In other words, labor received more than four dollars for every one dollar earned by capital in this State. It is but fair to say that labor every year makes more money than capital four times over in the department of manufacturing, take the United States as a whole.

"There are some employers, doubtless, who are cruel and oppressive and utterly selfish; but as a body they are enlightened and humane citizens, quite as much entitled to public sympathy as their workmen, either on the ground of justice, benevolence, or good citizenship. As a rule they do not act the tyrant, but are anxious to see their men prosper and ready to aid them in every way, with counsel, sympathy, and in all material things. They are, as a class, no better and no worse than other members of society of like intelligence who are engaged in lawful and laudable pursuits.

"It is only because there are hundreds of laborers to each capitalist, and therefore more votes to secure from their ranks, that demagogues take sides with them against their employers. There are good men among all classes, and bad men also. Let equal and exact justice be meted out to all and there will soon be an end to agitation in this direction."

CHAPTER VII.

I FINISHED my studies in both college and university, passed a first-grade examination and received the honors from both institutions. During vacations I always came home. I inquired of my mother about Effie on each occasion. She was away at school. This was to me a disappointment. I had hoped to see her. In the midst of society where beauty reigned her face came to me as I had often seen it during our acquaintance or at the hour of parting. Others charmed for a moment, but the instant I was alone her sweet countenance was before me. Often even in the midst of excitement I could see those mellow eyes looking into mine.

When I returned from school after final graduation I learned that her father, having greatly prospered in business, had built an elegant residence in another part of the city, on a beautiful location. The daughter was still absent. There being nothing to keep me at home, I spent some months traveling over the country for the purpose of gaining information by personal observation upon questions agitating the public mind.

About this time my parents, returning home from an excursion, were both fatally injured by a railway accident and were brought home to die. I remained with them day and night until they were released from suffering. They were buried side by side in the same grave.

Oh, the desolation of home when I returned from the funeral! My father was the best of parents. My mother had been to me as an angel from heaven. She had entered into all my plans and sympathies, soothed all my sorrows in childhood and youth, and in riper years was a bosom companion. She was to me both mother and sister. Every young man needs a sister to advise him, to smooth off the rough corners and polish him generally. My mother did this for me as deftly as any sister could. She romped and played with me in early life; in later years entered into all my higher aspirations and met the needs of the hour. I had no secrets from her. She learned my feeling toward Effie and was pleased. Her touch sanctified everything in the house and beautified all its surroundings. And now she was gone! No more her soft and loving hand should rest upon my brow! How cold to my touch! No more her tender voice would reach my ear! Turn which way I would, I met something that spoke of her. Her face shone out from the pictures on the wall, from every adornment, from every room. I seemed to hear her step, only to remember I should never hear it again. The silence was unbearable. Company I could not endure. I must get away. To remain in that silent and deserted home was a burden too heavy to bear. I went to Europe.

I visited all the principal cities; saw all the renowned places; went into society; was presented at various courts; accompanied parties of pleasure and adventure—nothing was left undone to dull and deaden the pain which pressed like a weight upon my heart. Success was only partial. In the midst of hilarity a face, a voice, an act of tenderness—something would recall my mother to me. Then I wished to go away and weep. This may have been a weakness; but for such a mother I was not ashamed to feel emotion.

For a time I could not endure the thought of returning to my desolate home. I remained away three years. Then there came a longing to see my native place and stand by the grave of my beloved parents. Amid all these years there had ever and anon appeared to me the face of Effie. In the most unlike places and times—in hours of peril, in moments of silence or excitement, alone or in company, in public halls, in the still hours of night—that sweet and earnest face came up before me. Why, I could not tell. Now that my thoughts turned homeward the greatest attraction in my native land was that well-remembered face and form.

A moment's reflection told me that she was no longer a child, but a woman grown. Had she forgotten me? Was she married? Should I ever see her again? Sober consideration led me to doubt on all these points. For all that, she was the one magnet among the living to draw me westward.

On reaching home the overwhelming sense of my loss came back upon me with crushing force: no smiling face to cheer; no welcome word; no kiss of love; no sweet embrace. Dear memories and precious tokens made the place so dark and dreary. I had to escape from its once dear associations or break down utterly.

I went into the city. Everything seemed cold and icy, and yet it was a warm day in early September. I went up one street and down another, to ascertain if familiar objects would gain some hold upon my mind and lead me out of myself. It was little better than passing through a cemetery. I stood by the grave of my parents. It was too much. Memory called up the past in all its sweetness and sadness, until I had to flee from the spot where reposed their sleeping dust.

As I passed along one of the streets on my return from the sad pilgrimage to the dead I met Effie's father. With pressing cordiality he took me to his home. I was then introduced to his daughter as one of my old schoolmates.

Such a vision of loveliness! It was perfection! I had seen the celebrated beauties of Europe and America; none of them could compare with this peerless but unaffected being.

But where was my little girl? Gone forever! I was so completely surprised and captivated by the exquisite loveliness and perfection of face and form that I fear I did not act well my part. With ready tact Effie came to the rescue.

"I remember Mr. North quite well as the schoolmate of early days. That was years ago."

"Does it appear long to you?" I replied. "To me it seems but yesterday."

I fancied she blushed slightly as she said: "We welcome you back to home and native land, and hope you will enjoy life with us."

This, as everything else she said or did, was unaffected. There was a simplicity and transparency about her entire demeanor as free from guile or duplicity as light from darkness. But the allusion to home recalled my loss, and a weight fell upon my heart and a shadow upon my face. As I spoke of this, in spite of myself tears filled my eyes. I asked pardon for the emotion I could not control. There was no need. Effie's eyes were suffused with the dew of tears. From that moment there was a bond of sympathy between us. I knew that in her I had a true friend. With consummate tact she led the conversation back to the days of our old fellowship, and recalled incidents of those times, some of which I had forgotten. But the worst was I forgot myself in her presence, and two hours glided by before I came to realize it. She said no apology was needed; that she was only glad if she had been able to lead me out of my sad sorrow for ever so short a period. On taking leave, Mr. Solon warmly invited me to call again.

I went from the house a new man. In these friends I felt the first touch of real and earnest heart-sympathy since my bereavement. There was no sham, no conventionality about it.

During the interview I frequently detected in Miss Solon traces of little Effie. In my dreams that night there was a sweet blending of the dear girl with the more charming young lady, always ending in the transcendent grace and beauty of the living presence I had met in the afternoon. I knew now that my destiny was bound up in that one who filled all the avenues of my heart. The more I subsequently saw of her the more I found to admire. In my eyes she was perfection itself. With rare and delicate intuition she perceived my needs, and like a ministering angel guided me into paths of self-forgetfulness. In her presence I could not be sad. Every new phase of her character added to the worth and goodness of herself. I soon loved her with a consuming passion. I never had learned until now the depths of my own nature. And yet her very perfection made me afraid. I was unworthy of the love of such a one; she was too far above me in purity and perfection. How dare I approach the sacred citadel of such a soul? Yet I did hope. I must hope. And I must dare all on that hope.

At last I did. I was accepted. I was then the happiest man in America!

After this Effie became more than ever to me. She held the place of mother, sister, and *fiancé* in my heart —the three dearest of all relations in life except that of wife. And there was a nearness and unity of heart that could not exist before.

Subsequently Effie told me that during all her time at school and afterward at home she remembered the little companion who used to walk by her side as a protector, who always took her part and anticipated and met all her wants. Her experience was the counterpart of my own. I think there never was a more complete and unreserved union of hearts than ours—a union that was more firmly cemented as the after-years came and went.

I was now lifted out of the valley of shadowy darkness into the broad sunshine of hope and joy. My life kept step to the music of love, and the brightest bow of promise spanned the sky of the future. But who can tell what a day may bring forth? Had I known what that future had in store for me! I must not anticipate.

CHAPTER VIII.

THE day was fixed for our nuptials. It was to be in the bright and beautiful May. After making the preliminary arrangements, I went home to happy dreams. It was midwinter. About midnight I was awakened by the alarm of fire. Springing up, I ran to the window of my room and looked out. The whole eastern sky was aglow with the light of a large conflagration. I hastened to the spot; the fire was in the direction of Mr. Solon's works. Alas, shops and warehouses were ablaze! The firemen were working with a will; all the engines of the city were on the ground. Herculean efforts were made to save the property; but the flames lapped and seared and flashed and roared and laughed in a wild revel of delight as they licked up houses and contents. In the midst of the din an awful cry rang out:

"A man in one of the upper rooms!"

An arm hung out of a window! Quicker than we can write it the firemen had a ladder placed. It seemed certain death to go to the rescue. A hero was there. He mounted through the smoke and flames to the spot and called to the man. No answer. He dashed in the window, sprang inside, lifted the insensible form, pushed it out, held to one arm, and followed. Down they started. It was like going into a furnace. The wild flames enveloped the man and his burden. An assistant rushed up to help. All reached the ground.

The breathless silence was then broken by a shout of joy and cheers for the hero, who was carried to the hospital in triumph, and though scorched, singed, and blistered, he came out after treatment undisfigured, almost unscarred, and honored by his fellow-citizens ever after.

The man rescued was past recovery; smoke and flame had done their work before the discovery.

This man was the cause of the fire. He had come along in necessitous circumstances some months before and out of sympathy Mr. Solon gave him employment. He returned this kindness by inciting the men to strike for higher wages. As this was a typical case, we give the leading points briefly. The stranger said to the men:

"Look at the difference between you and your employer. He is growing rich every year from the proceeds of your toil. Your sweat and blood go into his coffers in the shape of gold and greenbacks. It is your labor that makes his wealth. Without you he would become poor. He adds thousands to his possessions every year, while you who make all his gains remain poor. If you get ahead at all it is by such slow processes as will take a lifetime for you to secure a small competence for the days of old age. Yet this man revels in abundance all the days of his life. That abundance is filched from your brawn and muscle. His child has all that heart can wish or ambition crave. Your children are doomed to toil and privation, and can hope for nothing beyond the circumscribed bounds of poverty. Is this right? Do you intend to drudge on in this way to the end? Will you permit yourselves to be slaves of this man, who has the happy luck of possessing capital enough to run a business and get rich at your expense?"

These and similar utterances were continually dinned in the ears of the men, who had been satisfied and contented up to this time. These ultimately had the effect to cause a strike. Greatly to Mr. Solon's surprise his men came on Saturday afternoon and demanded an increase of pay. As soon as he could recover from the shock he said to them very kindly:

"My friends, I have been running behind for three months. The business has not been paying expenses. You can see for yourselves that the goods have accumulated in all the shops and storerooms until there is hardly space for storing more. I have kept you employed knowing what a hardship it would be for you to be thrown out of a situation at this time. Why do you come with such a demand at this season, when of all others it is impossible to increase your pay?"

"We think you can pay us better wages," said the leader.

"Why do you think so?"

"Because you are growing richer and we are not."

"I am not growing richer at this time, but poorer every day. It depends upon the uncertain contingencies of a future demand whether I ever recover from the present losses."

Then the new man spoke up.

"You are not getting poorer. You may not be receiving as much cash as usual; but here are the goods you have allowed to accumulate as so much wealth, which these men have made for you, and which only await the day of sale to fill your coffers."

"Suppose the day of sale does not come, or when it comes prices are reduced—what, then, will be the profits? I am taking all the chances for the sake of my men and their families. I could not find it in my heart to turn them out so long as it was possible for me to keep them employed; but as you have yourselves opened the way, and as it will be profitable for me to close down at present, I say to you, if you do not wish to continue to work at the prices I have been paying you are at liberty to leave me at once. I shall regret to part with you, but if you will go you must. I cannot increase your pay now. If you remain and times improve so that I can pay you more, I shall do so without your asking. Make up your minds now and let me know your decision speedily."

The men held a brief consultation by themselves and in a few minutes reported.

"We will gladly continue work at the present prices, and thank you for not sending us away. We never should have thought of asking an advance of pay but for this stranger, who has deceived and led us astray."

So the men remained. The stranger was paid off and dismissed. And he was the one taken from the burning building too late to save his life. He had been drinking in the evening, and either accidentally or purposely set fire to the place, with the result named. Mr. Solon had the remains buried at his own expense. His plant was almost a total loss.

Little did I think how this sad event was to affect my life!

CHAPTER IX.

I CALLED on Effie the next day. She was in distress of mind not caused by her father's loss. Feeling ill, she requested to be left alone and for me to call on the morrow. I did so. She was still under a cloud. The light of gladness in the eye was gone; the radiant face was beneath an eclipse. Evidently she was passing through a mental strain, and was not her own buoyant and cheery self.

"What is the trouble, dearest?" I inquired with the deepest solicitude, holding her willing hand.

She replied, "It is inexpressibly painful for me to say or do aught that will cause you pain; but necessity compels me. The fire has left father in such circumstances as must postpone our marriage indefinitely."

"Not by any means, love. You know I am amply able to care for you, and I am now more than ever anxious to do so. If you had not a cent in the world I should just as joyously make you the partner of my joys and sorrows as though you possessed millions. Your father's loss need be no barrier to our union as agreed upon, but may hasten the happy event, if only you will consent that it shall."

"I cannot," she said, and gave her reasons. Her first duty was to her parents. Her father's losses would reach a quarter of a million dollars. She must aid him by being his bookkeeper until better times. · I protested and proffered aid. She was sure her father

would accept favors from no one that would increase
his liabilities, and if he would she would not. I expressed surprise at this, but soon found that her high
sense of independence was sensitive, and not to be
placed in a doubtful position even by a lover. I had
to admire while I felt the pain of the declination of
assistance. I said:

"My dear Effie, you are worth a hundred of me, and
if I had the world to lay at your feet I should still be
your debtor."

She replied that this was very flattering, but only the
rhapsody of a lover. She remained firm, and I could
do nothing but acquiesce. I left her presence with
mingled emotions. Selfishness demanded the prompt
fulfillment of our engagement. Something higher in
me admired the courage and self-abnegation of this
peerless woman. I knew by the tremor of voice and
all visible signs how much it cost her to renounce self
and stand firmly by duty as she saw it. Even in my
troubled mind, battling as I was in a conflict, she had
placed herself on the mount of transfiguration.

Without dwelling upon this dark period of my life I
simply say that Effie remained true to her conviction,
and gave five years as the probable time of our proba-
tion. Five years! It seemed almost an eternity. What
should I, what could I, do all these years of waiting?

CHAPTER X.

I now come to the first distinctive event of my life which renders this record worth writing.

The bulk of my possessions was situated about a mile from the city. On the premises was a peculiar formation of rock covering over an acre of ground. It was about twice as long as it was wide—an oblong figure more resembling the work of a designing architect than a convulsion of nature.

A kind and gentlemanly stranger requested the privilege of making a room in this rocky hill for the purpose of establishing a chemical laboratory where he could conduct a series of very important experiments without being disturbed and where he would be certain to harm no one. I readily gave consent, and a few days after was called away on important business which detained me six months.

On returning home my attention was drawn to a pile of large rocks lying in front of the spot where I had given the eccentric chemist permission to fix his quarters. I had forgotten the affair entirely. This brought it to mind, and I went over to see what was done.

Imagine my surprise when the man took me into a room twelve by fifteen feet in size and ten feet high, cut out of solid rock. The thing seemed an impossibility. By way of explanation he took a bottle of peculiar-looking fluid, and with a tracing-pencil of his own construction drew a line across a block of solid rock two feet in thickness, and by repeating the process for ten minutes the stone was divided as smoothly as if it had been sawn asunder. This explained the problem but not the mystery. A simple mechanical contrivance enabled him to move the blocks as he cut them loose where he desired.

In a short time this room, which was delightfully ventilated, was elegantly furnished with hangings which deadened the sound. A smaller room at one side was used for the laboratory. The main room was a place fit for a prince. I desired the gentleman to give me his name. He said, "Call me the Chemist." So I knew him only by that appellation. He always appeared glad to see me, and took delight in showing me his apparatus and explaining his processes, which I did not understand. He claimed to be developing some wonderful discoveries, which I should be made acquainted with in due time. I paid little attention to these things, thinking them the chimeras of an enthusiast.

One day he requested an interview, which he said might prove of inestimable value to me. During the interview he explained to me the nature of a number of really marvelous chemical discoveries he had made. I need mention but a few of them, which are intimately connected with this history of strange events. One in particular was a preparation upon which he had spent years of labor and research with the most astonishing and incredible results. He had not yet given to this child of his skill a name, but

described it as a life-preserver during a period of suspended animation that it produced. He declared it
would put a person in an unconscious state, with an
entire suspension of all the life forces of the physical
and mental systems, and yet preserve these forces intact for an indefinite period of time.

The longest case of actual experiment was of ten
years' duration, on a mendicant who was suffering from
a painful disease. It was successful in all respects. He
had the preparation graded in strength from one hour
to one hundred years. I gave respectful attention to
all he said, but was not at the time very deeply impressed by what I heard. He and I were the only persons who had ever entered his retreat; and he assured
me I was the only person living besides himself who
knew of his secret. The mendicant had died from exposure before he could secure him for a twenty years'
trial. In the near future he proposed to furnish me
with a formula and full particulars for the compound-
ing of all his preparations, among which were a number
for removing stains from the human skin and all manner of textile fabrics, whatever the cause which produced them. All were harmless.

At his request, and to please him, I had an apartment
fitted up in my traveling-valise suitable for the purpose, which he filled with a number of bottles contain-
ing his products. He remarked:

" You will sometimes find these of inestimable value.
In case of emergency or unparalleled need, do not forget to consult these bottles for relief. I will place full
and intelligible directions with them."

I accepted his kindness because I saw it pleased him.
His earnestness made some impression upon my mind;

but the exciting events which followed drove this from thought and memory. A shelf near his bed and the laboratory proper had samples of his preparations ready for use at all times. These matters will prove of great interest hereafter.

One day, shortly before the fire occurred that has already been mentioned, the Chemist called me into his room, and said:

"I have a presentiment that something will happen in the near future which shall separate me from this dear spot. If anything befalls me, I bequeath all my belongings here to you. When they become yours you will learn to prize them as among your most valuable worldly possessions."

He then pointed out to me a secret place in the rock opened by a spring, invisible except to the initiated, where he always put the key to the outer door when he went away. He also showed me the drawers and other receptacles inside the rooms where he kept many things and all his valuables. I passed through this like one in a dream; yet I afterward recalled all that transpired. I told him not to yield to any morbid feeling or sentiment, but prepare to live many years to bless mankind. He protested that he was not morbid; that he might live, as I said; yet in obedience to an un-accountable impression he had done these things. He was perfectly calm and deliberate in all his acts.

I was called from home to a distant city on the following day on urgent business, and was absent three weeks. The day after my departure the Chemist was crossing the railway track near Mr. Solon's works, when an engine struck him, inflicting fatal injuries. Mr. Solon was near by at the time, saw the accident,

ran to the assistance of the unfortunate victim, raised
him tenderly in his arms, then had him conveyed to
his own home, where he received every possible care
and attention. Effie herself ministered to him in his
suffering. He died the third day, and was appropri-
ately buried by Mr. Solon.

CHAPTER XI.

EFFIE'S decision left an aimless life before me. What could I do? How occupy the time so many years? Like the troubled sea, I could not rest. To be idle was impossible. To be near *her* and yet so far away was unbearable. I must find something to do. Where was an opening for action?

At this juncture some new agitation of the hackneyed theme of labor and capital turned my attention in that direction. I would go into the field and make personal observation. My purpose was to visit all classes, and learn from each. Heretofore I had gathered an item here and there; now I would try to systematize.

I went among farmers first. Here I found a wide divergence of views. Some claimed that the farmer—the soil—produced all things necessary for life, and therefore should receive the first care and fostering aid of the government. In attempting to show how this could be done there were almost as many theories as men. All agreed on one thing, that *something should be done for the farmer.* These views were those of the agitators. One desired a sub-treasury; another wanted government warehouses and loans on grain deposited; others demanded government ownership of railways and of pretty much everything except themselves and their possessions. There was no end to schemes wild and visionary beyond belief had not my own ears heard them expounded. Unity existed only in the one thing named above. And these men were the staid and steady farmers!

I visited wage-earners. Their well-known theory is that labor produces all wealth, including that of the farmer; therefore the first duty of government and society is to protect and encourage labor, which is now oppressed and downtrodden. These claims have been so often discussed they need not be repeated here. The one discouraging feature was the tendency of so many laborers to lawlessness and anarchy. This was especially true of foreign-born workmen. I had heard of this frequently, but never felt its force until I came in personal contact with it. The more intelligent toilers discourage these tendencies and try to banish them. But they would not down. A large element in all the labor unions has unmistakable proclivities in this direction.

I learned most in private talk with single men or small groups. To gain their confidence I dressed like one of them. The bitterness of some of the men toward capitalists was appalling. Murder was in their hearts, with all the lesser crimes. I did not believe this before; I was compelled to believe it now. Agitators fermented the discontent and added fuel to the fires of hate already burning. I was sometimes almost paralyzed by the vindictive spirit manifested. I could quote utterances by the hundred, but the few words already written is a summary of the feeling revealed. I remained weeks among the various classes of laborers. Some of them are among the wisest and best citizens of the republic, an honor to themselves and their country; they are the real hope of our free institutions. The ones who make the disturbance are the ignorant, the agitators, the leaders who make money or obtain power and position by such means, and all who are restless and dissatisfied. I regret to say that these various classes number tens of thousands. With due consideration of all the stable and conservative forces of law, order, and the social compact, I am persuaded that these restless and vicious people are a menace to the well-being of society, and of a free government which opposes anarchy.

I next sought out individuals who had influence in various communities and interviewed them. Some of their prominent utterances are here grouped in a compact form.

One man said: "There is something alarming in this unrest of the people. When a single person raves or rides a hobby, it amounts to nothing; but when whole communities or bodies of men numbering thousands do the same thing, there is danger."

Another: "This turmoil will not last long. The good sense of the people is our sheet-anchor. Prosperity will silence discontent. When a few agitators are dead, or lose their grip, things will settle down to their normal quiet."

A merchant said: "The farmers and laborers demand everything. What is to become of the rest of the people?"

A farmer declared: "We have no use for middlemen and merchant princes and robbers. The sooner they are all cleaned out the better."

A laborer said to a farmer: "You want me to join you in efforts to secure high prices for your products. Why should I? High prices for you means expensive living for me. If you get a dollar a bushel for wheat, my bread will cost me twice as much as if you got but fifty cents for wheat. Your gain is my loss."

One said: "Who can divide between capital and labor? The farmer is both capitalist and laborer. His land is his capital. He tills it with his own hands. Both classes blend in him. Why should he antagonize either? The same is true of every mechanic who owns his shop and does his own work. It is the desire of every enterprising and ambitious laborer to secure capital. Why should he denounce the one who has already reached the goal for which he is striving?"

A commercial man: "Capital is conservative; it seeks stability. Agitation is all on the side of labor. It is in the ranks of labor that anarchy, socialism, and communism have their birth and are nourished. All the danger from revolution and upheaval comes from the side of labor. If the republic is ever destroyed, it will be overthrown by the agitators who corruptly use labor as the cloak to cover their aims."

A conservative farmer: "The most astonishing thing in the whole outlook is that farmers should join hands with the disorganizers. They have all to lose and nothing to gain by either political or social convulsions."

A loan agent: "Three fourths of the money loaned out on interest is owned by laboring men and women, or comes from their estates. Capitalists put their money into their own investments, and keep it under personal control. I know of no millionaire who is a money-loaner."

Many said: "Trusts and combines must go. They are the curse of the country." Others denounced banks. A general and unmeaning outcry against capital was heard on all sides. It was stigmatized as a tyrant, an oppressor, a robber. It lived and grew fat on the toil and blood of the poor. It is a blood-sucker, a murderer; and all the senseless twaddle of the demagogue.

Remarks similar to these were made by hundreds of men hundreds of miles apart, where there could be no possible collusion.

Conservative citizens everywhere discouraged all phases of this revolutionary agitation, and deprecated the array of one class against another. But pro-moters of confusion seemed to be in the majority in many places.

I presently struck a new lead. A gentleman rather energetically declared: "The worst thing that has ever struck this country is this new-fangled paternal-ism. Men who are in debt want the government to pay their debts in some way. Those out of money want the government to furnish them with funds. Those in need of transportation wish the government to carry them and their products for nothing. Every idler, vagabond, and tramp wants the government to feed, clothe, and make him rich. The farmer wants government warehouses and government loans with-out interest on his grain. He wants the government to make money so plenty that it can be gathered up as the Hebrews gathered the manna every morning. If a man is in trouble, he wants the government to come to his relief. If his soul is set on a fortune, the gov-ernment must get it for him. Every worthless, lazy, trifling pest wants the government to lift him into opulence. The wildest schemes are to be fathered by the government. In a word, the whole population are to be made kings, queens, and princes by the govern-ment. This notion is the curse of the land. It ap-peals to the baser elements of society. It holds out alluring promises to those who wish to get rich in haste without labor, to be clothed in purple and fine linen though they neither spin nor weave."

Another in the same vein: "'Looking Backward' has been the bane of this nation. It breeds a notion in the minds of thousands that somehow the government will be compelled by agitation to do for them what God, nature, and society demand they shall do for themselves. Its Utopian notions have taken root in many minds. Multitudes who never saw the book have received its teachings second-hand, and been poisoned by them. It is like the fabled basilisk: its very presence is death. Like the upas tree, it is fair to behold, but all who come within its shade are doomed. Its poison is more insidious than that of the rattlesnake, and it does not give warning of its bite until the deadly fangs have struck the fatal blow. It is the river Styx in this beloved land, and bears death upon its polluted waters."

"Why don't you destroy it, then?" was inquired.

"Kill it! How can you destroy a fog bank? You may smite it through and through with sword and javelin, and make no impression upon it. If it had any foundation or substance about it you could attack it. But who can fight a dream? Who run a-tilt against the baseless fabric of a vision? While you cannot hurt the fog, it infolds you and leads to disaster. The ship is lost in its fatal embrace. The man is bewildered by it. Sailors and men are alike powerless in its toils. So with this misleading book. It dazzles but to blind."

"That is a terrible indictment," said the other.

"I wish it was not true. I wish its *ignis-fatuus* light

could be blotted out, banished forever into the bogs that produced it."

"Surely if it is such a power there must be some method by which its evil tendencies can be counteracted."

"Give us the antidote. Its value will be untold."

I was astonished beyond measure.

CHAPTER XII.

THE experiences here recorded were not reassuring. The outlook was unpromising. The future presented to me an arena of turmoil and strife. Turn which way I would, there was no light for me. I knew Effie had all she could bear. I would not add to her distress. Better bear my own burden.

A heated political campaign was approaching. Deception and falsehood would run riot, and party spirit rule the hour. Patriotism would too often be swallowed up in partisanship, principle be sacrificed for party gain.

Labor troubles were rife. The daily press was a seething mass of foam and fury, lashed into commotion by its own unseemly strife. If party success could be achieved by unchaining the destructive forces of anarchy, there was no hesitancy in turning the key in the lock and letting these elements loose.

Magazine articles, from which something more sage and philosophical is expected, treated the profoundest questions of social economy with a flippancy scarcely worthy of the daily paper. Looking only at the surface of things, and falling in with the popular current, the most superficial reasoning was indulged in, and conclusions reached of the most erroneous character. No depth, no wisdom, no delving for fundamental principles, no probing of fallacies; only an effort to

gain attention by such methods as the demagogue
employs.

I turned away sick at heart. Was there no place of
safety? No secure retreat? No asylum of repose for
those weary of this clamor and confusion? Was there
no master-mind to point out a better way? Was the
reign of demagogues supreme? Were there none to
stand by truth and principle, "live or die, survive or
perish"? True men there were, but they were not
noisy. In the general tumult they were often swept
aside and out of sight.

As I contemplated the situation, the words of a gentleman I met in my late excursion came to mind. He
said:

"We boast of our refinement; but there is much of
the savage left in us. If there is a brutal prize-fight,
the papers are full of it; all the disgusting details are
given. It is rumored that two well-known pugilists are
to fight. If they do, all the papers will teem with particulars. These brutes will be made heroes; their movements will be reported; they will receive more attention than the wisest philosophers, statesmen, or divines;
and if the mill comes off, all the bloody rounds will be
heralded to the world with the utmost ability of repor-
torial skill. Remember my words, and see if they
come true. This goes to show that the beast is still in
the human breast. It may be as a lion chained, but it
is there. If there was no demand for this kind of
stuff, editors and publishers would not cater to the
barbaric taste. It is a sad truth that in our high civilization we are yet so largely savages!"

These strictures may have been severe; but who
will deny their truth? I was now in a humor to have
these remarks make an undue impression upon my

mind. If this roaring lion of savagery should be unchained, what dreadful scenes must ensue! Did not
the unrest on every side indicate the unfastening of
the fetters? When even the most sober classes of
men were moved to threaten violence, what would be
the results should the lower strata of humanity in our
large cities—half beast, half man—be turned loose?

I was probably morbid. I did not wish to mingle
in the strife. Where should I flee? At this juncture
the thought of the Chemist and his marvelous preparation flashed upon my mind. I had tried the com-
pound for short periods of time, and found its claims
were reliable. It had acted perfectly. I would now
venture to try it for a term of years.

How could I reconcile Effie to this? How part from
her so long? Under present conditions my presence
was almost as painful to her as my absence. So of
myself. If I retired from the world, no other mortal
should know the fact. Should I do this? The thought
came and was put aside many times. It kept returning. Finally it remained and became a purpose. I
made my arrangements. A friend was secured to manage my affairs until my return. I was to go on a journey, and be absent five years.

I must see Effie. How could I part from her? How
take leave? Could I keep my secret from her as she
questioned me and I looked into those truthful eyes?
No; in her presence I must say nothing of the long
absence. After the sweet interview I would write
such facts as I could. This program was carried out.

I lingered by her side—I could not tear myself
away. I was ready to abandon the purpose. She perceived my disquiet. What caused it? Could she not
guess? I felt the ground slipping from under me.

Concealment was not my forte. Her searching eyes were a ceaseless interrogation. I must go or tell all. I kissed and embraced her long and tenderly. Oh, the pain, the bliss of those moments! At last I broke away.

The next day I wrote to Effie, informing her of my resolution to go away, as I feared I should break down in a personal interview. I would be out of the reach of postal facilities, so that I could not write. This would be the last communication for possibly five years, the time she had fixed for us to wait. Whether she heard from me or not, she might rest assured that I should never forget her for a moment, and if alive at the end of the period named I should return and claim her as my own. She would now understand why I was so unlike myself yesterday, and took such a lingering and ardent farewell. Full explanations when I should see her.

This was the hard part of my undertaking. I placed the letter in Mr. Solon's box at the post-office, and then hastened to the room in the rock, lest even now my courage should fail.

After preparations for the final act were completed, I sat on the side of the couch and mused. Was not this foolish and cowardly? Why not manfully face whatever should come? Why desert Effie? This was the sore spot. I shrank and quivered. It was not yet too late. Stop now. I had the bottle in my hand. I set it down, arose, and paced the floor. Should I proceed? I was almost ready to say no. Then came the thought: "You have made all the arrangements. It will be silly to back out. What will the friend in charge of your business think? How can you explain matters to Effie? What will she think of your vacillation? You cannot now honorably retreat."

I hesitated no longer. Resuming my place on the side of the bed, I took up the bottle, poured out the required amount, and swallowed it. As I returned the bottle to its place the light shone fairly upon it, and I saw it was thirty-five years instead of five. In my haste I had taken up the wrong bottle!

What should I do? What would Effie think? She must conclude I had deserted her! The thought was worse than death. I would rush away and tell her all before the potion took effect. Alas, this was impossible! Already I was in its grasp. I felt its potency in every fiber. I had barely time to compose myself and extinguish the light, when, with the words on my lips, "Oh, Effie, Effie! my angel Effie! God bless and keep thee!" I sank away into unconscious forgetfulness.

CHAPTER XIII

My next conscious knowledge was a sensation somewhat resembling the prickling feeling which accompanies the return to a normal condition of an arm or a limb that has been asleep. There was no tingling or twitching, and no unpleasant sensations. It was as if something simultaneously let go its hold upon every part and fiber of the physical system, not suddenly in a jerk, but quietly and gradually. It required from one to two minutes for this mysterious agent to pass entirely away. As soon as it was gone I was fully awake. Memory sat upon its throne as consciousness returned. I was myself. It seemed to me but a few hours since I had gone to sleep. My first thought was of Effie, as my last had been.

"Thank God, she will suffer nothing from my short absence!" I mentally exclaimed. "Happily for us, the Chemist was mistaken; the potency of his preparation was a mistake or a sham."

And for this I felt unspeakably thankful. Reaching out my hand, I found the matches and struck a light. The air in the room was deliciously cool and inspiring. The automatic ventilation was perfect. It admitted air freely, while it excluded water, insects, and all unpleasant extraneous substances.

I quickly dressed. Up to this time I had been completely absorbed in myself and the immediate surroundings. Now my attention was attracted by a low

rumbling sound, conjoined with a slight trembling or
tremor of the ground. It was much like the passing of
a heavy train of cars on a railway. As there was no
railroad near, what could this strange sound mean? I
had never heard an army on the march, but it occurred
to me these sounds were such as an army would make;
but there could be no army in that vicinity.

I looked at my watch. It was a complete one, with
chronometer attachment. It had stopped at 10.27 A.M.,
April 10, 1892. I had retired April 9th, so the watch
had run until next morning. As I had been asleep
but a few hours, this must be the 10th, or at most the
11th. I would go into the city for dinner.

The first thing that caught my eye on emerging into
the open air was my own house, which was in plain
view. It looked old and weatherbeaten. Strange!
There must have been a fearful storm the past night.
But no evidence of a recent storm existed. I walked
beyond the range of the rocky hill and looked at the
city. What magic was this? The city had grown away
from recognition since yesterday—not a familiar land-
mark in sight! Was it enchantment? Alas, were my
eyes ruined? Had the Chemist deceived me, or was he
deceived himself? Must I go through life with distorted vision?

As I gazed in bewilderment upon the scene, there
arose one after another what had the appearance of
chariots. They floated off gracefully upon the air.
This was confirmation of the derangement of sight. I
well knew no such things as these had a real existence.
Each chariot had one, two, or four occupants, men,
women, and children. I rubbed my eyes. It did no
good. The sounds I had heard were dying away in the
distance. All in the chariots were going in the direction whence the sounds were receding. I turned to

look, but the hill cut off my view. These delusive sounds and sights clearly proved that my eyes and ears were sadly deranged. Was I a hopeless wreck?

I pinched myself to ascertain if feeling was normal. It was. Good! A flower was near. I plucked and smelled it. The aroma was natural. Better! I was half right so far. Now for taste, to see whether the majority of senses were right or wrong. I neared what to my disordered vision was the new portion of the city. I stepped with care, lest some trap might ensnare my feet or the illusion vanish. The pavement was solid. The fence was a firm fixture. The houses and streets were substantial. The yards in front of the nice houses were adorned with flowers and other evidences of taste. No need to pick my way so daintily. No fear of catastrophe! What wonder was this? Where were the fabulous stories of the Arabian Nights?

Presently a newsboy came along on the other side of the street, crying out: "Here's your evening paper! All about the great battle!"

The boy and his cry were natural. But what about a battle? I called to him: "Here, boy, let me have a paper." He ran over briskly. I received a copy and opened it—*The Evening Bulletin*. Then my eye caught the date line—"April 9, 1927." I feared my eyes were permanently injured. Glancing at the head lines, I read in bold type:

"GREATEST BATTLE OF THE WAR NOW IN PROGRESS!
IMMENSE SLAUGHTER ON BOTH SIDES!
VICTORY DOUBTFUL!
REINFORCEMENTS HURRYING FORWARD!
VICTORY OR DEATH THE MOTTO OF EACH ARMY!"

These stunning sentences fairly took my breath. Where was I? Had I been transported to some foreign

land? Or was this an extension of my hallucination?
In the midst of mental chaos I saw another newsboy
approaching, screaming, "*The Evening Telegram!* Latest
news from the battle-field!"

I had enough of the battle until I knew more of the
facts. Just then another chariot went up. I inquired
of the boy what those vehicles were flying in the air.
He looked at me with a peculiar facial expression, and
said:

"You don't fool me, mister!"

"I am not trying to fool you. I am a stranger here,
and do not understand the half of what I see."

He gave me a searching gaze, and seeing I was in
earnest, replied:

"You must be a stranger, and a greeny, too, not to
know what them things is. They is air-bugs."

"Air-bugs?"

"Yas; that's what we boys calls 'em. The big folks
calls 'em chariots and air-ships, and such hifalutin
names. But air-bugs is good 'nuff for us boys."

"What are they like, and how are they made?" I
asked.

"Oh, I can't 'splain them matters. Just go to old
Mr. Solon's shops, and they'll tell you all about 'em.
They makes the things there."

Then he ran away, crying the *Telegram.*

Mr. Solon's name recalled my bewildered senses in a
measure. I called after the boy to show me the direction to the shops.

"Five blocks away, right over there," he said, pointing in the direction I supposed the works to be situated,
if all this was not a dream. Pressing forward, I soon
saw a sign in large gilt letters:

"THE SOLON MACHINE-WORKS."

As I started for the office, my eye caught this legend on a building beyond:

"Established 1870. Rebuilt 1892. Enlarged 1912."

What did that mean? Were my eyes still deceiving me? I entered the office. A young man lifted his eyes from the ledger and gave me a pleasant recognition, then resumed his labor. As soon as opportunity offered I inquired for Mr. Solon. The man appeared to be somewhat surprised at the question, but courteously answered:

"Mr. Solon does not stay at the works now, and only visits them occasionally. He is quite feeble, and has practically retired from the active supervision of the plant. Perhaps I can serve you in his stead."

"Mr. Solon is a very dear friend. I should much like to see him. But you can enlighten me on one point. If my eyes do not deceive, I see what appear to be flying chariots in the air. I am told you manufacture them. What are they?"

He eyed me as though he doubted my sanity, and then said:

"Do you mean the chariots?"

"I presume so. Those things above the city. Yonder are some of them," pointing where they were.

"Is it possible you do not know what those are? We name ours, air-chariots and air-ships, according to the style of construction. Surely you must be familiar with things that are so common!"

I was greatly confused, and felt the blood of shame rise to my face and brow as I replied:

"I assure you I never saw or heard of them until this day. It may appear strange and inexplicable to you that I am so ignorant of what seems to be uni-

versally known.   Please regard me as a stranger just
returned after a long absence—a lineal descendant of
old Rip Van Winkle, if you will—and instruct me as
you would a child."

For a moment he appeared to doubt my sanity. Seeing I was at least harmless, he inquired what I particularly desired to know.   I said :

" All there is to learn.   To me these chariots are a
most wonderful invention."

" The first one was patented some fifteen years since.
They at once became popular.   The early ones made
were rather crude; since they have been greatly improved.   They are made of aluminum, the lightest and
toughest of all metals, and the only material suitable
for the purpose.   The propelling power is electricity
combined with magnetism.   I cannot explain the process intelligently, as that is not in my line.   Come and
see one of the chariots.   You will thereby get a better
idea of its construction."

We went into the shop devoted to their building and
examined one just completed; then followed the workmen, each having his special part to make, and witnessed
the process of putting together.   It was a revelation to
me.   When finished, the costly ones were remarkably
handsome.

There was a dynamo and a battery.   A circuit was
formed, along which the electricity operated by manipu-
lations I did not understand.   This was the motive
power.   I did not wish to further expose my ignorance
by making inquiries.   Every important piece of the
structure was hollow, light, and airy.   I could lift a
chariot from the ground capable of holding two persons.
The ships were the same except in shape.   When in motion they resembled a miniature vessel under full sail.

"Is it a usual thing for so many of these vehicles to be in the air at one time as I see to-day?" I asked.

"No. It is only on extraordinary occasions that so many go up at a time. These people are watching the army that has just passed through the city on its way to the front."

I was desirous to learn something about the war and the battle, but shrank from making manifest my great ignorance. If I could only get to Mr. Solon he would instruct me without wounding my sensitiveness. I inquired how far it was to his residence. He said about six blocks, and that he would accompany me there. Arranging his books, he came out, and we found a chariot ready in response to directions he had given when in the shop. We stepped in. My companion took hold of the polished handle to a lever, moved it forward a little, and held it steady. There was a slight noise, then motion. Up we arose and moved off. At first our course was along the street between the houses. Soon we ascended above the tops of the buildings and shaped our course at pleasure. The action was easy, graceful, and pleasant. In a few minutes we descended and halted before a fine mansion. My guide said:

"This is Mr. Solon's residence. I ought to tell you that they receive few visitors. A strange thing has happened to them. Their only daughter, a most estimable and lovely young lady, is either dead or in a trance, and has been so for many years. Nearly everybody thinks she is dead and ought to be buried. As there are no signs of decay and her appearance is natural, her parents refuse to permit or even think of this. I mention this fact to prepare you for any peculiarities that may attend your reception. Mr. Solon is a perfect gentleman, and will receive and treat you as such."

What emotions were awakened in my bosom by this recital! What a flood of feeling overwhelmed me! Effie possibly dead! Had my protracted absence killed her? Fortunately, no time was given for long agitation. While my heart was beating tumultuously the young man pressed a button in the door-check and the musical notes of a sweet-toned bell sounded within. To the servant who answered the summons my friend said:

"Here is a gentleman who wishes to see Mr. Solon. An acquaintance, I believe," looking inquiringly at me. I assented. I had forgotten to bring my card with me. The servant soon returned and invited me in.

As I entered the reception-room an aged gentleman came forward to receive me. "What name?" he inquired. At that moment the light fell full upon my face, and he exclaimed:

"James North, as I live! And we have mourned you as dead these many years!"

"Yes, it is I," I replied.

"You do not look a day older than you did thirty-five years ago, when you so suddenly and mysteriously disappeared. Where have you been all these years?"

There was a shade of reproach in these last words which cut to the heart. I responded:

"My story is a strange one—past belief in all respects. I scarcely know whether I am in the body or out of it—whether I and the things about me are a reality or a dream. I come to you for help. You look old, and speak of many years. It seems to me but a day since we parted. Tell me, is it so long? Have I really been absent thirty-five years?"

"You certainly have. It was 1892 when you left: it is now 1927, and about the same time of the year."

"Then it is no fantasy! The Chemist was right. I have been sleeping these thirty-five years—at least, have been unconscious all that time!"

This was said more to myself than to Mr. Solon. He caught at the words and demanded with what to me seemed needless emphasis:

"What is that you say about the Chemist and a long sleep? Speak! It may be life or death to Effie! Tell me quickly!" And he grasped my arm. I had never seen him so moved. The mention of Effie's name recalled what the young man had said. I was as greatly agitated as her father.

In as few words as possible I told my strange and weird experience. At its conclusion Mr. Solon ejaculated:

"Thank God! I am now sure Effie is not dead but asleep."

"What is it about Effie?" I almost demanded. I was too profoundly affected to stand on ceremony. He answered:

"The most wonderful thing in the world! Let me commence at the beginning. You remember the tragic event which terminated the life of the Chemist. While he lay upon his dying bed Effie's kindness to him won his heart. Her presence acted as a solace. Perhaps it awakened cherished memories of other days. A little time before his death he took from his pocket three small bottles filled with a transparent liquid, and gave them to her, saying:

"'These will be of great service to you. This liquid will produce quiet and restful sleep when all other means fail. One drop from this bottle will induce twelve hours of refreshing slumber, no matter how greatly the nervous system may be disturbed, or how

persistent the insomnia.' Of another bottle he said,
'This will produce days and weeks of sleep.' Of the
third he said, 'This will cause years of insensible quiet.
You will find directions for using on each bottle.'

"Before he could say more a paroxysm of pain seized
him. He never recovered to resume the subject.

"Effie tried the weakest preparation to secure rest
with perfect success. The others she had no occasion
to test. She keenly felt your absence and silence, notwithstanding you had prepared her for these. She
never doubted you for a moment. Her faith in you
was implicit. She did not despond. She strove to be
cheerful and generally succeeded. While she remained
my bookkeeper the occupation of mind and thought
acted as an antidote to depression. Her services were
of great value to me, for a time almost indispensable.
My business prospered beyond any former period. At
the end of four years I no longer needed her, and was
glad to relieve her from the labor she had so cheerfully
given. When released from care and responsibility
her mind was free to think of herself. Then she realized more sensibly your absence. She said little. She
was mostly bright and cheerful. But it required an
effort; it was not the spontaneous outgoing of a joyful
spirit. The glad songs that made melody in the house
became less frequent; the elastic step lost its buoy-
ancy; the bright and sunny smile only occasionally
lighted her face; the eyes lost some of the soul-
light from their depths; the delicate peach-bloom
was driven from the cheeks by the pale lily. These
changes were so gradual only a parent's love would
detect them.

"We became anxious, her mother especially. She
was never moody or morose, only pensive. When she

saw our uneasiness, she rallied and tried to be her old self. Even this cost her an effort. Our sweet, dear daughter of other days seemed lost to us. How we longed to hear from you, if only a word to tell us all was well! But a silence like the pall of death hung over your fate. There was no ground of assurance. Only hope remained. And on what a slender thread that hung! If alive, you certainly would send some message during all these years. It was a terrible strain! Effie's faith in you never wavered, but of your fate she could but be in doubt. 'Hope deferred maketh the heart sick.' As the five years' limit drew on she grew more anxious. In spite of the striving for self-composure she unconsciously became restless. The effort to hide her feelings tended to increase the unrest. One day her mother found her weeping over your farewell letter. At first she endeavored to hide her emotion, but finally broke down and sobbed on her mother's bosom, saying, 'Oh, if I only knew that James is alive! I know he will come back if he lives. But this suspense is terrible! I do not know how long I shall be able to bear the strain!'

"That evening she took some of the quieting remedy. By some mistake she got hold of the wrong bottle, and feeling more than usually depressed she poured out double the prescribed quantity and swallowed it. Something in the taste or action of the medicine arrested her attention. Looking closely at the bottle, the label and directions upon which had become dimmed, she said to her mother, who stood by:

"'O mother, I have taken from the wrong bottle! It is greatly stronger than the other. I see it is marked "Thirty"! What if it should be thirty days! If it should be thirty years do not let me be buried. They may say I am dead, but I shall not be. If anything is wrong, promise me that I shall not be put in the grave until decay tells that I am certainly dead.'

"'Rest assured, dear, you shall not be buried so long as there is a hope that life remains, if it is thirty or fifty years.'

"'Thank you,' she said, holding her mother's hand. 'I feel wondrously strange! Something seems to take hold of me all over. I am completely in its power. It is gentle and soothing, mysterious——'

"The words died on her lips, and in a moment she was unconscious. She remains so to this hour. We have been in tribulation; but your experience gives me hope. It lifts a burden from my mind."

I had listened with breathless interest. My soul was on the rack. The intensity of feeling was almost unendurably painful. I paced the floor in distress, bitterly reproaching myself for causing Effie such suffering. Was she dead or only asleep? The intensity of feeling caused me to tremble with fear even in the face of my own experience. A feeling of dread came over me. Had I murdered the one being who could make my life worth the living? The thought was too terrible. I could not endure it. As soon as the narrative was ended, I inquired:

"Where is Effie now? Can I see her?"

"I will call her mother. She can answer you better than I."

In response to the call Mrs. Solon entered the room. She was startled to find me there. In the words of her husband, she said:

"Not a day older! How impossible it seems! Yes, you may come with me and see Effie."

I followed her up to Effie's room. No pen can describe my emotions. My soul was moved to its utmost depths. Had Effie passed beyond the reach of mortal fear or hope? Was I left stricken, smitten, alone in the world? Or was there life and hope and bliss for me?

CHAPTER XIV.

I was born on the 9th day of April, 1865, the day that General Lee surrendered the army of Northern Virginia to General Grant, and thus ended the cruel War of the Rebellion. I had placed the destiny of my life at the disposal of Effie Solon on the 9th of April, 1891, and was accepted by her to my unspeakable happiness. It was on the 9th day of April, 1892, that I retired from the world and commenced the long sleep.

And now, after the most remarkable experience that ever befell the lot of mortal, I was about to meet that loved one again, after the separation of an ordinary lifetime, under circumstances so strange and unnatural as to be past belief, but of such thrilling interest as to absorb all the faculties of soul and body.

I had not yet ascertained the exact length of time Effie had been unconscious; neither had I taken account myself of the present date. While I had seen it on the evening paper, and possibly might have heard it mentioned, I was so confused and confounded then that it made no lasting impression upon me. Now I stood on the brink of destiny, with the quivering balances of fate poised in trembling doubt before me. Life or death. Shall I step into the light of one or plunge into the darkness of the other?

Mrs. Solon preceded me to the bedside. There lay the idol of my heart, still and motionless as if already coffined for the grave. So pale and silent! The first thought was of death. It smote me as a blow from some unseen power. A closer scrutiny of the matchless features revealed them apparently unchanged in every respect, save the pallor of which her father had spoken.

"How natural!" I exclaimed.

"Exactly as she looked when she closed her eyes thirty years ago," said her mother.

"So long as that? Do you remember the exact date?"

"I do. It was April 9, 1897, in the evening."

"Is not this April 9th—to-day, I mean?"

"I believe it is. I had not thought of it before."

"What time in the evening did that occur?" I asked.

"Being depressed and weary, she had prepared to retire for the night a little earlier than usual, I think."

"It will be thirty years, then, in a short time, when she ought to awake, if nothing is wrong."

"Do you think she will come to life?"

"In the light of my experience, yes."

"It seems impossible."

"Did not the ancient Egyptians embalm the bodies of their dead so as to preserve them for thousands of years? If a dead body can be kept for centuries, cannot a body which retains all the life-forces be preserved for thirty years? The life principle ought to keep it from decay so long as it remains, even if in a dormant state."

"Looking at it in that light, it does seem possible. I have wavered between hope and fear all these years."

"The dread suspense will soon be over. If she is not dead, life will manifest itself this night, unless there has been some mistake or miscalculation. If she does not awaken, hope is gone. Her appearance is favorable. She resembles one asleep, not one deceased. Only the unbreathing inaction and the white face point to dissolution. There are no signs of decomposition."

"That is what has kept me from utter despair."

We lapsed into silence. I wondered why or how Effie had selected my birthday for this sleep. As she had only intended to be at rest for a few hours, this must have been a mere coincidence without design. I was not certain she knew that April 9th was my natal day. Had He, without whom not a sparrow falleth, shaped these events?

The evening shadows had now gathered; the lights had been turned on. At most, two hours of waiting suspense! I craved the privilege of holding the position by the bedside nearest my beloved. This privilege naturally belonged to her parents; but they were so changed by age, Effie might not recognize them. I was the same. My request was readily granted. Mr. Solon remained below; the mother and I were sole watchers in that mysterious presence. At first we conversed in subdued tones. The strain upon nerve, brain, and heart was too great. Voices were hushed. Silence reigned. The stillness became intense. Though we breathed lightly, this seemed to fill the room with sound. I could hear my own heart-beats; I fancied I heard those of my companion.

The hands of the clock pointed to nine. The crisis was at hand! Effie would soon revive or—— I would not put the alternative. I could not endure the thought. The profound quiet without and within was alike. All nature appeared to be in sympathy with us in this hour of supreme trial.

Nine o'clock! I arose and stood in breathless expectancy where the eyes of the sleeper would open upon me first of all. No sign of life! The ticking of the clock marked the seconds. They seemed to be hours; ages were compressed into minutes. How long must this agony last? Half-past nine! No change. Could soul and body endure this tension without snapping asunder the chords of life? Nine forty-five! Death still reigned supreme. A pressure gathered about my heart; I feared for a moment it would stop its pulsations.

Then I suddenly remembered Mr. Solon had said that Effie poured out a double dose when she took the potion. Horrible thought! Would she sleep thirty years more? The suggestion sent a chill through me like ice. I mentioned my fears to Mrs. Solon. She was startled. Could it be possible? I paced the room with clasped hands and aching brain. Must I wait thirty years longer? It could not be! O God, spare me this!

One minute to ten! Something drew me to the bedside. I stood there with eyes riveted on the face of the lovely sleeper. Oh, if life would only return! As I gazed with bended head I fancied there was a quiver of the eyelids. Was it more than fancy? A moment longer and there were slight twitchings on face and brow. Another second and the eyes opened, then closed. No recognition. It seemed an eon, but was only a moment. The eyes opened again. A twilight pause. Then full intelligence shone in eye and face. I was bending low over her. One word she uttered:

"James!"

"O Effie, Effie!" was my enraptured response. Then with an irresistible impulse I rained kisses on brow and face and lips, and pressed my cheek to hers.

Mrs. Solon gave a faint scream, which brought Mr. Solon upon the scene. The joy of that hour was too sacred for other eyes to see or ears to hear.

Effie's first words of observing composure were:

"How old father and mother look! I surely have been asleep but a few hours, yet they have the appearance of great age."

Her experience was such an exact counterpart of my own it need not be repeated.

Presently our long fast was broken by partaking of an appropriate repast. Mr. and Mrs. Solon retired.

Effie and I, having had sleep enough to last us at least another twenty-four hours, spent the night in converse so full of all that was exciting and endearing that morning came all too quickly for our joy. It was a bright spot in memory. She accepted the explanation of my retirement. If she thought the act unreasonable or unjustifiable, she did not say so. We were too happy for anything but thanksgiving and love.

CHAPTER XV.

EFFIE and I were the lions of the day after the story of our long sleep became known. Scientists, philosophers, ministers—all classes desired to see us, to talk with and about us. The ubiquitous reporters were greedy to be first to get the facts. The notoriety was exceedingly unpleasant and annoying, but had to be endured. Persons came hundreds of miles to see us. Aside from a knowledge of the Chemist's wonderful discovery, they learned nothing to pay for their trouble.

I was deeply anxious to learn the facts concerning the war and other things which had startled me since my return to life. I knew I could rely upon Mr. Solon's ripe experience, calm judgment, and wide information, and lost no time in seeking from him the desired knowledge.

The great battle near Chicago was undecided. A cessation of fighting had taken place by agreement of both armies, each side waiting for reinforcements which were being pushed forward. The dead also had to be buried and the wounded cared for. I inquired:

"What is all this fighting about? How long has the war been in progress?"

"Your two questions will require two answers," said Mr. Solon. "What the fighting is about the wisest philosopher may not be able to tell. The causes which have led up to this sad and deplorable event may be named. You remember the agitation of the labor-and-capital subject years ago. As one result of it my property was burned down. That was a mere incident, however. There were hundreds of others, some like it, others different, but all having the same common origin.

"The laboring classes had real grievances which were not properly recognized and redressed, largely because they were too impatient to await the remedy. At times they were wild and unreasonable in their demands. Capitalists were made to feel that the working people were their enemies, and hence that they must be on the alert to defend themselves. You remember the incipient stages of this antagonism. It was marked on one side by strikes, on the other by lockouts, etc. I need not rehearse the history. Instead of bridging the chasm between the employer and the employed when it was small and could easily have been done by proper and mutual concessions, the antagonism was permitted to grow and increase until it became a wide and deep gulf, which it now appears impossible to bridge over or pass.

"For years it was thought the great conservative population, termed the middle classes, composed largely of farmers, well-to-do mechanics, and successful laboring men, would hold society to its moorings, and prevent any widespread violence. But this stay has been swept away.

"The farmers, who were not succeeding as well as they thought they ought to succeed, became dissatisfied, and formed organizations of their own, secret and oath-bound in character. The object at first was to assist and benefit themselves as a class. Afterward these became political bodies, planning in secret for the destruction of those whom they regarded as in any manner opposed to them. Their former staid characteristics appeared to leave them as soon as they became agitators. Action and reaction being equal, they swung away from their former stability to the opposite extreme, and became the most violent and extreme of the discontented population. No other class of people proposed and advocated more radical, extreme, and visionary schemes. Nor was any other class more selfish in its demands. Their aims were all for their own benefit, regardless of the interests and rights of others. High prices for their products, no matter what the cost to consumers, nor how great the hardships imposed upon the laboring poor. This, however, was characteristic of all other classes of agitators and producers.

"For a time there was an effort made to unite all the laboring elements in one combination. But the common laborer, who depended alone upon his day's wages for a living, soon learned that he was always a buyer and never a seller of the products of labor. Hence, if he aided the farmer to obtain high prices for his grain and produce, he thereby increased the cost of his own living. He was between two fires, the manufacturer on one side, the farmer, including stockraiser, on the other. If he aided either one of these to advance prices, he taxed himself to pay the increase. Why should he do this? The manufacturer told him that competition gave him the lowest possible prices for his goods and wares; that his true policy was to increase and strengthen manufactories, for by so doing he not only cheapened the prices of the articles he consumed, but at the same time multiplied the number of employees and the certainty of finding constant employment.

This looked reasonable. But some farmers and others came along and told him to open competition to the world, thereby widening the field of operations and gaining new markets. Let the world, and not simply the United States, be the theater of action. The others said: 'If you do this you compel our laborers to compete with the almost pauper labor of the Old World. You cannot control their markets or have any voice in their domestic or national policy. You simply place yourselves at the mercy of those who have no care for you, and over whom you have no control. You had better keep your interests confined to your own country, over whose government and policy you can exercise supervision, and not give away your birthright for a mess of pottage, and the pottage become sour before you eat it.' The other side replied: 'Such a view is narrow and is only devised in the interest of the few at the expense of the many.' So the contention proceeded. It already existed in your day, and only became warmer and more bitter with the increasing heat.

"The laboring classes became bewildered and divided. There must always be a buyer for everything sold. As there are more purchasers than producers, it looked as though the buyers and the sellers would be the natural antagonists. This would have placed all producers, manufacturers, farmers, miners, etc., on one side, and all strict consumers or wage-earners only, on the other side. This project was started. But it fell to pieces for the reason that many producers were also consumers, and every consumer a producer. The problem was too intricate for solution. Even the day-laborer was a necessary adjunct to production, while he was a constant consumer. It was found impossible to untangle the inter-involved skein. Society is too much a unit for any clear-cut division of its parts.

"One of the worst features of the whole controversy was that arising from the fraudulent methods devised by capitalists to increase their wealth at the expense of the masses. Not satisfied with the slow and steady processes of lawful and legitimate accumulations, they resorted to watering stocks, combining in trusts, syndicates, and forcing markets, and fixing prices. They were 'in haste to be rich,' and so fell into snares. The stocks of railways and other corporations were watered from two to ten times their real value. The excess went into the coffers of the rich manipulators. The people were taxed to pay the interest and dividends on the fraudulent increase of stock. Railroad fares and freight rates must be enhanced to meet this manifold multiplication of fictitious capital. Thus all the produce of the country was compelled to pay tribute to the railroad princes. Those who reaped the benefits of this class of transactions did not put their own money into the investments, but sold the added stock to other parties, who were denominated 'innocent purchasers,' or holders of the same, who must be protected in their rights, and were so protected by the courts.

"You can readily see what a vast field for fraud was here opened. Practically there was no limit to its dimensions. Its boundaries embraced nearly everything. The people rightfully complained of the burdens of taxation thus illegitimately placed upon them by these gigantic schemes of capital fraudulently used. It was a ground of complaint against which there was no defense. It was practical robbery on one side, and being robbed on the other.

"I give it as my opinion, whether it is good or worth-

less, that if Congress and the States had passed acts
outlawing all watered stocks, and giving the holders,
if they really were 'innocent purchasers' of the same,
the right to trace up the matter and get their money
wherever it could be found, the same as stolen goods
are restored to the owner when traced to any hands,
and so compelled the millionaires to disgorge their ill-
gotten gains, such action would have largely tended to
quiet the discontent, allay the agitation, and prevented
the present deplorable condition of affairs.

"But this was not done. The demagogue's cry,
'The rich are growing richer and the poor poorer,'
gained force and plausibility by these vast accumulations of wealth through illegal means. Capital finally
became so potent that it was said to 'control legislation
and own the courts.' At first this was a mere play upon
words. Ultimately it became apparently a truth of
history. The masses became more and more indignant.
Agitators were in the zenith of their glory. No one
could foretell the future.

"This was the development on the side of capital.
I mean of illegitimate capital; for that which was
actually employed, putting down dollar for dollar for
all it occupied and sought returns, was conservative
and dreaded agitation and anarchy. The great mistake
of the laboring classes was in not properly discriminat-
ing between true capital, their real and best friend,
and the false capital that defrauded and oppressed
them.

"On the side of labor the conflicting elements for
a time seemed to preclude the possibility of united
effort. The cry against capital was too ill defined to be
successfully maintained. 'Who is a capitalist?' was
asked, with an assurance that no conclusive answer

could be given. The man with a million dollars was
envied by him who had but a hundred thousand; the
latter by him who had but ten thousand; and he by
the one with a single thousand; while the last was envied by him who had a hundred, and so on till the one
who had a single dollar was envied by him who had
nothing. Where did capital begin or end? How could
elements thus at variance be merged into one common
cause? Where could the line of division be drawn?

"I think no one has or can solve this problem. The
cry of 'capital,' 'monopoly,' 'tyranny,' 'robbery,' 'oppression,' and the like, were all made to play a part.
But the real secret of the success of the disorganizing
movement is to be found in the desire, growing
stronger and wider every year, *to get something for
nothing.* That desire used to manifest itself in the
purchase of lottery tickets, in the various gambling
devices, in getting goods at less than cost or than
their true value, in catching at every chance adver-
tised, whether by responsible persons or otherwise, to
get something valuable without paying an equivalent
for it. Rascals and swindlers took advantage of this
characteristic of human nature, and pandered to it
by advertising schemes to secure plunder. Merchants
catered to it by proclaiming forced sales, bankrupt
stocks, foreclosure sales, and any and all other devices
which could be invented to secure customers. I need
not linger to recount all these phases of public taste
and desire. I do not pretend to be philosopher enough
to analyze all the elements which have contributed
their parts to form the great combination that is now
in arms. I think all I have named can be counted on
as contributing to the sum total.

"This one thing I may say, that finally the discordant elements grew stronger and more numerous. The attraction of numbers became a force. Numbers gave influence. Demagogues were drawn to the source and center of power. Better men were also influenced by different motives to join the procession. Weight of numbers and incessant activity gave momentum to each movement. One of the mysteries connected with this whole business, which I have observed from its inception to the present hour, is this: that while the universal cry of all the agitators was for 'reform,' yet there was not an unsuccessful rascal in the whole country that did not join in the cry. More remarkable and inexplicable is this other fact, that these rascals became leaders in reform movements, and the loudest to denounce those who had been more successful in life, whether these latter were honest or dishonest; for, as I have previously said, many of the wealthiest of men were really the greatest rascals in the land; and but for them and their fraudulent methods and oppressive acts, there never could have existed the present condition of affairs. Now it looks very much as if all the accumulated wealth of the nation would be swept away, and the rich robbers become the victims of popular frenzy. The end no one can see, but the outlook is gloomy and unpromising."

"How are matters in Europe?" I asked.

"Ah, you have been out of the world so long. I had forgotten that fact for the moment. This upheaval began in the Old World. There were real grounds for the uprising there. The people, having been held as little better than serfs from time out of mind, had the right to assert their manhood, demand its recognition, and some opportunities to make life worth the living. The land there, as you know, was nearly all held by nobles, whose estates were entailed and could not be alienated or divided among the heirs. The people had no fair chance. Only the most resolute and fortunate could succeed. It was not so in this country. The laborer of yesterday was the millionaire of to-day. The millionaire of this generation or his children became the laborer or laborers of the next. The wheel of fortune made changes with every revolution The agitators from the Old World placed the capitalists of America on the same footing as the hereditary lords, dukes, princes, etc., and denounced them as roundly. These foreign agitators were the originators and fomenters of the discontent and disorder here. Others, catching up their ideas and theories, aided them. But I am digressing.

"Europe is revolutionized. It is almost a vast and bloody desolation. London and Paris are in ashes. St. Petersburg, Berlin, Vienna, and other cities are heaps of ruins. Monarchy is dead. Alas, that anarchy was not buried with the thrones of kings and despots! Nobilities are blotted out. The people are in power; but they are not using their power wisely. In every nation it has been too nearly a repetition of the French revolution of 1793; in some respects, worse; more property has been destroyed. Discord, and social and political chaos, prevailed almost everywhere for a time. Good order is not yet restored. England and Germany appear to be faring better than the other countries. Russia has been little better than a wide field of murder, rapine, brutality, and cruelty. She became a ghastly charnel-house, and is not yet greatly improved. Italy much the same."

"And what is the real situation at home?" I queried. "How could war be inaugurated on our soil? What were the authorities about, and what are they doing now?"

"You are quite an interrogation point; but I will try to answer your questions in a body. The leaders of the great political parties coquetted with the agitators. Especially was this the case where one party was strong and the other weak. The latter usually sought an alliance whereby to secure the spoils of office, and readily coalesced with anything to gain this end. The spoils system as abused was at the bottom of nearly all our political evils. This action of the political leaders gave the demagogues an importance and influence they otherwise never could have attained. Party ties were broken, or so loosened as to retain but little hold upon the voter. The cohesive force of political organizations was shattered. Under some circumstances this might not have been an evil, possibly a blessing; but with the disintegrating elements permeating society and politics, the tendency was toward anarchy, and could scarcely lead in any other direction. The antagonism was between stability and revolution. Reform, because of its use as a term to cover all kinds of corruption and venality, became a by-word, a mockery. Still it was employed to delude the unthinking and discontented. The rogues of all parties who desired office, and could obtain nothing on their merits, resorted to shams under the name of reform to win their way. The unfortunate, the discontented, the lazy and indolent, and all who desired to get something for nothing, were attracted by the plausible theories of deceivers, and flocked to their standard. All who claimed that the 'world owed them a living,' whether they earned it or not, became 'reformers.' Thus it transpired that the disaffected, the disappointed, soured, and morose elements of society, no matter from what cause, drifted into the ranks of those who made great pretensions and promises, and predicted a political millennium when they came into power. Finally these carried a few States. The measures they advocated and the laws they enacted were not calculated to increase confidence in their methods or themselves. But those with sores of real or imaginary grievances still rallied under the banner of large pretensions, however barren of fruit.

"In the last presidential campaign, that of 1924, they elected their President and a majority of the Lower House of Congress, the Senate having a majority the other way. They tried to pass Utopian and anarchical laws, which the Senate defeated. Finding the Senate was a barrier to all their visionary schemes, they raised the cry 'To arms!' and so the war commenced."

"Why did the President not stop hostilities at the outset?" I asked in amazement.

"I am not certain that he could have done so had he been the right man in the right place. I think, however, if a Jackson or a Grant had been at the head of the government, he would have placed an iron hand on the hostiles, and quelled the movement at the start. But the President is a repetition of Mr. Buchanan at the opening of the Rebellion. He deplores the condition of affairs, yet has not the nerve to lay hold of his power and wield it to put an end to the strife. He has nearly two years yet to rule, or not rule, and by that time the whole country will be desolated."

"You have a dismal view of the future," I said.

"I can have no other. The forces are nearly equal. The radicals would be at a disadvantage in military leadership but for the fact that leaders from the Old World have come over to aid them. They have experience. Indeed, but for them I doubt very much whether there would have been any fighting at this time, if ever, in this country. But these foreigners are here, and give glowing accounts of the wonderful things which have been done in Europe, and urge the disaffected ones to take up arms and maintain their rights and their cause. So the war is upon us."

"Will it be bloody?"

"How can it be otherwise? All civil wars are bloody, and the most dreadful that ever cursed mankind. When brother is arrayed against brother, and a 'man's foes are those of his own household,' then, truly, is the bitterness of war."

"Is there no hope for peace?"

"I see none."

"How is it at the South?"

"The same as here. There has been a complete revolution there since your day. Immigration set in that way. The new South outnumbered the old. The negroes have been partially scattered. Those that remain are adjusted to the new order of things, so that the old trouble has nearly disappeared, and things run smoothly. The colored people are divided in the present struggle much as are the whites. I think more of them are for conservative measures than for radical action. The race has greatly improved in intelligence and refinement."

"Have the implements of war greatly improved since my acquaintance with them?"

"Yes; so much so that battles are simply scenes of carnage. There is no chance for one general to take advantage of another now as formerly, because of the chariots. Each army is supplied with these, and there are as many of them up in the air overlooking the field of operations as are necessary to observe each and every movement. Each chariot is supplied with a telephone connecting with headquarters, and every maneuver of the enemy is promptly reported by the observer, who is a skillful tactician. Hence the commanders know all the time what is transpiring and just what to do. This being the case on both sides, there is but one recourse left, and that is to fight it out by hard blows, man for man, and life for life. It is frightful to contemplate; but these are the cold and remorseless facts."

"I remember they tried balloons in the Civil War, but they were found impracticable, if not dangerous. I should think now that the guns of the opposing forces would be leveled at the chariots and destroy them."

"That was done at the outset. Now the chariots are covered with a coating of mail so smooth and hard that an ordinary bullet or ball will glance harmlessly from the surface. By an adjusting process they can be moved so rapidly this way or that, and remain such a short time in one position, that the heavy guns cannot be trained upon them. At first the occupants of chariots on the opposing sides rushed upon each other and fought duels in the air. On one occasion both were killed; on another, both were wounded; then one would be killed and the other wounded. Vivid and exciting descriptions of these 'battles in the air,' or 'combats in the clouds,' have been published, and eagerly devoured by all readers. Now the chariots are armor-plated, so that fatal encounters need not occur; and by common consent these air-fights have been discontinued."

"That sounds like a romance."

"In your day an impossibility; now a reality easily explained."

"So wonders never cease."

CHAPTER XVI.

I WAS very desirous to learn more about the chariots or air-ships, so as to be able to operate them. Effie had never seen one. I wished to take an excursion in the air with her as *companion du voyage*, and did not want to run any risk of accident, and I made known my desire to Mr. Solon, and he kindly consented to become my instructor. He had both chariots and ships, one of each at his home, of the latest patterns and improvements. They occupied the buggy-house of former years, the buggy and carriage being things of the past. Mr. Solon said:

"During the last decade of the nineteenth century a very important discovery was made and published to the world concerning electricity. Its peculiar province and work in the economy of the universe were set forth and explained. This gave a new impetus to investigation. While the discovery did not tell what electricity is, it told what it does, and something of the how and why. This enabled investigators to pursue more intelligently their lines of research into the peculiarities of this wonderful force of nature, and better results have been attained. By the use of electricity and magnetism combined in action, a propelling power has been secured which enables us to navigate the air. This could not have been accomplished, however, if aluminum or some similar substance had not been discovered and utilized about the same time. Now let us examine this chariot," he said, leading the way to it.

"The framework is all of aluminum. It is the lightest material we have that is strong enough to meet the requirements. This is a battery, very compact, but very powerful. Here is the dynamo, and here a magnetic battery of great strength. These, all active and in harmonious combination, by their connecting parts, which are easily adjusted, furnish the motive power. They are under complete control of the operator. Here, under this leaf, which runs the length of the chariot, are little wings. They work rapidly and noiselessly, but with perfect efficiency. These are all necessary to the successful working of the apparatus. At first the vehicle was connected by wire with a generator or dynamo on the ground. From it a large number of chariots could be sent off and supplied with motive power. But they were limited in their trips by the length of the wire connecting with the dynamo. Now we carry the power with us, and there is no limit to its use, or to the distance we may go. The supply is inexhaustible. This is an ingenious piece of mechanism, something after the mode of construction in a watch or clock. It is wound up and set going, and keeps all the machinery in action as long as the connections are maintained. The whole is under complete control, and can be shut off and thrown on more readily than an engineer can operate his engine. Get in now, and I will show you the movements while we take a ride, so that afterward you can handle the chariot with ease and perfect safety."

Without illustrations showing the parts it is impossible to give the reader a fully intelligent description of the chariot or its working machinery.

We seated ourselves for a ride, Mr. Solon having wound up the machine and made everything ready under my eye. We went some miles into the country, sailing low and high. At first Mr. Solon did all the engineering. Then he placed the handle of the lever in my hands, and assisted me to learn all the movements. At the end of a couple of hours I felt myself master of the situation, and we returned home, where I learned how to house the chariot easily and to stop its operations.

The following day Effie and I took a delightful excursion far into the country. We enjoyed our aërial voyage hugely. It was a new experience, and its novelty added zest to the pleasurable sensations. The view from our highest point of elevation was magnificent and indescribable. The city was beneath us, and every part as distinctly visible as could be. The landscape stretched away in every direction, until in the far distance earth and sky met and kissed each other. Beautiful? Describe it, who can? Busy life everywhere; herds feeding; spring flowers blooming; the face of the ground putting on its mantle of green; the distant hum and murmur of business, of conversation, of insect life, came to the ear in subdued cadence with a strange fascination. The eye and the ear were both greeted by strange experiences, which contributed to the exhilaration of the hour. It was with reluctance that we finally turned our faces homeward, promising ourselves more of these enchanting excursions.

I did not feel entirely satisfied with Mr. Solon's explanation of the situation of public affairs, and so on the evening of this day I remarked to him:

"Your views of the disturbed condition of society and the culmination of differences in open hostilities do not seem to me adequate to the occasion. There must be some moral as well as political causes at work."

"Certainly," was his reply. "I confined my remarks before almost exclusively to the political questions involved, and their bearings on business interests. There is a moral side to the subject, and it is really the vital point in the whole matter. Formerly our people had a profound respect for the decisions of a majority in the cases of differences of opinion. That decision was accepted and acquiesced in without hesitation or murmuring; but this desirable and necessary feature of public sentiment in a 'government of the people, by the people, and for the people,' has been so weakened that it has lost its former potency for good."

"How could that happen?" I asked in some surprise.

"Like most revolutions of public opinion, by small degrees. It is plain to see now what was not so manifest at the time of the incipient stages of this deplorable change. Men ceased to respect and obey the laws when the laws did not please them or seemed to conflict with their interests. The debtor class sought to evade the contracts they had voluntarily made, claiming that necessity compelled them at the time of the contract to make the best terms with the capitalists they could, and that the money-loaner took advantage of their necessitous situation to exact enormous and unjustifiable interest on monies loaned. This, no doubt, in some instances was true. Claiming its truth, the debtor declared he was acting on the broad basis of what was really just and right in refusing to pay as he had agreed—first the usurious interest, then all interest, and sometimes both interest and principal. From this beginning, with some show of justice in it, the principle of repudiation widened out and took in all matters in the domain of exchange. All purchases where the buyer felt he had paid too much for an article, whether

he really had or not, were not held by him as binding.
You can readily see how this notion of each man to
be judge of all matters where he was interested would
demoralize business and destroy confidence between
man and man.

"Then there has been ever since your time a kind of
public acquiescence in the idea that it is not wrong to
beat a railroad company or other corporation out of its
just dues. Men sometimes prided themselves on getting the best of these institutions. The public tacitly
sanctioned the fraud, though it was no better than
theft or robbery. This weakening of the moral sense
soon extended from corporations to individuals. Men
would exact more from the government or the public
for the same service or thing than from a fellow-citizen,
and think it all right. It was hardly considered wrong
to defraud the government. This debauchery of morals
also reached into other arenas.

"But the worst feature, probably, was the disrespect
for and disregard of law. Every man felt himself at
liberty to transgress such laws as he did not like. This
had a very small beginning. As already intimated,
usury laws, as all acts requiring payment of interest
came to be termed, were finally regarded by the debtor
class with great disfavor, and were violated without
reluctance. The law for the observance of the Sabbath
was habitually violated. The laws against gambling
and lotteries were all set at naught where it could be
done without detection. The same could be said of a
number and variety of statutes. One class of violators
might have produced little general effect; but where so
many enactments were trampled upon, it could not do
otherwise than breed contempt for law, and especially
for all laws distasteful to any individual or set of persons.

"But the most disastrous example of law-breaking was that set by men engaged in the traffic of intoxicating liquors. Not because each particular case was worse than others, but for the reason that such great numbers were engaged in this business. It did not make any special difference what the law was which tended to restrict or control the traffic, all were disregarded much alike. More ado was made over laws prohibiting the sale of intoxicants, for the simple reason that this class of laws was more difficult to violate without detection. But all restrictive legislation was tabooed or only nominally regarded. Where license laws prevailed, whether high or low, but more especially where they were high, they were complied with in a sense. Men would secure a license and pay the fee. But nine tenths of the saloons were controlled by the wholesale liquor-dealers, who furnished the supplies and owned the fixtures, but operated in the name of some other party or parties, who were named as the saloon-keepers. When the saloon which had the license did not pay well enough, or when it was run for the purpose of securing an exclusively respectable trade or patronage, which of course excluded the old topers and habitual drunkards, then a joint was provided to catch these unrespectable drinkers. This joint was frequently operated by the man who held the license, under the direction of the wholesale dealer, in a side or back room, or under ground. Sometimes it was separate from the licensed establishment entirely. It was always and absolutely illegal. But the bosses of the trade were interested in the sale of liquors to all classes, and so prevented the prosecution of these joints or their keepers. They did not seriously interfere with the more aristocratic saloons, as their customers were not desired in them as patrons lest they should drive off the respectable drinkers, who would feel themselves insulted and outraged by beastly drunkenness around them. The business was engaged in solely for the money that could be made by it; and to make the most all classes of customers was the end and aim. You can take in the situation at a glance. The licensed saloon was gorgeously decorated and made as attractive as possible. Here the drunkards were manufactured. When fully graduated they were sent down to the joint for final extinction.

"This wholesale violation of law was winked at by the politicians for selfish purposes. The liquor-dealers made more money and made it faster than any other class of men in business. They spent it freely to secure their trade and traffic. The office-seekers of all parties fed the saloon-keepers and courted the influence of the liquor barons, who controlled an army of voters. Each and all parties were afraid to attack this potential influence. In many places, especially in the large cities, it held votes enough to decide an election and defeat or elect the candidates of either party where there was anything like an equal division of strength between them. They bought up legislators and members of Congress, bribed courts and juries, procured perjury by wholesale, and run things generally with a high hand.

"There could be but one result to grow out of this persistent disregard of law, and that must be disastrous. The anarchist claimed the same right to violate the laws he disliked as the liquor men, the gamblers, or any other class of violaters. 'Whatsoever a man soweth that shall he also reap.' Those who trampled upon the law have been 'sowing to the wind,' and now they are 'reaping the whirlwind.' These great principles must remain true forever. The sowing time has been of long duration; the harvest will be proportionately great, but it promises to be short and destructive beyond precedent.

"I am not speaking of these causes of the present condition of things as expressions of my own opinions on the real merits of the matters presented, but as a statement of the simple facts of history as they now stand out clearly in view. You can moralize upon them as you like. I have only given you prominent examples of the demoralizing forces whose tendencies during many years have culminated in the present upheaval of the foundations of social order. It looks, too, as if political institutions would be subverted, and lawlessness run riot over the land.

"I have given you nothing new. All these elements of destruction existed in your day; they have only developed and grown strong. Now they seek for the mastery, and God only knows what the end will be."

"The picture you present is a dark one. With the moral foundations removed, the prospect of an amicable adjustment of differences vanishes."

"The outlook is a cloud without the silver lining. Our city is probably the least disturbed of any in the country; so far, it has escaped the turmoil of the past and the tribulation of the present. The reasons for this I will give you at another time."

CHAPTER XVII

THE following facts in relation to my home city, I learned from Mr. Solon. He said:

"As soon as I got fairly on my feet after the fire, I resolved to turn over a new leaf in business. Always sympathizing with the laboring classes, I tried to have my workmen feel I had an interest in their welfare. The strike which led to the fire was unjustifiable in every sense of the word; but the event caused me to think more seriously upon the joint obligations of capital and labor. I wished to adjust my business upon the broad principles of right, and brotherhood between man and man. I read and thought much. I was familiar with all the trite sayings about the mutual dependence of capital and labor, and the special rights and privileges of each. Muscle on one side, money on the other. Must these natural friends be made enemies?

"So far as I was concerned there should be no warfare. I had heard of proprietors of plants sharing profits with their workmen. As far as I knew, these methods prospered. But there still remained the separation of classes and interests. After mature deliberation my plan was for a union of all parties and interests. If capital and labor are natural friends, why not consolidate for mutual welfare? I was willing to trust my workmen. They were honest men: I would keep no others. Most of them were intelligent. The organization I should propose would be a departure from those in vogue in that it should be *mutual* and not *exclusive*, embracing *both* capital and labor.

" Having arranged the general plan, I left the men to fix the details. When completed the constitution and by-laws were a model of simplicity and comprehensiveness. The officers were few and only such as were necessary. We had no autocrats. No man, or committee, was clothed with supreme power. All business was done by the body. Committees were assistants only. Our society was for mutual protection and benefit. Brotherhood was its motto. Nurses and other aids were provided for in case of sickness. A fund was set aside to assist those disabled by illness or accident, and a pension fund for the aged and infirm. All these were well guarded to prevent imposition.

" The men named three years' steady employment as the requisite for membership. Probationary members were admitted at the end of three months. These had no vote or share in the profits, but possessed all other rights and benefits of the order. The workmen fixed the price of labor, from the lowest to the highest skill. Inducements were held out to every one to become more skillful. Skill was the goal of every man's ambition, because it paid. Without adequate incentive there can be no improvement. The men also named ten per cent. per annum as the amount of interest I was to receive for capital invested. As insurance and taxes were to be paid out of this it was not too much.

" All net profits were shared equally by the members. The natural selfishness of men was developed in this matter. The skilled workmen thought they ought to receive more of the profits than the others. There was some prospect of trouble in the settlement of this question. By unanimous agreement it was referred to me for adjustment. I said to the skilled workmen: 'You have already provided pay for your skill in fixing the prices of wages agreed upon. If now you get pay again in profits, you will be paid twice for the same thing. This you can see is not right.' The point was clear and acquiescence readily given.

"A library was provided, filled with choice books on all subjects, and arrangements for its care and oversight. A lyceum was also instituted. As far as possible we provided for our own moral, intellectual, and physical needs. No intoxicating drinks were permitted in our organization. Total abstinence prevailed. The men voluntarily renounced the use of tobacco in any form. I was elected presiding officer year after year, until by reason of age I declined a reëlection. Our elections and terms of office were annual.

"We have never had a serious jar of dissension, and no disturbance among us. We are a complete society in ourselves. Our interests are a unit. There is no conflict between capital and labor. Like man and wife, the two are one. I own the plant. My ownership is conceded and respected. I can dispose of it at pleasure; but no sudden change to damage the men is allowable. The men own themselves and dispose of their labor at will. No discord, no expulsions from the union except for cause.

"Our profits vary from year to year, according to the demand for our goods. The per cent. of profit is small. It is a cardinal principle of our order to be unjust in nothing, including prices for our wares; they are as low as can be afforded. The highest dividends yet reached amounted to one fifth the wages paid for labor during the year. They are always satisfactory. The bookkeeper is mutually agreed upon. He selects his assistants. They audit all claims and accounts and ascertain the amount to be distributed as profits.

"We have prospered greatly. It could scarcely be otherwise when every man employed is a part of the concern and personally interested in securing the best results attainable. I do not know whether this plan furnishes a solution of the labor-and-capital problem or not. I did not propose it, nor was it adopted with that end in view. It was simply our method of unification. It suited us. It has kept us harmonious. No agitators, reformers, demagogues, or anarchists are permitted to come among us. No men leave us, except to better their condition. Some of our men have received lucrative appointments; others have been elected to office.

"The great success of our enterprise caused others in this city to follow suit more or less perfectly. As a result we have no labor troubles. No enemies have been made who desire revenge. Hence we have escaped molestation since hostilities commenced, and are likely to escape until all the land is involved."

"You seem to have made Utopia a reality," I said.

"By no means. We are neither Utopia nor poetical Arcadia, but simply a community of human beings with all their faults and foibles. There are envies, rivalries, and jealousies existing among us, and plenty of selfishness. The grosser elements, which result largely from bad habits and inflamed passions, have been largely eliminated. We have men and women with five talents, two talents, and one talent. These do not always see, think, and act alike. It would be an unpromising dead-level if they did. Where there are differences there may be bickerings; but there is always the promise of improvement and progress. If the man with one talent rejoices that there are other men who can accomplish more and do better than he, when he has done his best, then will harmony grow out of variety, and the best results be attained by diversity in unity."

"What is the present condition of the great cities?" I asked.

"In most of them, deplorably bad. They are hot-beds of crime. Pauperism prevails to an alarming extent. Politicians have ruled and plundered them so long and continuously they are financially stranded. Virtue and integrity in official positions are almost unknown. The burdens of taxation are nearly unbearable, yet have to be endured. The better class of citizens either have not the power or lack the courage to free themselves from their bondage. Municipal administrations are theaters of reckless extravagance, unblushing corruption, and well-nigh open robbery. Honesty and economy are things of the past. All the large cities are hopelessly crushed with debt, both bonded and for current expenses. Payment of the principal is not seriously considered. It is barely possible to meet the interest as it falls due. No remedy is visible."

"You draw a dark picture."

"The picture is there; I simply unveil it. There are tens of thousands of good people in those cities, some of them the excellent of the earth; but the majority is composed of the baser population. Large numbers of them are men who neither fear God nor regard man. Crime runs riot. The police are either in league with the criminals or afraid to suppress them. The millionaire and the beggar look each other in the face daily. The palatial residences of the rich, and the garrets,

cellars, and hovels of the poor are but a stone's-throw
apart. The contrast maddens the vicious who are destitute, while it is unnoticed by the men of princely
wealth. Mammon rules the hour with the majority on
one side; desperation grows more reckless and daring
on the other. The outcome can scarcely be otherwise
than direful."

" You speak despairingly."

" I am usually hopeful and see the bright side of
things; but with war raging in the land, men's passions
at fever heat, fraternal blood flowing like water, the
hungry and wicked poor on the outlook for plunder
and revenge, I confess the light on the dismal scene does
not appear."

" Let us labor and hope for the best. Good may yet
come to our country."

" I presume there is some compensation for all the
ills we are heir to; but in this case they are invisible
to human eyes. At my age I have no desire to witness
scenes of carnage, rapine, and devastation; no desire
to see fratricidal strife where brother sheds his brother's
blood. Before these eyes behold such acts, such deeds
of crime, I pray that I may be laid quietly away in the
silent city of the dead."

CHAPTER XVIII.

THE latest intelligence from the seat of hostilities was of the most exciting nature. After the first day's fighting the two main armies had suspended active operations, as previously stated. The fearful fatality, made certain by the number buried, seriously impressed all parties. The number slain exceeded all previous estimates.

As the President was not a party to the war, and the governors of the various States had either remained neutral or taken sides according to their personal or political predilections, there was no really recognized head of either side. The generals in immediate command were in actual control—a condition greatly to be deplored.

Before the truce expired a new aspect was put upon matters. Two young men, former friends, now rivals for the hand of the same lady, proposed this unique method of settling the national quarrel. These men represented the opposing forces. They would champion their respective armies, and in personal combat decide the differences at issue. Which one should prove victor in the duel, his side should dictate conditions of peace. All the circumstances combined to favor the proposal. It would save bloodshed and great loss of life and property.

117

The two men were of the same age, size, weight, and strength. They were permitted to arrange the time, place, conditions, and weapons of the combat. They met. Each knew it was to be a fight to the death. The magnitude and peril of the undertaking had a powerful and subduing influence upon them; they were awed into a feeling which precluded all levity, even forbade enmity and made them feel as kin. Their old friendship, which had not entirely died out, was revived. Possibly in this newly awakened sensibility they might have receded from the stand they had taken, but for the fact that by jeopardizing their single lives they might save thousands and tens of thousands of their fellow-soldiers from early and bloody graves. This thought made them resolute. In the most calm and deliberate manner they arranged all the details of the encounter, as far as these could be anticipated and provided for.

The strangest and most exciting part of the whole transaction was the fact that they decided to conduct the combat in mid-air in chariots, where the battle would be visible to all who desired to be spectators. The chariots were to be exactly alike in all respects—bullet-proof, with a shield of armor to protect their persons. The contest must therefore be decided by skill rather than force—skill in handling the chariot, or in taking advantage of any mistakes either might make.

After the preliminaries and conditions were all determined by the parties themselves, they were reduced to writing by the leaders of both sides, signed in triplicate, one copy given to the general of each army, and the third deposited by mutual agreement in the safe of a bank for reference in case of any mishap to the other two.

It would require at least ten days to have the two

chariots constructed according to the plans agreed upon, and then two days' practice for the men to become fully masters of their respective craft.

This wonderful event was heralded over the country and the world. The most intense excitement prevailed everywhere. Hundreds, and even thousands, resolved to witness this strange and weird duel in the air, so unlike anything in the history of the world.

Ordinarily I have no taste for things of this kind; I never desired to see a fight between two men, or even two dogs; but I determined to be one of the observers of this anomalous event. It even had a fascination for me. I think it was the romance and not the tragedy that drew me to the scene. I asked Effie if she would accompany me, but she declined. While she partook of the general excitement which everywhere prevailed, she did not wish to see the fatal affray. She interposed no objection to my going, but rather sanctioned it.

Of course I went by air. It required two days to make the trip, as I lay by over-night and was in no haste. I was there on time.

I saw the two men as they met and shook hands before ensconcing themselves in their respective war-chariots. They were splendid specimens of solid physical manhood, handsome, muscular, intelligent; nothing low or brutal in their appearance. I could perceive no sign of bitterness in their looks or acts; there was no bantering or boasting on either side—no tendency that way. As they parted hands and turned away, I saw stamped on each face an expression of iron determination which said more plainly than words, "Victory or death." I knew that at least one of these men would never see the light of another day, or, if he did, it would be with a mangled body, maimed for life.

At ten o'clock A.M. the signal was to be given. Then the men were to commence the ascent. No act of hostility was to be engaged in, until they were five hundred feet in the air. The chariots were beautiful—polished until they shone like burnished tinsel in the bright sunlight. When inclosed within them the men were invisible from without, except in favorable positions. They had windows of plated glass of a peculiar tenacity and toughness, so that they would resist a ball fired from a revolver or other small-arm. Through these they could look out and see everything going on around them.

There were more than two thousand chariots or ships present whose inmates had come from a distance to witness the great event, and as many more from regions nearer by. The air was full of vehicles. The arena allotted for the combat was directly over the ground between the two armies. It was marked off by boundaries a thousand feet in diameter, and no ship or chariot was permitted to pass these bounds; nor were the combatants to go beyond the lines during the contest, but as high as they pleased.

I understood that the young lady who had so interested these young men was one of the spectators, and that this fact was known to them. This gave additional interest to the occasion among the spectators, and doubtless inspired the principals with a resolve to do or die, or both.

I took a position a little over five hundred feet from the earth, where I could take in the whole of the one thousand feet. Around me in every direction were chariots and ships stretching away in the distance. It was a display of such strange and wonderful import as would under other and different circumstances have engaged my whole attention; now the more striking event absorbed my entire being. Every fiber of my system was wrought up to the highest tension; the intensity of feeling was painful when the mind was not occupied elsewhere.

The antagonists took their positions. There was no haste or trepidation on the part of either. A momentary suspense. Every eye was on the two chariots. Two hundred thousand spectators held their breath and waited. A movement. Then the chariots were maneuvered rapidly and most skillfully, as if to gain some advantage of position. No results. The action of one was so promptly met and checkmated by the other that nothing was gained or lost. By mutual consent they took a rest. Two hundred thousand people breathed easier for the time, and the painful tension was somewhat relaxed.

Then the chariots moved again. A series of most rapid and dextrous evolutions followed. Suddenly there was a simultaneous flash of pistols from their respective port-holes, and two reports blended in one. No harm was done. The smoke rose up and rolled away. Another period of active movement, then two more flashes and reports, with the same result as before.

One of the rules adopted was that no cheering or other noise or sign of approval was to attend the combat; it was to be conducted in silence. All the occupants of air-vehicles were charged to observe this rule. All on *terra firma* were held by the discipline of armies to the utmost quiet. The stillness at times was oppressive; it was like the calm which precedes the earthquake or the cyclone.

Another rest. Then a fiercer onslaught than before.

The chariots were hurled against each other with frightful violence, and the crash of the collision was heard far away. This was followed by another simultaneous discharge of revolvers. This time the bullets met midway, mingled by the shock into one mass, which fell sullenly and swiftly to the ground beneath.

At this stage of the contest the combatants withdrew from each other a short distance, resting in watchful attitude, as if devising some new method of attack. Anon a series of most skillful maneuvers to gain some advantage held the speechless attention of all beholders. The effort to secure favorable results on either side failed. This was succeeded by attempts to dive under, or fly, or leap over each other; but each was too wary to be caught, and the attempts were abandoned as fruitless.

The skill displayed in these rapid and constantly changing movements was little short of marvelous. As the combat deepened the belligerents became more eager and earnest to bring it to a close. Endeavors to catch on the fly, to strike amidships, to find some vulnerable spot, were made with a rapidity and swiftness that caused dizziness to watch the adroit thrust and apt parry of each side. In spite of the strictness of the rule to observe silence, a murmur of applause, like the hum of insects, arose above the silence. It was promptly hushed.

The skill of the two charioteers was so perfectly equal that a drawn battle seemed to be the only probable, if not the only possible, termination of the contest. No such thought as this, however, found a place in the mind of either of the principals, if judged by their acts. It was with them a battle to a decisive conclu-

sion. With them a drawn battle meant a double death.
Another hour passed without essential change.

"Long time in even scale the battle hung."

At length, after having failed to win by skill, the
duelists began a regular assault. The chariots were
hurled against each other with such vehement force
as to threaten their utter demolition. As they came
together on one occasion, the larger port-holes were
opened, and pistol-shots fired in rapid succession, until
the six chambers of each revolver were emptied. For
a moment the smoke enveloped the scene, the chariots
were hidden, the result unseen. Then a breeze drove
the smoke away, and no harm could be discerned.
Each had failed to send a ball through the port of the
other on a fatal mission, and the chariots were un-
harmed.

Distant thunder now announced the coming of a
storm, in which heaven's artillery was to play a part.
If the combatants noticed this fact it was not percepti-
ble to those who were spectators of their actions. That
the vast multitude of onlookers were not indifferent to
this coming event was evident from their manifested
anxiety.

Presently the chariots moved wider apart, as if to
withdraw from the further prosecution of what gave
promise so far of a bootless encounter and a hopeless
attempt to reach definite results. Not so. Like two
mighty birds of prey intent upon the destruction of a
foe, they suddenly flew upon each other with a fierce-
ness hitherto unseen, unfelt. The crash of the shock
rang out so loud that distant ears heard it clearly, and
a louder attempt at applause was only checked by the
stern orders of the officers in command.

How long could the chariots resist such rough usage? The storm drew near, yet so excited was every one that its approach attracted no attention. Twice, thrice, were the chariots thus hurled like cannon-balls against each other, without visible effect. Then they withdrew still farther apart than before, and put on all the power at command. I could see the faint blue of the electric flame as the dynamos were worked to their fullest capacity.

Just at this moment a fleecy cloud, white as the vapor of steam, the advance-courier of the coming storm, came down like a flying shroud, driven by a gust of wind, and enveloped the chariots. For a brief time nothing could be seen in this environment of cloud but the lurid flames of electricity flashing out amid the gloom. Evidently the occupants were keeping up the power to the utmost. The scene was wild and weird beyond the power of language to express. The hush and suspense were such as had never fallen upon such a scene. Ah, no such scene had ever before been witnessed by men! As suddenly as it had floated down upon the field of strife, the cloud was lifted up on the wings of the wind and carried away. There rested the chariots, ready for instant action. A combat amidst the clouds!

I instinctively prepared for something unusual, decisive. A moment they poised, as if in the balances of fate, then, like two engines at speed of a hundred miles an hour, they rushed together with a clash that rang out over all the region around, loud and fierce. The shock was too great. The metal yielded. The chariots were broken in pieces, hurled bottom upward, held a moment in air, then fell to the earth with frightful rapidity.

I had set my machinery in readiness for motion almost instinctively, and before the broken chariots were half-way in their descent I was speeding down toward the spot where the shattered vehicles must reach the ground. Hundreds of others followed my example as soon as they could get ready.

Just as the two dismantled chariots with their human freight struck the soil, a piercing scream of agony rang out, so full of unspeakable anguish it almost chilled the blood. I was told it came from the young lady who, in a sense, had been the cause of this strange event. Happily she fainted away and became unconscious before her eyes gazed upon the scene which was soon unfolded.

It was a horrible sight we looked upon. Both men were quite dead. Whether killed by the shock in air, or by the fall and concussion, could not be told. They were badly bruised, and mangled masses of flesh and bones, yet their faces were but slightly disfigured. Each countenance wore the same stern set of determination which I had observed at the outset, but no bitterness or mark of revenge was visible. It was a drawn battle; and what a terrible one!

All sense of surrounding things appeared to be lost in the one tragic event which absorbed all thought, all interest, all sympathy. But the storm, unmoved by human woe or joy, came on apace. Hundreds rushed to the spot where the ruined chariots and dead men lay, while thousands were held back and in check by rigid discipline. Before an intelligent effort was made to remove the remains of the dead heroes, a bolt of lightning flashed out of the depths of the cloud, and, as those who saw it said, divided, one fork striking the flagstaff of one army, the other the opposite; both, with their respective flags shivered into shreds, were hurled in torn fragments to the ground.

The superstitions regarded these two events, the fierce and indecisive battle of the men, and the destruction of flagstaffs and flags at the same time, as an augury or an omen of the outcome of the war should it continue, and as a warning to cease hostilities which should not be disregarded. These prognostications were not without their effect upon both sides, and a truce of thirty days was agreed upon for the purpose of coming to an amicable settlement of differences if possible.

The young men were buried with great honors in one grave, over which their friends erected a fine and costly monument.

A strong and persistent effort was made for peace by the better men on both sides of the contest. Success would have attended their endeavors but for the unreasonable demands of the extremists, who insisted upon unconditional surrender. A settlement on honorable terms to all would finally have been reached but for the element of irreconcilables, who, having nothing of their own, could lose nothing, and had all to gain. These insisted that the capitalists were alarmed and would yield to a full and complete division of property if firmly held to it; but if they would not, then push the war and compel them to do so. These extremists, who never should have been listened to for a moment, ultimately prevailed, and a peaceful termination of differences failed. Nothing then remained but to resume hostilities and fight it out to a bloody conclusion, even if the whole country should be desolated by the ravages of war.

CHAPTER XIX.

I RETURNED home soon after the aërial combat, and awaited the result of the negotiations already mentioned. When the inevitable became known, I resolved as far as possible to keep aloof from the struggle. I had no reason to participate on either side. I detested war. I saw no justifiable grounds for this brutal strife among brethren. That it would be a long and sanguinary contest none could doubt. I dreaded the idea of witnessing the scenes of carnage, the dead and dying, the destruction of life and property, and general devastation. There surely could be no adequate compensation for all these horrible deeds. No human foresight could penetrate the dark and dismal future.

I determined to turn my effects into cash as far as possible, and be prepared for any emergency. I had mapped out a plan of action, which could not at present be put in execution. I must wait. Time was an important factor in this matter.

I had one hundred thousand dollars in government bonds. They were now out of date. Would they be redeemed at this late day? By inquiry I learned that the bonded debt had been paid off long ago; all outstanding bonds had been called for. I confided to no one that I possessed these bonds, and determined to go to Washington to ascertain if I could realize on them. At first payment was refused. The bonds were a curiosity. None had been seen by any of the heads of the departments. I pressed my claim, which all could see was just. Finally, investigation revealed the fact that these identical bonds had been called for, and money appropriated for their redemption. A full cabinet, advised by the attorney-general, approved their payment. They were paid in full, with interest to maturity. I returned home much gratified over my success. This was the last of the national debt caused by the War of the Rebellion.

In the meantime active hostilities had been resumed at the end of the last truce; all the horrors of internecine war were being enacted. The strife was extending on all sides; more and more the people were being drawn into it. Before the battle near Chicago was fought to its bloody conclusion, that city was set on fire by the baser elements of its own population and utterly destroyed. So rapid was the spread of the flames that thousands of people were caught in the conflagration, and great numbers perished; others rushed into the waters of the lake to escape the fire, and were drowned. Pestilence followed, taking off more than the fire, the waters, and the armies combined. They who had fired and plundered the city soon paid for their wickedness by the ravages of the disease to which they fell victims. Little good had they of their ill-gotten lucre.

New Orleans and other cities of the great Mississippi Basin met with a fate similar to that of Chicago. Then came the cry, "On to New York!" This city was regarded as the head center of capital and the aristocracy of wealth. It was the peculiar aversion of the masses who espoused the cause of labor. Wall Street was the especial abomination and object of hatred of the levelers. Chicago and her gamblers in grain, produce, and stock had been wiped out; now New York must follow, with a more terrible punishment, if that were possible.

It is not the purpose of these pages to follow and record the events of the fratricidal war which desolated the country from center to circumference. So great and fierce became the struggle, some divines declared it was the great battle of Armageddon which John describes in Revelation. When New York fell, it was pronounced the fall of Babylon. One minister read as his lesson on Sabbath morning selections from the eighteenth chapter of Revelation, and applied the same to New York. Of course this minister was on the side of labor, and desired that what he read might apply to the fated city. This incident goes to show how bitter was the feeling existing, and how little of the spirit of Christ was manifested even by those claiming to be His messengers—teachers sent by Him to proclaim to men the gospel of peace and love, "good-will to men," and forgiveness to enemies.

CHAPTER XX.

Turning from the arena of strife, the more personal thread of this narrative will be resumed. While the events were transpiring in the great national theater which made of our country a vast arena of turmoil and devastation, Mr. and Mrs. Solon became more and more feeble. Effie was made heir in her own right of all the . Solon estate, real and personal.

Meantime, by consent of all parties, Effie and I were married on the 9th day of April, 1928. This happy event was like sunshine amidst the surrounding darkness. It was the consummation of our earthly hopes, the crowning glory of our love.

All the employees of the Solon works united in a request to have the nuptial ceremony performed in the church, that they might witness it. Our personal preference was for a private wedding in the presence of a few chosen friends; but we knew this request came from the hearts of the people who made it, that it was an expression of respect and affection for Mr. Solon and his family, a compliance with which would greatly gratify them. The request was granted. The ceremony was simple and impressive. Then came hearty congratulations from the army of workmen and their families, which we knew were sincere. It was a happy hour, and a precious memory never to be forgotten.

Two years later Mr. and Mrs. Solon died, a few hours apart, and were buried together beneath the monument already erected on a beautiful lot in Sunset Hill Cemetery. They had long desired to leave the world together, and this wish was realized. They also escaped being witnesses to the fearful and ghastly ravages of the fratricidal war which raged so fiercely over the land. Our city still escaped.

The remains of these dear ones were followed to their last resting-place by every person connected with the establishment Mr. Solon had founded. They brought rich floral tributes to decorate the church, the caskets, and the grave. Hundreds of eyes were wet with tears as the minister spoke of the good couple who had exchanged mortal for immortal life. I had never witnessed such a scene—so many people mourning as for a dear friend. It was heart-felt grief—no hired laments. It was a tribute of love few kings of all the ages have received. It was the spontaneous homage paid to a noble man.

After the solemn rites were over and Effie and I were seated in our quiet home, I said to her:

"How is it that all these people are so attached to your father? They desired with one voice to be present at our wedding; now they turn out in a body to attend the funeral. They weep as for one near and dear to them." She answered:

"My father always treated his workmen as his equals. He was their companion and counselor. He listened to the story of their troubles; he sympathized with them in their sickness, trials, and bereavements; he wept with them when they wept; he shared their joys and joyed with them; he made their welfare his constant concern. He was one of them in their organization. He never held them off or made them feel that he was better and more to be respected and reverenced than they were.

He shared as one of them in the dividends of the business, because they said he gave as much time and labor
to the concern as any man connected with it.   He never
used these dividends for himself; they were all devoted
to benevolences of some kind.   If the families of any
of the workmen were sick, the doctor's bill would be
sent in receipted; if there were deaths, the undertaker's
bill was paid and the receipt passed over.   Family
supplies would be furnished in cases of long illness or
other disabling misfortune.   In special cases not provided for by the general fund, nurses would be hired
and paid.   If a family was in need, or if not in need,
which has been a rare occurrence, if a little aid in a
pinch would tide over a difficulty, ten, twenty, or fifty
dollars would find their way into such a household and
bring relief.   Two were thus made happy, the giver and
the receiver.   Father enjoyed aiding those in need as
much as anything else he did.

"It was a long time before the recipients of these
kindnesses learned who their benefactor was.   Father
followed the direction not to let one hand know what
the other did in such matters.   He would have been
glad if the secret had never been divulged; but it was
impossible to hide the facts permanently.   When the
men and their families learned who the unknown benefactor and watchful friend was that always came to their
aid in exactly the right time, they became more deeply
attached to him than ever.   I am fully persuaded they
would have risked their own lives to save his.   They
would receive favors from him when their pride would
have refused to accept the same aid from others.
Somehow it did not seem like charity coming from him,
but more like assistance to a child from a loving and
thoughtful parent.   They could not refuse a benefit

from him, because they felt sure it would cause him regret and rob him of a real source of happiness.

"These are some of the reasons why these people are all genuine mourners now, and why they desired to see us married and give us their benediction on that event. It was not idle curiosity but sincere regard which prompted them on that occasion."

"I see. I understand, too, why it has been suggested that proper affiliation and sympathy between employers and employees would solve the vexed problem of labor and capital. If every employer had done as your father did with employees, this terrible war would have been an impossibility. Talk about these men who wept at your father's grave taking up arms to destroy him! As well think of you and me going to war! How much better every way, how much less expensive to both labor and capital, such a course, than this war and wholesale destruction of the accumulation of generations, leaving out the frightful slaughter of human beings—of brother arrayed in deadly feud with brother. Why were not men wiser?"

"You forget," said Effie, "that as all employers were not like father, so all workmen were not like his. It requires both sides to be composed of the right material for the outcome to be as in this case. Bad laborers are as much in the way of beneficial achievements as are bad employers."

I saw the point. Men are what they are, what they have made themselves. The war was on. Passions were at white heat. There was no prospect of peace anywhere in sight. Reflections on what might have been could do no good. What should we do—we two, who had no interest in the quarrel, no hand in bringing about the trouble, no hatred or revenge to gratify?

Should we wait until disaster reached us, or should we escape? Where could we flee? What avenue of escape was open to us? Where could we find a peaceful refuge? Europe was unsettled and bristling with arms. The New World was a volcano. The islands of the ocean might be disturbed by the turmoil at any time. If we could "take the wings of the morning and fly to the uttermost parts of the earth," could we secure rest and peace there? Life was before us; but what a life! And we were strangers to all that had wrought this change of a generation; we were not a part of the surging tides of commotion lashed into fury on all sides.

It did not take me long to reach a conclusion as to what was best for us to do. But would Effie consent? There was one place of refuge, and one only, so far as human foresight could penetrate the unseen future. As soon as time dulled a little the edge of grief over our double loss of parents, I would broach the subject to Effie. My plan was for us to take another protracted nap, and wake up when the war was over.

Not to prolong the matter or weary the reader, when the time came I spoke of the plan to Effie. At first she shrank from the ordeal; but it became less and less repugnant as she thought upon it. When I finally pictured the wave of desolation coming to our own home, with its possible fatal results to one or both of us, the thought of her seeing me or of I seeing her the victim of brutal and maddened passion swept away the last vestige of opposition or even of reluctance. Anything was better than the awful chances of this ghastly war.

We at once commenced preparations. The business of the works was intrusted to the foreman and bookkeeper, with instructions to carry out Mr. Solon's methods to the letter. How long we might be gone was uncertain; and we gave no hint of our purpose. Until our return all things must go on as before. In case of death or removal their successors must carry out the same instructions and have everything in shape to render a just and faithful account of the steward-ship.

We turned as much property into cash as possible, selecting gold and greenbacks as the most desirable representatives of value. The funds were safely deposited in the room of stone in the hill. We also placed there the most elegant and latest improved patterns of an air-chariot and air-ship. When all the preliminaries were arranged and everything was in readiness, we paid a farewell visit to the grave of Mr. and Mrs. Solon, shed tears of love and regret over their sleeping dust, not knowing but the graves of the dead might be obliterated by the violence of war. We took leave of our friends, and in the quiet of evening, taking care that no one should see us, we repaired to our cozy quarters in the solid rock.

Once within the sacred spot—sacred to us because of the many delightful hours of love-life we had enjoyed there—we sat down to consider and converse for the last time before passing into a long forgetfulness. The length of time we should sleep was discussed. As we both had vivid experience on the subject, there was really no dread or terror at the prospect before us. On the contrary, as we contemplated the perils and repulsive scenes from which we were escaping, there was something of pleasure and gladness in our ability to do so. This may not have been sturdy bravery, or free from selfishness, but it was in its way gratifying. Effie suggested ten years as the duration of our sleep. I favored a longer time. Ten years might not end the war. If the war itself should be ended, the damage and waste it should cause could not be repaired in twice ten years. Effie said:

"Fix the time to suit yourself, only do not let it be too long."

This was satisfactory to me. I had the duration of the period of repose fixed in my own mind, but did not wish to name it to Effie. She would regard it as too long. Having much to say, the hours of converse reached far into the night before we felt like saying good-night. Purposely I prolonged the sweet hours of delight until I knew it was morning. I desired it to be morning when we should awake. Everything being arranged and placed in order, I prepared the draughts, each taking one, which we were to swallow simultaneously. Composing ourselves, the potions were taken; then, quietly resting upon our pillows, with "Good-night, love," on the lips of each, we entered the land of forgetfulness.

CHAPTER XXI.

My first sensation after the loss of consciousness was the same as in my previous awakening. This was simply a repetition of my former experience until fully awake and in possession of my faculties. The first thought was of Effie. She had awakened at the same moment. It was dark within those solid walls, but we said in the darkness, "Good-morning, love," at the same time touching hands, as though it had been the sleep of a few hours. I struck a match and lighted the lamp. Effie's first remark was:

"This has been but a short nap. You did not administer a very potent draught, I guess."

"So I should believe, but for my former experience; but if I made no mistake, and I am quite sure I did not, it is just seventy years since we said 'good-night' and went to sleep."

"Seventy years!" she exclaimed, almost in affright.

"Yes, seventy years. It was 1930 then. I determined to wake up in the year 2000. So here we are. Shall we go out and look at the world?"

"Of course. What else can we do?"

"If the change is as great as it was for half the time in my former experiment, we shall recognize very little of anything we see. I am prepared for almost any sort of surprises."

"I too. I hope the war is over."
137

"Oh, it must be, long, long ago. If it had continued these seventy years all the people would have perished."

We dressed very deliberately and with some care, not knowing what might greet us on entering the arena of active life.

"I wonder if the fashions have greatly changed in these seventy years. They must certainly," remarked Effie as she put the finishing touches to her toilet. The instinctive thought of dress natural to women came into her mind.

"Quite likely," I replied; "though at the end of thirty-five years gentlemen's attire had not so materially changed as to draw marked attention to my costume." Effie looked so charming in any fashion of dress I felt that every one who saw her must admire.

"I should prefer not to appear odd," she said, half to herself, half to me.

When ready we sallied out to see what was to be seen. Quiet reigned. There was little noise or confusion. We passed on into the city. There was not the change I had expected to witness—nothing comparable to the changes of the thirty-five years of my former absence. There was more sameness in everything. The houses were all much alike; the surroundings almost fac-similes one of another. There was no hurry, no rush of business, no bustle of any description.

"It must be Sunday," I said. "It is entirely too quiet and still for every-day life."

Effie made no reply; she appeared to be absorbed in thoughts or meditations of her own. I followed the direction of her eye and saw two ladies moving along the street. After a moment she said:

"The style of dress is different. I shall appear antiquated in my garb."

I presume the ladies will understand Effie's feelings better than I did. I fear my sympathy for her in this trying hour was not very deep, perhaps not what it ought to have been.

We passed on into the heart of the city and met more people. I noticed the attention of the ladies was attracted toward Effie. I felt it was her beauty they were admiring. She was handsome as a peri, and none of them was comparable to her in my estimation. She understood the situation better, as this remark proved.

"These women think I am dressed like a fright. See how they are all gazing at my costume."

"It is your beauty, not your dress, that attracts their notice. I am proud of you."

"Oh, fudge! Women are never attracted that way by the beauty of other women. Don't you know they always inspect to criticise each other?"

"No. Is that the way you do?"

"Possibly a little. I used to follow the custom, but was cured of the practice by a lecture from my mother in my younger days—at least, nearly cured."

"I presume I shall never understand your sex," I remarked musingly. We moved on. Presently I inquired: "Would you not like to visit the old home?"

"Yes, of all things I would, if it will appear natural."

"Nothing seems natural. There must have been a complete revolution of things since we left the world. Yonder comes an elderly gentleman. He can tell us, perhaps."

As he approached I asked him:

"Can you point us the way to Mr. Solon's residence?"

The man looked confused. The question was either

a surprise to him, or he was at a loss for an answer. After a little pause, he replied:

"I think there is no man named Solon in the city. I have a faint recollection of having heard the name when I was a small boy. There used to be large machine works over there," pointing to the right, "known then as the 'Solon Machine-Works.' I can just remember the fact. But all that is changed now. The government, you know, owns everything, carries on all the business of the country, and so individuals have dropped out of business existence, and are no longer proprietors of establishments."

"Did I understand you to say the government owns everything now?" I asked.

He looked at me as if doubting the sincerity of my query or my sanity, but seeing my evident honesty in the premises, he answered:

"Yes, everything. Where have you been not to know this? I perceive now by your dress you are not exactly like the rest of us. It has been such a long time since the government took possession of everything in the country, I am really astonished to find any one ignorant of the fact."

"Please excuse my ignorance. I presume the former residence of Mr. Solon is now owned by the government and is not in private hands."

"Certainly. Nothing is in private hands. When peace was declared all things were made common and passed into the possession of the government. When a very small boy, I used to pass an elegant edifice known then as the residence of a Mr. Solon. It is so long ago I had forgotten about it when you first mentioned the matter. It now comes to me like a dream. I had not thought of it for years. I think you will find the place in that direction," pointing where I knew the dwelling was if standing. " But you are too young to have ever seen Mr. Solon. He has been dead many years. Let me see—it must be seventy years since he died. I think it was in 1930; and you cannot be much over thirty years of age."

" Thank you, sir," I said, seeing the conversation was drifting into a channel I did not desire to have it take. " We are greatly obliged for your kindness and will trouble you no further."

The reader may be surprised that I should ask a stranger concerning a place I was entirely familiar with. My desire was to obtain information of the situation of affairs, and not of localities. Nothing appeared natural. I had learned more than I expected, and yet knew enough only to be bewildered. What business had the government with Effie's home? I kept thinking, but said little.

We set out in the direction of the old home. How different all things seemed from what they were when we left the city—yesterday? So it appeared to us. As we looked this way and that, saw the impress of age and the wear of time upon everything visible, we could well believe that threescore and ten years had passed since our feet had trod these streets the last time. Some old landmarks could be recognized, though changed.

When we reached the old home the landscape was in a degree familiar; but the house had been remodeled to some extent, so as to render it as far as possible to conform to other residences. Its stately proportions and elegant design could not be obliterated, only modified. It was still the most elegant and finely constructed building in the vicinity. The beautiful surroundings, the trained flowers and ornamental shrubbery of other years, were in a state of neglect and decay sad to look upon.

Ellie gave a sigh as the transformed appearance of her home took from it all the attractions which made it near and dear to her. The flowers she had trained with such care were gone. No trace of the work of her deft fingers remained. All the associations which made the place sacred to her were missing. Looking on the scene was much like standing by the grave of a loved friend.

"Let us leave here," she said. "There is nothing left for me to love or cherish. Only if I could have possession again I would soon restore it to the dear old home once more. And why is it not mine? Who had the right to wrest this property from me? By what authority or rule of right could I be dispossessed of my lawful inheritance? What has the world come to? Has the government become a wholesale robber?"

"I presume we shall have to wait and learn," I said. "It all seems so strange, so unnatural, and we are such utter strangers in this our native land, it will require patience and self-denial, perhaps, to adjust ourselves to the new order of things. I remember how I felt after my first adventure; and the change now appears to be far more radical and overwhelming. If all the old gentleman says is true, I suppose you own about one hundred-millionth part of your own property, and I the same of mine. It is idle to speculate until we know more of the facts. Possibly the government owns us as well as our property. We shall have to learn that also."

We had been walking away from the vicinity of the place once called home, and were now some little distance off. I said:

"Let us get something to eat, and then go back to our home in the rocks. That is still ours, and they cannot take it from us until they find it."

"Yes, it is time we had something, for the stomach's sake, after our long fast. I had forgotten all about that need, but since you mention it I believe I do feel a sense of hunger. And I really long to get back home and find time to think. I am getting lost and must find myself."

Our personal adventures in getting a meal were annoying to us, but not of general interest. We found that neither gold, silver, nor greenbacks was current money; government scrip was the only currency. We had none of it. Our money would not be taken as pay for the dinner we had ordered and eaten. We were embarrassed, confused, and knew not what to do. A gentleman came to our relief, and paid for our meal in his scrip, taking a five-dollar gold piece in exchange— as a curiosity, he said.

Perplexed by our ignorance of the existing order of things, we hastened back to our retreat. Once safely there, we sat down to consider the situation. Yesterday, as it were, we were rich; to-day we had not wherewith to procure food. Yesterday we had homes; to-day were strangers in our native land, and aliens from our own homes. We had been despoiled, robbed of everything, and were penniless with thousands in our safe. What should we do? What could we do? If I could only find employment to meet our pressing needs! But if government possessed everything there was no one left to give employment. We had not learned the true status of affairs, that the government owned us as well as our property, and would give us food, clothing, and shelter in exchange for work. We were too confused to seek for proper information ; possibly too proud to expose our ignorance, more probably too sensitive. The situation was serious. The longer it was contemplated the more apparent its desperation appeared. It was cold, stern reality that stared us in the face—an apparition that would not down. Suddenly a ray of light penetrated the gloom, as I believed, and I said to Effie :

"I think I see the way out. I have a large amount of greenbacks ; so have you. These are promises of the government to pay. I do not believe it will repudiate its own obligations. At any rate I will test the matter. I remember my bonds were taken up and paid for when presented out of time. Why not the greenbacks?"

"You may succeed. Better try, at any rate. But everything is so strange and so changed, I have my doubts. Anything is better than suspense. One thing, however, must be provided for : we must both live while you go to Washington."

"I can arrange that. You go to sleep for a period of five days ; I will be back by that time. I will provide for my own wants."

This was agreed to and carried out. When I reached Washington I scarcely recognized anything, so complete was the change. The city was there, the brick, stone, and mortar, much as I had seen it. But the machinery of government was altogether different. The red tape was about the same. The departments bore but little resemblance to their former appearance. The whole aspect of things was changed inside and outside of the government buildings.

I had great difficulty in getting a hearing at all. At first my proposition for the government to redeem its promises was treated almost with contempt and derision.

It was declared that an entirely new era and new order of affairs had been established; that all old obligations had ceased with the acceptance by the people of the present system of things. I went to the President, a clever but not very brilliant man. He was kind, but gave me no encouragement. Finally I succeeded in getting the executive council together—in my day termed a meeting of the cabinet. Here the whole question was discussed. I explained my situation: how I came to be here on the stage of action so young, and yet over a hundred years old; how my property and that of my wife had been taken without our consent, and without any consideration or equivalent, leaving us destitute. Now it was proposed to take from us all that remained of value. I need not repeat all that transpired. Suffice it to say that finally it was concluded to give me government scrip for my greenbacks, which was done to the amount of one hundred thousand dollars, with the understanding that the scrip was to be used for personal and family demands, and not for speculation. I was also requested to say nothing concerning the transaction, which would lead to inquiries and put the administration to the trouble of making explanations. I had no desire to do this. All the government desired was to keep matters free from embarrassment or entanglement.

I was then told that a case somewhat similar to my own had just come to light in Boston. A Mr. West had been found after sleeping over a hundred years under mesmeric influence. The fact had become a great sensation. I was advised to visit this centenarian, who was near my own age, and compare notes with him. The interview would doubtless be of much interest to both of us, and possibly to the world at large.

This piece of information was of deep significance to
me, as it removed the concentration of attention which
must otherwise rest upon us, and divided it.   I knew it
would be gratifying to Effie also.

My mission so successfully accomplished, I returned
home without delay, reaching there a few hours after
Effie had awakened.   She was greatly rejoiced at my
success.   The situation was relieved of all difficulty.
Life now presented cheerful aspects.   I mentioned the
case of Mr. West, and Effie agreed with me that a trip
to Boston was the very thing to do.

CHAPTER XXII.

HAVING resolved upon the visit to Boston, and there being nothing to detain us in our present locality, we at once commenced preparations for the journey. We had no property to look after, no business interests to provide for, no friends to leave—nothing but a few personal matters to engage our attention. It required but a few hours to make ready. But we resolved before setting out to make some excursions into the adjacent country, and visit scenes and places of other years, if we could find and recognize them. Little, indeed, was there that had the appearance of former days. Change was written even on the face of the landscape. There was small comfort to be derived from what we saw. No dear associations remained to draw parting regrets from our hearts.

The evening before the day fixed for setting out on the eastern trip was spent in quiet conversation. So full of excitement and strange adventures had been the few days since our awakening, that real enjoyment in each other's society had, in a measure, been excluded. We had scarcely been our real selves. Now, with nothing to intrude or disturb, we could enter into each other's feelings in soul communion.

It proved one of the most happy evenings of our life. The rest of the world was changed almost beyond recognition. Customs, manners, phases of life, personal responsibility, the relative positions of men to society

and public affairs, of women to domestic economy and
home associations—all had undergone a complete revolution; whether for weal or woe, time must determine. In the midst of this sea of confusion to us, it
was a source of exquisite comfort to find in ourselves
something stable, unchanged, the same as when we knew
the world before. Out in the great world we were
exiles on our native soil. Here we were at home and
knew all that was about us.

One who has never passed through an experience
like ours can form no just conception of the sensations
produced, nor of the unspeakable pleasure in finding
one safe and secure anchorage in a haven of rest and
peace. The rest was so refreshing, the peace was so full
of comfort. That evening was an oasis in a desert, an
era in our lives.

We had discussed the merits of the air-ship and
chariot, and finally decided that the latter would be
preferable for our purpose. Of course we should voyage in the air. Every detail had been carefully looked
after, and we were ready. A night's refreshing sleep,
possibly the last we should enjoy for a season, and with
the early morning we were off.

Without accident or incident worthy of note, we
reached Boston. It was with some difficulty we found
a public house. The people did not appear to be well
posted in local matters, or to take any interest in our
welfare. We finally succeeded in reaching a hotel. At
least that is what it would have been called in our day;
but "Government Inn" was the name by which it was
known. It was quite an ancient title for a house of
entertainment, but we were too anxious to find a place
of rest to moralize on names or appearances.

There was no bustle, no rushing of porters, no an-

swering the calls of guests as in our time, no excitement or tumult.   Everything appeared to be neat, clean,
and in good order.   We were shown to our rooms.
There was nothing attractive about them ; no display ;
no evidence of an effort to outrival some other house.
The furniture was plain and substantial ; good enough
as far as it went, but neither profuse nor ornamental.
It was quite unlike the fashionable hotels of a hundred
years ago.   I was not yet prepared to pass judgment
on the change.   It might be for the better ; it might
not.   I would wait and see, not only in reference to
public houses, but with regard to all that came under
my observation.   Hasty conclusions were not always
wise, and I wished to be correct in the estimate I
formed of the existing civilization as compared with
the old.

As we were to become a part of the existing order of
things if we lived among men and did not choose to
become hermits, we must familiarize ourselves with the
customs and usages of society as we found them.   We
discussed the matter and prepared ourselves as well as
we knew how to become denizens of our own country.
What a thought!   What an experience!

The table of the "Inn" was, like its other appointments, well and substantially supplied, but lacking in
much that formerly characterized public houses.   There
was quiet everywhere.   This was most agreeable to us.
The servants were attentive but not obtrusive.   There
was no hurry or commotion ; no jostling of each other ;
no rattling or clashing of dishes.   You selected from
the bill of fare what you wished.   The prices were
named opposite each article.   You knew what you were
getting and its cost.   The charges were very reasonable.

During the afternoon I sought an interview with the

gentleman I supposed to be the proprietor. He told me he was only the overseer appointed by the government. The house and all pertaining to it belonged to the government. He had no interest in it. He was employed to conduct it, and received his salary or wages, nothing more. In this he was on the same footing as every other citizen. His responsibility extended no further than to prevent loss or damage to property as far as in his power, and to see that the house was properly kept. It was neither a laborious nor a worrying position.

"Do you have many guests?" I inquired.

"No, very few. There is no call for much travel. Every person is furnished so much for living expenses, which amount is fixed at such a sum that little is left for travel or outside disbursements. If any one travels much his rations are cut short, and most people prefer plenty to eat rather than expenditures in travel. There is no business, calling people from home. All the business of the country is done by the government, and government inspectors or agents and employees in the transportation of produce, etc., are the only class of persons who have occasion to pass from one part of the country to another."

These particulars were drawn out by a request on my part that he would enter into details as if giving information to a stranger who was entirely ignorant of the customs and usages of the people. I did know a little, but scarcely more than enough to confuse my ideas of things, and I desired to learn all that was possible without exposing myself.

"Why does the government make no provision for traveling on the part of the people?" I asked.

"It cannot. If people should be furnished facilities

for transportation at public expense, the whole population would be on the go. Business would be suspended, and famine and starvation would ensue. People would rather travel .than work, and if it cost the same, or the government furnished the means and paid the expenses, no work would be done."

"I see. But will not this lack of intercourse between the different parts of the inhabitants tend to alienation and separation?"

"Perhaps it will. It is not my business to look after those things, and I do not trouble myself with matters which do not belong to me."

"Will you be kind enough to refer me to some one who is well informed on all these matters, and can aid me in my research after knowledge?"

"Yes, sir, with pleasure. There is Dr. Leete, one of the best informed among our citizens, though he is something of an enthusiast. He can give you a large amount of desirable information on general and special subjects. He has now under his care a young man who is said to have been in a trance or sleep of some kind over a hundred years. He will doubtless be glad to assist you as well. But the man who is most thoroughly posted, and the one who has the widest range of knowledge, is Mr. Hume, our chief of police. What he cannot tell you is scarcely worth the knowing, so far as Boston is concerned—and the whole country, for that matter."

"Thank you. How can I find these gentlemen?"

"The doctor at his home; Mr. Hume at police headquarters."

The gentleman kindly tendered his services to give me an introduction the next day.

CHAPTER XXIII

THE chief of police proved to be a remarkable man, a little over fifty years of age, full of vigor, and looking much younger. He was genial and social. Coming to him for information, he proffered all the aid he could give me. It did not take long to learn that he was a man of no pretensions to superiority, but of a wide range of practical information, and a full comprehension of the social and political affairs of the country. He was unobtrusive, modest, almost diffident, but a man of keen insight, close observation, and untiring research. I remarked on my first interview that he probably found little time or opportunity to heed calls that distracted his attention from official duties. He replied:

"My official labors are by no means onerous. The whole plan of our government is based on the supposition that people who are properly fed, clothed, and housed will naturally be virtuous; that pretty much all the crimes and evils of former times resulted from hunger, cold, or privation; that poverty was the fruitful source of disorder and lawlessness, and the abolition of poverty also abolished misdoing. That is the theory on which our police system is established. Hence I have no heavy task put upon me as its chief officer."

"Does the theory hold good in practice?" I inquired.

"It does not. But as this theory prevails throughout all departments of the government, high and low, I have a very inadequate force at my disposal, and so much leisure on my hands. As you investigate the facts you will learn more about these matters."

"Does the pay correspond with the work performed?" I asked.

"It is presumed to; but practice and theory are frequently at variance. People under our system of government are paid because they exist, and not primarily because they labor, though between certain ages they are required to work. The fundamental basis of our economy is that every human being is entitled to a living, and must have it, whether it is earned or not."

"I remember such a sentiment existed in the nineteenth century. It found expression in the words, 'The world owes me a living,' which was often supplemented by the declaration, 'and I am going to have it.' But the general verdict of men then was that the world owed no man a living unless he earned it, if he was not physically or mentally disqualified to do so. It seems you have adopted the one and discarded the other."

"Not entirely discarded. It is held that every one should and must labor. It is presumed that the labor will compensate for the living. So it might, if all people were perfect. As they are not, the theory, of course, is as imperfect as the people who are depended upon to make it good."

"I perceive the point."

"You speak of remembering the condition of things in the nineteenth century. Of course you mean you have read of that century, not that you experienced the things you allude to. You cannot much exceed thirty years of age.'

"I have unwittingly betrayed myself prematurely. Perhaps it is just as well."

I then related my experience, so marvelously strange to men, and now become so simple to me. Mr. Hume looked incredulous, but being a gentleman did not call in question my statement. I requested him to test me by mentioning any occurrence or event from 1875 to 1892. He did so. The result removed every possible doubt from his mind. He then mentioned the case of Mr. West, who had been the wonder of Boston the past two months. I said I had heard of him at Washington, and that one object of visiting Boston was to see him. In company we went to see this gentleman at Dr. Leete's, where we received a royal welcome.

Mr. West and I found so much in common to converse about, as though events of over a hundred years old were just transpiring, that the others listened with silent and absorbed attention. It was far more thrilling and instructive than any romance. It was like holding up a mirror before those present into which they could look and behold the events of the nineteenth century passing like a panorama before them. We spoke of the Italian and Chilian embroglios, and of the Bering Sea negotiations with Great Britain, as events not yet settled. The things fresh in our memory were unknown or dimly called to mind by our hearers, who knew of them only by tradition or the history that imperfectly recorded them. It was more than an hour before we found a stopping-place, and then our auditors requested us to continue; but we declined on the ground that we should have other opportunities for this recreation. I made known my desire for information concerning the present. Mr. Hume then referred me to Dr. Leete.

I found him enthusiastic in praise of the existing order of affairs. He confirmed what Mr. Hume had already said, that society and government were founded on the fundamental principle or idea, that people were to be supported because they existed, and that if furnished with the necessaries and ordinary comforts of life, they would be virtuous and happy. The doctor's notion was centered in the belief that the craze for wealth in former times had led to the robbery of the poorer classes of their natural rights, and that hunger and nakedness and exposure drove them to crime. He claimed that most of the crimes and misdemeanors of the nineteenth and previous centuries were direct results of poverty, or necessarily grew out of the condition of things which made poverty a fact.

I suggested that many of the worst criminals were above want and of more than ordinary intelligence. He admitted the fact, but contended that these persons were either influenced by their environments or in haste to get rich. The doctor expatiated for several hours on the theme in which he delighted. I was highly entertained, but was not converted to his views; I desired to see and know more before reaching settled conclusions. As his views are fully set forth in his conversations with Mr. West, they need not be repeated here. From his side I found him a ready and willing helper in my investigations at all times.

I was presented to Mrs. and Miss Leete, and at my earnest solicitation Mr. West and Miss Leete accompanied me to the Inn to call on Effie. This was the beginning of a delightful acquaintance and friendship. From this time onward we were not entire strangers in the city.

CHAPTER XXIV.

HAVING made such an auspicious beginning, I began to look about me seriously for the best and most reliable sources of knowledge. I was not long in seeing that Mr. Hume was the most careful and impartial observer of customs and events of any with whom I came in contact. He was also a philosopher. He could give reasons for his opinions. He did not deal in assertions. He did not make use of unsupported affirmations. He never suffered himself to be led to conclusions by the superficial appearance of things. He tried to find a solid basis for convictions and beliefs. He was not enthusiastic. In converse with him I referred to Dr. Leete's fascination with the present order of things, national and social. He said:

"The doctor is perfectly captivated with matters as they are. He really thinks the world is almost a paradise. There are some things he does not know, and other things he will not know. In your day, as in all past ages, there were optimists and pessimists. The doctor is an enthusiastic optimist: he sees only the good and ignores the evil. His gaze is so absorbed in the silver lining to the cloud that he does not see the cloud at all. He believes everything is lovely and pure, partly because he is so himself. In this sense his views are creditable to his heart and life, if not to calm judgment. He sees only that which is to be approved, and all his observations are rose-colored. He thinks we are practically living in a restored Eden. If he occupied my position for a time, he would be compelled to change his notions quite radically. He does not believe mankind has a disposition to sin outside the demands of the stomach and the comforts of life. If these are supplied, men and women will be happy and contented, is his theory. He has always been favored in life. He is a fine physician, and greatly beloved. Though past the age of service, he still has patients by the score, if not by hundreds. This very popularity makes him enemies. Other doctors are jealous. Men in other callings dislike him because he is a general favorite. There is an undercurrent of feeling bordering on hatred toward him. He is in some danger of personal violence. I have tried to put him on his guard; but he believes nothing of the ill-will toward him, and treats all suggestions of personal peril with indifference, if not with contempt. Never having done or wished harm to any one, he cannot conceive how any one should desire harm to him.

"While the doctor is in danger, yet his age is a protection. Few persons are base enough to lay violent hands on a person of his years. His daughter is in most danger. She is noble, pure, and good, and is very popular with the better class of people. This is especially true of young men. This popularity has excited the ire of not a few of her own sex, who regard her as a thorn in the flesh because she is so generally liked, particularly by the gentlemen. I have warned her father. He treats the matter as unworthy of attention. He loves his daughter intensely. He cannot think any one is so depraved as to do harm to a being so innocent and lovely as Edith, whose whole life has been devoted to making others happy. No care or precaution is taken by the parents or daughter to prevent harm. I am not a little anxious concerning the outcome.

"Mr. West has been a center of attraction since his advent became known, partly because of the strange adventure which brought him among us. His evident partiality for Miss Leete and the report that they are to be married have added fuel to the smoldering fire of dislike. She is really hated by a number of young ladies and by some of their mothers for no reason except the fact that she is amiable, beloved, and popular. I shall not be surprised to hear of some trick played upon her, or some injury or violence done to her."

To my inquiry if he could not prevent such an occurrence he replied that his force was inadequate, and if otherwise he could not anticipate a crime. It must be perpetrated before it could be punished.

Leaving personal matters, I inquired how the war ended. Mr. Hume stated the facts.

"I may say it was fought out to exhaustion; both sides were worn out. The difference between capital and labor, rich and poor, comfort and pauperism, was practically wiped away. All were poor—almost poor alike. The wealth of the country was obliterated. The cities were in ruins; the rural districts were vast areas of desolation. What the war had not destroyed was used to obtain provisions and clothing, etc. All the great and minor fortunes had faded away. These were the objects of the special vengeance of the rabid element in the ranks of labor. The tilling of the soil was practically abandoned. Provisions became so scarce that the armies could not obtain adequate supplies. The troops became clamorous. Mutiny was threatened. As a last resort the labor army was led to attack Washington with the avowed purpose of plundering the treasury and burning the records. This the other side resolved should not be done. It would be an irreparable loss to have the archives of the nation turned to ashes and its capital blotted out. So at the seat of government—though there was no government except in name—the last attack was made. The fighting was long and desperate, and the mortality correspondingly great. But the city was preserved. A truce was agreed upon because it became an absolute necessity. This was followed by the permanent cessation of hostilities. There was no money in the treasury, and nothing for the hungry soldiers to plunder which could avail to re-relieve their straitened condition. Peace was followed by the adoption of the present form of government. There was little to gain or lose by either side. An agreement was reached after months of deliberation by mutual concessions."

" Why does Dr. Leete say the present order of things was secured without war, or the shedding of a drop of blood ? "

" That is one of his peculiarities. He follows Professor Smiley, who has written an elaborate work on the subject, in which he takes the position that the war with all its horrible attendant and direful realities was the outgrowth of the old civilization—a direct consequence of its barbarous origin and unnatural heritage; that all which took place previous to peace must be charged up to the nineteenth and preceding centuries. The new civilization dates only back to the new era, and is responsible for nothing beyond that epoch, which, he claims, is the great event of all time."

" That is rather strange logic. I can remember as far back as 1875; and I know that during a period of seventeen years from that date to 1892 there were a number of strikes and other troubles between laborers and capitalists, wherein blood was shed. The Haymarket tragedy in Chicago became historic in my time. It is therefore clear that blood was shed almost from the inception of the controversy and antagonism between capital and labor."

" All of which is true. Within ninety days after your first retirement in 1892, the bloody riots at Homestead in Pennsylvania, at the mines in Idaho and Tennessee, and the strike at Buffalo, N. Y., when many lives were sacrificed, many maimed, and large amounts of property destroyed, tell the same crimson story. Troops had to be called out at all these places to suppress lawlessness and murder. These facts clearly point to a trace of human blood from the commencement of the strife to the close of the war. Our fathers ought to have been warned in time of the impending disaster; but they were not, or if warned they heeded not. It seems like trifling with the clearest lessons of history to say that this astounding revolution was secured in perfect peace; but we shall have to let our friends have their way and enjoy their sweet illusion. I guess it does no harm. The professor and the doctor desire to clothe the present social and political fabric with clean and unspotted garments of angelic purity; hence they saddle all the crimes and ills of the race to what they are pleased to term the dead past. Being dead and buried, they claim it does it no harm to be made responsible for the mistakes and woes of mankind in those times."

" That is quite benevolent and consoling to the existing order of things, whether true or not. But I am seeking knowledge. Was there no compensation for the losses of the war?"

"Possibly there were. Men will differ in opinion on that point. Two things were accomplished which rendered the present order of affairs possible: the very poor all perished; the rich were reduced to poverty. While I do not regard the present form of government desirable or permanent, yet the leveling process named has made it possible for a better government in the future. No estimate of the cost of the war has ever been made; it was so fearfully destructive of both life and property no one seems to have a desire or disposition to ascertain the sum total. Those who fell in battle were but a small portion of the whole number that died. Famine and pestilence carried off their tens of thousands, while the battle-fields slew their thousands. No census was taken in 1930 or 1940. The census of 1950 showed fifteen millions less population than the census of 1920. This indicates a loss of sixty-five millions of people. But as some removed to other lands to save life and property, immigration almost ceased, and births were not nearly so numerous as in times of peace and quiet, the true loss of life would be less than these figures, which was the number of inhabitants in the nation in 1892, when you retired. But after making all due allowances, the loss of life was away up in the millions, so high as to make one shudder merely to think of those terrible years when the grim Reaper gathered his human harvest. The contemplation of that crimson chapter of our history is so appalling, with your permission we will turn from the black list of death to something less repulsive."

"Gladly. Is there much foreign immigration to this country now?"

"Very little. There is no demand and no place for foreigners."

" Is not that fortunate for us?"

" Doubtless. It was largely the foreign element that led to discontent and hostilities. If only native-born citizens had inhabited our country, I am persuaded we should have had peace to the end. The early republic owed much to foreigners of the better class; but when the criminal and pauper classes came over in such vast numbers the evil days began."

" I have seen the outward appearance of things; as now existing they look attractive. Are there any hidden or invisible under-currents not so pleasing?"

" I am sorry to say that beneath this exterior of loveliness there is hideous deformity—scenes too dark to depict. In your day, under gilded trappings of wealth there were horrible realities unseen by the mass of men. The same is true to-day. There are ten thousand drunkards in Boston. Distilleries and breweries are not permitted to exist except as run by the government; but there are a number of private manufactories of intoxicants underground, much like the moonshiners in your day. These furnish liquors to those who crave them."

" Why are they not suppressed?"

" Because nobody is empowered with authority to do so. As I said, the theory of government is that there will be no crime where there is no physical want. As want is kept from all—or supposed to be—by the direct act of government, it is presumed there will be no desire to violate the laws, or to do any wrong to society or to each other. The first generation after the war was so busy repairing the waste and providing for the wants of all, that there was really almost no need of law. The necessity laid upon that generation kept the people so active they found little time to study or execute wickedness. They had had so much turmoil and war, they wanted rest and peace. It was not then, as now, so many hours a day, and then rest. All the day long was a scene of toil. It was twenty years before the existing system assumed its present features and became the established order. This generation has much idle time on its hands, and it is as true now as when Watts sang it of old:

> "'Satan finds some mischief still
> For idle hands to do.'

"I regret to say that some of the men who drink take the portion of wives and children, furnished by the government for food and clothing, and spend it for the coveted beverage. Hundreds of children go hungry to bed almost every night from this cause. I have reported the facts to the authorities at Washington, but no attention seems to be paid to the subject."

"It appears to me there must be a serious defect in your system somewhere."

"True. It has always been so in all systems. Laws are made for the prevention and punishment of crimes and misdemeanors. 'Thou shalt not' is the language of all law; but every age has witnessed the violation of laws by the vicious. Murder, theft, robbery, and other outbreaking or violent crimes are provided for in theory and in law, though hardly expected in fact. But these secret sins are left to 'grow by what they feed upon.' They are practically unrestrained. Gambling is indulged in. There are secret places where this vice is carried on to any extent the players desire. Counterfeiting is also one of the secret sins of the city. It is easier to counterfeit our government scrip than it was the greenbacks of your age. No one can tell how much counterfeit scrip exists.   You can see at a glance how easy it would be for a skillful workman to make a fac-simile of a piece of scrip."

"Does not the government keep a record and register all the scrip it issues?"

"Certainly; but what of that?   Suppose I have a piece of scrip of a certain number and date.   Before it is all used up I make a counterfeit of the same date, number, and value, and take it to some depository of supplies where I have not been in the habit of purchas-ing, or to a different department of the same depository, where the clerks are not posted, and present the spu-rious scrip. It could not be detected. I could purchase what I desired with it without being suspected. My wife could use the genuine at the same time until it should be exhausted, and do it innocently.   This is done all the time."

"That is as bad as it was in my day, if not worse."

"Why should it not be?   Human nature is essen-tially the same in all ages.   Circumstances modify the actions of men, but do not make them other than men. This leads me to another point.   Licentiousness runs riot in the secret recesses of Boston.   In your time some women were driven into lives of crime and wretched-ness by want, hunger, cold, lack of shelter.   All good people deplored their misfortune.   But in every age there have been the Mrs. Potiphars, the Helens, the Cleopatras, and the thousands of others who chose to do evil without compulsion.   They exist in this city now.   There was a class in your day called 'free lovers.' That class of people is not dead nor asleep.   There are several secret cliques or societies of them in Boston. One of them is now in session.   Without the knowl-edge of these people, or of the gamblers and distillers,

I have secured telephonic communication with their various assemblies. If you will sit at this instrument you can hear them in secret discussion, not imparting but comparing their peculiar views."

I took the place designated, and while listening heard sentiments expressed and avowals made which respect for the feelings of the reader forbid to be repeated here. Nothing exceeding these utterances, in lack of virtue or in open profession of free-love principles and practices, ever disgraced the nineteenth century. I remarked to Mr. Hume:

"These people must belong to the abandoned classes, who care nothing for the good opinion of respectable society."

"On the contrary," he said, "they are mostly persons who pass in the best circles of society, and pose as virtuous members of the same. They suppose that they are unheard except by themselves, and so appear in their true character in these secret meetings. It is the natural outgrowth of passion on the part of men and women who have plenty of idle time on their hands and are not disposed to use it for purposes of self-improvement."

"I confess this is a startling revelation to me. It is surprising, shocking, basely infamous!"

"There is no possible excuse for such lapses from virtue; and I am not surprised that you are astonished by this revelation."

After some further conversation, Mr. Hume proposed to introduce me to a friend of his, a farmer of rare intelligence, who, he assured me, would be glad to enlighten me on some phases of our civilization and polity as these affect agriculture. I was delighted at the prospect of this new opening of a channel of information on so important a topic.

CHAPTER XXV.

On the day agreed upon, I took Mr. Hume in my chariot for the proposed visit in the country. His attention was particularly attracted to the chariot. He remarked that he had never seen one so complete and perfect. I replied that under governmental supervision great improvements ought to have been made.

"There is where you are in error," he said. "Under our system of operations there is no adequate inducement for persons to improve or invent machinery. The inventor has no personal interest or right in the product of his inventive skill more than his neighbor. All he gets is a diploma or medal, and these are empty considerations. Government owns everything, including products of the mental and physical powers of her citizens—in fact, owns the man himself. He is a mere machine, or a part of it; the crank or belt which run the whole affair is the government. Individual freedom, in the broad sense, that a man is master of himself, his time, talents, and labor, is not known. If it ever existed, it is a thing of the past; it died with the surrender of the man to the government. Hence there is almost no improvement in any direction. The telegraph, the telephone, aërial navigation, electrical machinery, and all else, remain practically as they were when the government swallowed everything. Railroads have deteriorated. There being no general travel, and no call for it, the roads are used almost exclusively for freights. Until children and youth are twenty-one years of age, they are required to go to school. From twenty-one to forty-five the people belong to the government for work, and are required to put in eight hours of labor each day. They have no choice but to give these eight hours of time to the public in labor during each twenty-four hours. They cannot work and travel at the same time.

"They own nothing at the end of forty-five years. Government owns the houses they live in, all the furniture and appurtenances thereto belonging, except a few decorations and a few books, when residents choose to furnish these at their own expense. Public libraries are accessible to all the people, and so books in private libraries are few. The people have no excess of funds with which to purchase anything. A Bible and a few standard books are provided for each house, and remain in it. After the age of forty-five the people are simply pensioners on the government. As a matter of equity and right, the pension is fixed at such an amount as will only properly keep the person comfortable—no overplus to expend in travel or gratification. To overstep this rigid rule would be to break down the whole structure of governmental rule. Even if a bounty was offered for extra service, it would lead to endless strife and jealousy, and ultimate revolution. One iron rule must be observed impartially: all must be treated alike—the same requirement of time and service, the same pay for these. These must be gauged to a fixed standard of economy, not of extravagance or waste; to provide for the needs and not the pleasures of life. This is the reason there is so little communication between the remote parts of

the country. We are becoming estranged from each
other. The people of Boston know as little from personal intercourse about the people of the great central
area of the continent as they do of the inhabitants
of South America or Africa. Our citizens scarcely ever
see a stranger or a citizen of any other State, except he
be a government employe. What the outcome will be
no one can foresee. There still remains the telegraph,
which gives us the general news all over the country;
but it is getting to be much like intelligence from a
far-away and alien land. What common interests
have our people here with those of Texas, Kansas, or
California? None whatever, except that which comes
through the government exchange. We have no business connections with those distant people, and, in point
of fact, none with our next-door neighbors. New York
and Pennsylvania have no interest in common with us.
There are no intermarriages, no social communications,
no ties of any sort to bind us together as one homoge-
neous brotherhood.

"There is no hurry anywhere. A man gets the same
pay for his work if he is deliberate as if he is in haste.
Our railroad passenger trains, when they run at all,
never exceed twenty-five miles an hour; freights are
lazily carried along at ten to fifteen miles per hour.
Railroad men, like others, put in eight hours a day;
at the end of each eight hours' journey there is a
station and a relay of hands. No speed is necessary.
It requires a large number of hands to keep the railroads and the service of trains properly in order.
Everything works by rule, but it is the iron rule of
the machine, which excludes all freedom, enterprise,
or aspiration. Everything is a dead-level, so to speak
—so much work for a living, which is given in exact

measure to each one. Such a system excludes emulation, shuts out ambition, and abolishes hope of preferment or distinction."

"Dr. Leete does not look at the condition of things in that light. He claims the incentives to ambition and excellence are as great now as formerly."

"I know he does. But the facts are against his fancy-colored theory, which is the outgrowth of his own happy and exceptional experience. He does get some private perquisites for his professional services; but even in his case there is nothing left for him to expend in extensive travel or other costly luxuries. What people spend for extras is taken from wages or pensions, and cuts off that much of their only revenue, regarded at best as only fairly sufficient for the necessaries of comfortable living. You can readily see where the clear-cut facts point. It is just as impossible for one person to travel much, or expend much in any direction, as it is for one to be rich and another poor. Equality is the one idea upon which the entire fabric of government and society is constructed. 'Liberty, equality, fraternity' is the motto, and the effort is to make it a reality. That it fails in every way and at every point, except where the government dispenses to the people, is evident. But most persons do not look beneath the surface to see what the real facts are. They feel that something is wrong, yet do not perceive the source of the wrong. Some hold their peace for policy's sake.

"In your day visitors went at such hours as pleased the parties themselves. It is not so now. The eight hours belong to the government; in them no visiting is permitted. All social intercourse must be had during the hours devoted to recreation and sleep. If we should reach the home of my friend before five o'clock, he would not dare to stop work and receive us until that hour which releases him from obligation for the day. This clock-work reaches to all departments of human life and action. Honest men are faithful; dishonest ones are not. The treadmill drudgery of the eight hours' compulsory labor whets the appetite of the evil-disposed to run into excesses when released from the grasp of the cast-iron rule."

We had now reached our destination, and received a hearty welcome at the farmer's home. The family consisted of Mr. and Mrs. Acre, and their son and daughter. When Mr. Acre saw my chariot he said:

"That is a fine rig. The government turns out no such work as that. I have seen nothing so complete, costly, and elegant. How came you to possess such a rare gem of beauty and convenience?"

"There is a long story connected with it, which I beg to delay repeating until a future time," I said.

Mr. Hume then stated the purpose of our visit, and our host replied that he would gladly render me any assistance in his power, which would be small compared with what Dr. Leete and Mr. Hume could furnish.

CHAPTER XXVI

MR. ACRE continued the interview.

"Dr. Leete and Mr. Hume have enlightened you on the fundamentals of our system, and I need not repeat. The system is one of ownership and servitude. No man can dispose of himself as he would; he simply obeys orders. It is called a paternal government, but the name does not mitigate its rigor. It has some advantages. No one is to be in want. That many are in want is not the fault of the government, but of individuals. Employment and pay are both sure. No actual want except as the result of criminal conduct; no tramps nor beggars; no paupers of the old style; houses for all, comfortable living for all provided—these are blessings which arrest the attention at once. They are attractive. They give our civilization an exterior polish that is pleasing to behold. Alas that this beauty is only skin-deep! If only all people were good and honest, true and virtuous, the evils of the system might not appear."

"If I understand your polity, it aims to deal with all persons exactly alike. How can that be unjust which is equal?"

"It is only equal in name, not in fact. There are multiplied methods by which men evade the just requirements of the government, and defraud it and the honest portion of the community as completely as if they stole from or robbed them. The worst feature of

our system is that it puts a hardship upon its only
true supporters, while it permits the treacherous and
tricky to defraud almost at pleasure."

"I do not see how that can be."

"I presume not. Even close observers like Mr.
Hume would hardly discover this defect in his calling.
Dr. Leete would never see it, and would not believe it
if told him. He is infatuated with the exterior, and
never delves beneath the surface. The intent is right.
In theory all people are treated alike; in practice they
are not. Let me illustrate. I am given forty acres of
land to cultivate, and am required to work eight hours
a day all the year round. Every hour is devoted to the
cultivation of crops, care of the harvests, removing the
products, or preparing the soil for the next season's
crops. I try to be faithful. No other forty acres of
land in this region makes better returns than mine.
Here is my neighbor Briggs over the way, who has
the same amount of land, equally as good in all respects as mine; he has the same implements and help
furnished him for use in cultivating the farm; yet he
produces less than half as much as I do each year.
Why? He is lazy and indolent. When he does work
it is not with industrious zeal, but in a lounging, slip-
shod manner. Much of the time he pretends to be
sick. I do not wish to judge harshly or wrongfully;
but the facts must tell. He goes to bed—claims to
be in much bodily suffering. Dr. Leete, good-natured
and unsuspecting soul, comes out to see him, examines
the case—never suspects deceit or duplicity—finds the
man sick; gives him a certificate of illness, which is
good for perhaps a week, with medicines or prescrip-
tion. The doctor goes home. In one hour Briggs is
out knocking around, cursing what he does not like,

and idling away his time, doing nothing to benefit himself or the rest of the world. He has ten children and about one nurse all the time, making thirteen in the family. We have two children, or four in the family. He draws supplies for thirteen, I for four. My farm yields one hundred per cent.; his, less than fifty per cent. He gets three and one-fourth times more for his time than I do, while I pay back over twice as much as he does—a difference of one hundred per cent. in profit, and of three hundred and twenty-five per cent. in expenses, or a total of four hundred and twenty-five per cent. Is there justice or right in that difference?"

"I confess I do not see any. I had not thought of the inequalities in that light. Cannot the government provide for such cases?"

"How provide? If a man is detailed to watch every farmer it will require as many detectives as laborers, and these are to be fed, clothed, and provided for as others, so that nothing can be gained."

"Is not this an extreme case?"

"No; I wish it was. I know of twenty other similar cases which have come under my own observation. It is safe to say that not more than one half the farmers do faithful work. I am now placing the number at the extreme limit of best advantage. The other half are more or less derelict in duty, most of them badly deficient. It is not an inviting picture; but it is true to life. Read the returns for farms in Massachusetts, and you will see that I have been liberal and over-charitable in my estimates.

"But bad as this feature of the working of our system is, there is another still worse. To make this plain and intelligible, I must state a few primary facts.

There are but three original sources of production, namely, the soil, the mine, and the water. The husbandman, the miner, and the fisherman produce or develop all the resources of the world in their original forms or conditions. Then come the forge, the loom, and other appliances, which, for brevity, may be termed representatives of all transforming processes. Here, then, are four classes of people who do all the valuable or productive labor of the world. All other labor, if it may be dignified by that term, is for personal comfort or self-gratification, and adds nothing to the possessions of mankind. Now look at our cities, filled with vast numbers of people, nearly all of whom are mere consumers. They produce absolutely nothing, and live off of other people's toil. And they live finely. Look at the magnificent public buildings in Boston; and all the other cities are like it. Who paid for these costly structures? They did not come by chance. They represent an immense outlay of human energy; but not one in four of those who enjoy them ever did an hour's labor toward their erection. These, more than three fourths of the denizens of our cities, are the recipients of blessings secured by others. Every brick and stone, every piece of timber, every ounce of mortar, represents the toil of the working classes named. They are the price of blood, for it takes life to accomplish these results, and the blood is the life. These build, but others inhabit. The toilers produce the fruits of the ground, the riches of the mine, the stores of the deep, and transform the same, while the others 'eat, drink, and are merry.'

"What do four fifths of the people in the cities do? They cook, wash dishes and clothes for themselves and one another, and nothing else. They toil not, neither do they spin, in the sense of production. They do not produce or develop an ounce of the food they eat, or a thread of the clothing they wear. They are simply paupers, fed and clothed by the government from the stores which others bring into existence."

"That is an entirely new aspect of the case," I said, struck with the force and originality of the statement.

"It is the only truthful view. Tell me, if you can, what the people of the cities do to provide their own support?"

"Dr. Leete says they are servants and served by turns, and all work."

"Work at what? Simply to minister to one another's wants or comfort out of the abundance we who really do labor furnish ready to their hand. They only live to consume; and their enjoyment is like dancing upon the tender and bare nerves of the toilers, who face the storms of all seasons, the heat of summer and the cold of winter, the dangers of the mine and the main, that they may have the wherewithal to feed and clothe themselves, live in comfortable houses, and sing in merriment over their easy lives, free from care or anxious thought. I wish to emphasize what I have already said, that these people are only pensioned paupers of the government, who live upon the fat of the land, and never do an hour's labor toward the production of their own living.

"I know that Dr. Leete and others who have lived in cities all their lives think that serving each other is labor. But in the true sense it is not. The doctor talks about equalizing labor among all classes. Only a denizen of the city, who knows nothing about the real facts of the case, whose experience and observation have been confined to cities all their lives, where serving and served are the chief ends of life, could ever have conceived an idea so wide of the truth as it is, or of actual realization. As well assert that it rains alike on all days in the year, or that it is cold and warm alike every hour of the three hundred and sixty-five days. We farmers have to go out in the sun and rain of summer to till the soil; in the cold and snow of winter to feed the stock, and see that nothing goes to waste. If the grain or hay is down and a rain is coming on, we must strain every nerve to secure the results of our toil. Some indolent farmers, like Briggs, do not care, and permit the crops to be damaged or destroyed by the storms. But the conscientious farmer makes all possible effort to preserve that which is likely to perish. How can a man in the city, under cover and well provided for, do any amount or kind of work to offset this experience of the farmer? The rain and snow, sleet and hail, overtake the farmer in his toil. He has no great awning, like a continuous umbrella, to shield him from the inclement weather. He endures the pelting of the elements in all seasons, and under all phases of their visitations. But the paupers of the city can walk dry-shod and in perfect safety under their great canopies, every foot of which is constructed out of the proceeds of the sweat and toil of those who really do labor and suffer for the preservation and comfort of the race.

"No man raised on a farm, or delving in a mine, or periling life on the sea, would be guilty of saying that the labor of the country is equally distributed. It is only one who belongs to the pauper class, or who has spent all his life among that class, who can sit down at his ease, smoke his cigars, and expatiate on the equitable distribution of labor among all classes and to each individual. If any kind of work required but ten minutes to offset the eight hours of daily labor, the doctor says it would be so adjusted. When he can control the winds and the clouds, calm the tumult of the seas, or remove all danger from the mines, he may talk in that strain; but not until then. Suppose that during the ten minutes of toil the mine should explode, the ship go down, or the cyclone sweep the farmer away, how would the doctor compensate for the loss of life, or make eight hours of easy labor its equivalent? No, sir, the paupers should be put to some occupation of real industry where they would learn at least the rudiments of true labor."

"Then you favor abolishing the cities?"

"Most certainly I do, as at present constituted. What are they good for? What purpose do they serve in our economy? They are excrescences on the body politic, and hot-beds of vice socially. It is in the cities that nine tenths of all crimes are committed. In your time they served a purpose: they furnished markets; they were places of exchange; they were business centers, and were useful in many ways. But they were cancers even then that ate out the virtue of the people. Now they are of no use whatever. They are not marts for the sale of produce; there is no produce for sale. They furnish no means of exchange, for nothing is exchanged. Government does all this, dealing directly with all the people. This can be done better without the cities than with them. Each manufacturing establishment can be selected as the site for a depository where the raw materials can be delivered and goods served to the people. Compel the paupers to become producers. If the number is so great that less time need be spent in labor from each one to furnish needed supplies, then let fewer hours be devoted to toil.

"But the whole system is wrong. I am a radical on this point. There can be no improvement, no development in progress, where there is no adequate incentive to action, as you have probably heard Mr. Hume remark. Our agricultural implements are no better than those in use fifty years ago. The genius of progress seems to have folded her wings and retired from among men. Occasionally, at rare intervals, some one stumbles upon some new thing, or some improvement of the old. But who will devote time, talent, labor, and money, or the scrip which represents it, thus depriving himself and his family, if he has one, of the comforts of life, for the purpose of devising some new thing, when the thing itself is not his after he has found it, but belongs to me as well, and to no one in particular? As the government owns him and his invention, he will not trouble himself to invent."

"Dr. Leete speaks of prizes or awards to those who excel in any line," I said.

"What do these amount to? It is simply being gazetted as a successful person in the particular department of labor or enterprise where he belongs. I have had this honor repeatedly as the one who excelled as a farmer. But it is empty as the wind. The name is read and in an hour forgotten; the medal is seen to-day and to-morrow is remembered no more. The fickle multitude shout, 'Hosanna to our King!' one day, and the next cry out as vociferously, 'Crucify Him!' He who spends his vital or mental force to secure such empty applause and ephemeral notoriety has little appreciation of their real value. They have in them no quality which can stimulate human industry or skill."

"I fear you are a pessimist," I remarked.

"I think not. I endeavor to look at all matters

calmly and rationally. Can you point out wherein I am in error or a pessimist?"

"Not on the spot. Your statements are rather stunning in their character; and certainly you do not lack force in giving expression to them. Do you wish to return to the old ways?"

"I do not fully understand what you mean by 'old ways.' My impression is that the old ways were gradually improving all the time. Much that then existed is better than what we have now. The removal of motive for personal activity has proved a great loss—in fact, it is death to enterprise and development. The lack of intercourse and communication among our people is proving disastrous. But I will not attempt an enumeration of the lame places in our system. It is too defective all over to require analysis. When a man loses his personal identity and becomes the tool or instrument of another, whether that other be a man or a government, he is too near a cipher to ever become a power in the world. If he were a slave and still had an interest in and control over the products of his genius or skill, there would be hope for him. But even this privilege is denied to American citizens under our economy."

"Your estimate is gloomy indeed. Have you no plan of improvement, or no substitute?"

"I do not dignify my notions into the realm of plans. It seems to me that the benefits of our system can be retained in connection with the blessings of a system which secures personal freedom and the right to enjoy the fruits of one's own toil, whether of mind or body. If the government has the right to demand and command the services of all its citizens, surely it has the right to dispose of its pauper population by compelling them to work for the common weal, as others and myself are compelled to work. If I understand the facts, the change from individual to united effort was made almost exclusively for the benefit of the poor, or to banish poverty from the land. If the government had set apart a portion of its public domain while yet under its control, and then made all the paupers and the poor who were able to work go to such reserved lands and make their own living, the remedy would either have removed or greatly mitigated the disease. It kept thousands of Indians on reservations and fed them from the proceeds of the toil of the white population. This last feature was a manifest injustice, unless by some process of reasoning, not clear to me, this policy and procedure were designed as payment for the land, to which the Indians had a very questionable title. It was not placed upon this footing, so far as the records show. Why did the government take such care of the Indians and not provide for its own poor? If it could compel Indians to go to certain specified districts of country, why not compel the unprovided poor of the white population to do the same thing? I am unable to see why one of these policies might not have been adopted as well as the other. I am aware that the theory of government then was essentially different from what it is now, and was not in the line of this suggestion. But self-preservation and wide benevolence both appear to me to demand such a policy, or something kindred to it; and self-preservation is nature's first law. Possibly my present environments disqualify me as a judge in the premises; and yet the possibility of these existing environments is a factor to be taken into consideration of the subject. Certainly such a course would have been preferable to the wholesale destruction of life and property by a fifteen years' war, during which both the wealthy and the poor of the land disappeared.

"There was still another method by which the poor might have been relieved, and all the real benefits of our system, combined with the advantages of the old, been secured. A tax for the poor could have been devised by the use of which employment could have been secured in some department of industry, if such department had to be provided by the government. Those who possessed wealth could much better have devoted a tenth of it to provide for the poor than to lose it all in the hope of saving it intact."

"I am afraid your plans are too visionary. They certainly would have been considered so in my time."

"If they are more visionary or revolutionary than the one which makes the government owner of the man and the products of his labor, I fail to see it."

"Possibly not. But to me, just from the nineteenth century, they appear novel and scarcely practicable. But, of course, I may be wrong. Do you think the present condition of things is permanent?"

"Not by any means. It is the most difficult thing in the world to make machines of men. Already the murmurs of discontent can be heard on every hand. I am sure the thrifty farmers are ill at ease. They do not fancy being placed on the same level with the idle and careless ones. There is growing discontent in every direction. If you will accompany Mr. Hume on some of his excursions through the city, you will find that even among the paupers there is dissatisfaction. And of all others they ought to feel themselves highly favored. They are daily and yearly receiving something for nothing. Instead of being thankful, they claim this as their right, and are the most self-impor-

tant class of all our population, which fact does not
tend to harmonize opinions and feelings."

" You predict a change, then ?"

"Yes; in less than five years there will be changes
and modifications, if not an actual revolution. Labor
is now organized, not against capital, but in opposition
to pampered pauperism in places of ease. But it is
doing its work quietly."

I thanked Mr. Acre for his kindness in giving me the
benefit of so long an interview. After a pleasant visit
with the family we returned to the city.

CHAPTER XXVII.

In accordance with Mr. Acre's suggestion, I sought an early opportunity to accompany Mr. Hume through the city.

We first visited the magnificent public edifices, which were the pride of Boston. I need not dwell on their elegance; the reader can picture as well as I can describe them. The vast awnings were delightful retreats from the heat or the rain. As we examined these buildings and their adornments, my companion said:

"These are some of the costly structures of which Mr. Acre complains so earnestly."

"What is the object of such lavish expenditures?" I asked.

"Simply to adorn and beautify the city. It is to gratify the pride of the citizens."

"Then I do not blame Mr. Acre for feeling indignant."

"One half the labor and expense would meet all the requirements both of comfort and usefulness."

"The other half goes for æsthetic taste, I suppose."

"More nearly for ostentation. They were erected years ago, when there was prosperity, and when there were funds to expend. No new structures are now in process of erection because no means are left for such purposes."

This last remark made little impression at the time, but afterwards was vividly recalled to mind. When the grandeur and glory of the city had been observed, Mr. Hume said:

"You have seen the beauty and splendor of Boston; now we will look upon its wretchedness and squalor."

I found no tenement-houses, no rickety stairs to climb, no damp and reeking cellars to explore. Outward appearances were not unpleasant; until the inner veil was drawn aside nothing repulsive was encountered.

Then I saw sights to chill the blood. Children nearly naked ran to hide; women half-clad sought to escape observation; little ones crying for bread; fathers beastly drunk! I cannot find it in my heart to depict the scenes of wretchedness and misery which I beheld. Except in the matter of houses only, which could not be sold, what I saw was a repetition of the degradation of the nineteenth century. I inquired indignantly:

"How can these things be, under your paternal government?"

"Simply because these men and women are selfish and sinful."

"Why are they not punished?"

"We have no laws provided for such cases. It was confidently believed they would not and could not exist under our beneficent economy. I have reported the facts to the government repeatedly, but without results. I am simply directed to do the best I can until a remedy shall be devised."

"This is dreadful! Fathers drunk, and wife and children ragged and hungry; parents both drunk, and children naked and starving! Does Dr. Leete know this state of affairs?"

"He does not believe these evils exist."

"Why does he not investigate?"

"I have frequently invited him to accompany me as

you are doing, but he is either too busy or has no inclination to do so. I sometimes think it will do no
good to destroy his dream of human happiness by these
exhibitions of depravity, suffering, and wretchedness."

"I think he and every citizen ought to know the facts
and remedy these terrible wrongs if possible."

"Did knowledge of wrongs enable you to remedy
them in the nineteenth century?"

"Only to a limited extent. But the conditions now
and then are so different."

"True. But men are the same. Taste and passion
are the same. Men cannot be reformed by either bread
or law. There is no moral quality in either of these.
You doubtless recall many instances in your time when
there would be a black sheep in this family and that—
a devil, as it were, coming from a company of angels.
Then again there were white sheep coming from bad
families, like angels coming from a company of devils,
so to speak. Yet these black sheep and white sheep
had the same care, shelter, food, clothing, and parental
care as the others. No philosopher has ever been able
to account for the difference. But there it is, a stern
fact, known and seen of all men. It is the same under
our paternal government, only, there being one great
family, the black sheep are multiplied a thousandfold.
You have witnessed some of the results; I will now
show you more. As before stated, I have not succeeded
in getting Dr. Leete to look upon these evidences of
want, suffering, and sin, because of his disinclination
to see or believe anything that is not desirable in our
social order. And then, too, 'where ignorance is bliss
'tis folly to be wise.' We will now look in upon the
gamblers."

It would be a waste of time and space to narrate all

our adventures in the dens where men lost and won as
of old.   It was a repetition of the same deeds as made
men mad in the nineteenth century.   The gamblers endeavored to escape in some instances, in others to hide
the evidences of their nefarious practices.   But Mr.
Hume knew them.   Their devices were confiscated and
destroyed; numbers of them were arrested and fined.
For the time their operations were terminated; but
they would soon rally and try again.   The private stills
and breweries were also raided and captured as far as
discovered, and destroyed, the operators punished.

Deplorable as were the evils of drink and gambling,
the orgies revealed at night under cover of darkness
were still worse.   The former led to physical and
financial distress, the latter to moral ruin.   People of
whom better things would be expected were found engaged in riotous living, to depict which would defile
these pages.   I was horrified at the revelations.   My
very soul was made sick.   I finally begged my guide
to take me from such scenes of debauchery and crime.
I almost felt a loathing of my kind as I escaped with a
shudder from the presence and dominion of "her
whose steps take hold on hell."   I breathed freer when
I reached God's pure air once more.

"And this is Boston in the year 2000!   This is Dr.
Leete's Eden!   Heaven save the mark!" I exclaimed.
Mr. Hume replied:

"Not Boston proper, my friend, only underground
Boston."

"It matters not what name or qualification you give
it; it is the same old hell upon earth of former times.
The glory of the new era grows dim; its gold is tinsel;
its beauty vanishes.   It is the illusive fruit of Sodom,
enticing to behold, turned to bitter ashes on the lips."

"I am afraid you are too severe. You have been too suddenly awakened from a pleasant dream. Human nature, as I said, is the same as it was in your day, no better, no worse. Our mistake has been in presuming that appliances which have no moral qualities or properties in themselves could, nevertheless, impart these to men. This is nothing new. It has been a mistake of the ages, even of the church at times. It is more manifest in our case because it is on such a wide scale. You must not do us injustice."

"I would not be unjust to the meanest creature God has made; but what am I to think of the morals of a community whose most favored members are guilty of these excesses?"

"It is nothing new. Were not kings, queens, and princes guilty of like conduct through all the past centuries? Were not the rich of your day often as bad as these?"

"True."

"Yes, true, because the master passion of the human heart when once unchained becomes master of the man. Our people have plenty of leisure and no care for bodily needs or comfort. Under such favorable conditions what but disastrous results could be expected?"

"This is such a rude shock to me that I must have time to reflect. I had earnestly hoped for better things. I was largely inclined to the optimistic view of the new dispensation. The kaleidoscope is broken; its fragments lie scattered at my feet. I must find time and place to collect and replace them under the new light."

An incident occurred during the day which I now relate because of its after-consequence. Mr. Hume entered a building to transact some business; I took a seat by the door, inside. Two ladies passed by, between whom I heard this fragment of conversation:

"I think she will not carry her head so high after we are done with her."

"What will Mr. West do when he sees her?"

"I think the sight will dampen his ardor, and——"

They passed out of hearing, and the remainder of the sentence was not heard by me. Before I had time to consider the purport of this conversation Mr. Hume was ready and we resumed our way. As I stepped into the street my eye glanced in the direction the women were going. I saw them enter a house. Prompted by I know not what, I made a note of the street and number. Five minutes later the incident passed from my mind completely, and probably never would have been recalled but for subsequent events to be narrated hereafter.

CHAPTER XXVIII

EFFIE and I received a very cordial invitation to visit again Mr. Acre's family. We selected a beautiful day and set out early in the afternoon, intending to explore the country in several directions. Neither of us had been favored with an opportunity to see the environments of the city.

Many of the views were enchanting. We ascended to an altitude where the distant ocean was distinctly visible as it spread out away in the far distance and kissed the bending sky. Few vessels were in sight on its placid bosom. There were no evidences of commercial activity; no smoking steamers hastening into port or speeding away to other climes; no vessels in the harbor loading and unloading their cargoes; no indications of trade and traffic. How different from the nineteenth century!

Away off to the northward were the dim outlines of the Green Mountains; in all directions places of historic interest. The scene was exhilarating.

Presently we turned our attention to the fields and farms beneath us, and descended to get into closer proximity to them. It required no skill of the specialist to discover the truth of what Mr. Acre had said about slovenly farming. I could detect good and bad cultivation and care at sight. My early experience gave me this advantage. Only a small proportion of the farms

189

were in first-class order; more were in a fair condition; a majority were discreditable to the occupants; while large numbers were in such miserable plight as confirmed the worst estimate Mr. Acre had placed upon them. With equal facilities on the part of all, the disparity was much greater than in my time.

We were welcomed with open hospitality, and Effie found new friends of congenial tastes. At my request Mr. Acre enlightened us again.

"As I said to you the other day, there is great inequality in the distribution of the burdens of labor. The people of the cities have all the ease, those of the country all the hardships. You have seen the elegance and splendor of the city. Do you see any of it in the country? No; you find only plain accommodations here, without ornament or adornment of any kind— nothing to cultivate a taste for the beautiful. The buildings are fairly convenient and plainly substantial. We produce; the denizens of the city cook and eat. We not only produce the food of the nation, but we do our own cooking and washing; in the cities the cooking is done by wholesale and the washing and ironing by machinery. If close by, farmers can avail themselves of these advantages; but when a few miles distant it is very inconvenient, if not impossible, to do so. Farmers' wives have no easy time with their work. Eight hours with them often lengthens to ten or twelve when they cultivate refinement or have æsthetic tastes to gratify.

"It is this great disparity between the comforts of the city and the hardships and privations of the country that causes such a rush of people to the former. This tendency has produced its legitimate effect. With all its care to provide food in abundance to meet all the demands of consumption, the government finds itself embarrassed to keep up the supply. Young men incline to choose occupations in the cities for the reasons already given; and who can blame them? As a result the crop reports show a steady relative decline, while the census returns show a steady relative increase, of population in the cities. There can be but one of two outcomes—a scarcity of food, or a compulsory distribution of labor. Already this alternative is staring the government squarely in the face. For twenty-five or thirty years, while the country was recuperating and the rebuilding of the cities required hard labor, this tendency did not exist or was not observed; but now it is too apparent to be mistaken. Our policy is one for the growth of cities and not for the development of the farming interests. The food supply must be looked after."

"Why not appropriate the cities exclusively to the old people retired on pensions, and have the rest all distributed for productive and mechanical labor?" I said. "Certainly this would be more equitable and judicious than the present methods?"

"It has been suggested and will doubtless be carried out in time, perhaps soon. When we have the census returns for this year completed and analyzed, some action will be taken. I am expecting much valuable and useful information from that source.

"There is one other element of hardship in the farmer's lot which at first does not appear. It is only learned from experience. Government can make no provision for permanent family homes. Next year I shall be forty-five, and my time for the occupancy of this house will expire. It then reverts to the government. My son will probably succeed me. That is the rule where all parties are agreed, and is found to operate well. This will break up our happy family relations."

The tears came into Mr. Acre's eyes, and his lips quivered. His wife saw his emotion and came at once to his side; she had heard the last words uttered, and knew that a sore place had been touched. As a comforter she placed a hand on each side of his head and said cheerily:

"Never mind, dear. We shall be left to each other, and some home will be provided for us."

"Yes, but all these cherished associations will be cut off," he replied. "Here we have spent all the years of our wedded life; here our children have been born and grown up. We have tried to make home attractive for their sakes and for ourselves; and now so soon it will all be over."

He spoke with deep emotion, and the tears that had stood in his eyes, held back by force of will, now slowly rolled down his cheeks. Unable longer to master her own feelings, the wife's cheeks were also wet. I looked at Effie. She also was crying. Every eye in that house was full of tears. After a time I found command of myself and said:

"This is an entirely new feature of the case to me. Cannot such a calamity as the breaking up of families be averted?"

"How can it be? The government can never know how many children there will be in a family; and even if it did know, how could it provide homes for all of them? If my son is my successor here, which we all expect, we can remain with him until he is married. But to keep him single until we died would be more cruel than for us to find a new place to live. The order of nature is reversed by our artificial society. Instead of the parents retaining the homestead, as you used to call it, but which is no homestead at all under our economy, the children, or one of them, remains in possession, and the parents are turned out of house and home and sent elsewhere. The land is cut up into forty-acre tracts and less. If there are ten children in the family, it would require ten houses, or one to each four acres, to accommodate them with separate homes. Another generation equally prolific would require one hundred additional houses, and the forty acres would be a village. Any rate of increase would soon blot out all the farms of the country, and no tillable land would be left. Necessity compels the old occupants to be sent out."

"Under the old system of things families were separated when the children grew up and were married," I said.

"True; yet where father and mother lived was always home to the children. Now there is no home association. One married son or daughter may succeed the parents, and the rest are dumped out in the cold, or sent to some strange place to live. That dear old song, 'Home, Sweet Home,' is largely a legend of the past. Separation is now compulsory, not voluntary, and that makes all the difference in the world. It is the difference between freemen and slaves."

"I understand now, as I did not then," I remarked, "what you said the other day, when you designated the people as slaves, and the government as the one great master. I fear I shall never be able to love this system of government. Every new development renders it less attractive."

"It becomes more apparent also why the city is preferable to the country as a place of residence. At the end of the forty-five years there, no necessity may arise for a change of residence. The occupations do not require it as here. Dr. Leete will doubtless retain possession of his present residence when his daughter marries. She will find the new home, or possibly reside with her parents, as she is the only child. He never can know the sad experience of the farmer, and is utterly disqualified to pass judgment on the question of our civilization as it affects us."

"I never should have guessed at these facts, but as you state them, I perceive the impossibility of their being anything else but facts. Nor do I see any way to avoid them or their painful accompaniments."

"And the reasons for the popularity of city life are also made more and more apparent. Farms will have to be cut down to twenty, ten, and even five acres in time. But that does not change the results. When the time comes the occupants must go; the actual farmer must be the resident on the farm."

"I perceive the logic of the situation. But is there no compensation?"

"In a sense there is. Government is bound to furnish every citizen a place to dwell in, whether it be called home or not. In that all have houses to occupy, our system is an improvement upon its predecessor. It feeds all in theory also; but, as you have seen with Mr. Hume, some go hungry, despite the good intent of the government."

"Yes, I understand that now; yet it seems to me a remedy ought to be provided."

"Not until humanity ceases to be selfish."

"You said the other day there would be changes made soon. Of what nature are they?"

"I do not feel at liberty to explain now. One thing,

the able-bodied paupers of the cities will be compelled to engage in some productive labor, and the cities given up largely to the pensioners. The necessity for an increase of food-supplies to keep pace with the growth of population is upon us and must be met. But, as I said to you the other day, there must be even more radical changes before satisfactory results of a permanent character can be attained. Change or stagnation must come; and stagnation is the prelude to death. I do not think we shall die."

Much more I desired to ask my host; but the time for our departure had come, and with a sense of indebtedness for the cordial hospitality of our entertainers, whose society had been to us a rich treat, we bade them adieu.

CHAPTER XXIX.

THE following day I visited some of the factories to see how they were managed. I learned nothing of importance. No new method and no improvement on old ones were visible. There was no energy, no push, no enterprise. Slowness seemed to prevail everywhere, and in all departments of endeavor. I appreciated better Mr. Acre's remark about stagnation.

On returning to our room I found Effie in a state of great excitement.

"What is it?" I asked.

"Have you not heard about Edith Leete?"

"No. Anything serious?"

"The most fiendish act of its kind ever perpetrated upon a human being. She is utterly disfigured. Her former beauty is turned into hideousness. I cannot describe it; you must see for yourself. She is totally prostrated; so are her parents. Mr. West has not seen her yet, and she cannot bear the thought of his seeing her."

"Is the disfigurement or deformity permanent?"

"It is said it can never be removed. But come with me and see her. The doctor desires it greatly. Comfort them if you can."

We were at Dr. Leete's in a few minutes. At first Edith would not permit me to see her face; finally she removed the thick veil from over it. I was startled at the sight. On one cheek was the picture of a creature, half human, half fish, similar to the representations of mermaids of old. Its face was a gross caricature, but retained enough distorted resemblance to give assurance it was intended to delineate Miss Leete herself. On the other cheek was an ogre looking toward her with a kind of leer and gross admiration. The mermaid figure was nude from the waist upward. On the neck, with its head reaching up and over the chin, was a third figure, evidently intended as a caricature of Mr. West. Beneath, on the lower part of the neck, just at the base of the last-named figure, this legend was painted in distinct letters:

"Mr. West sees Edith making love to another."

Any movement of the face caused the figures to grimace at each other detestably. It was a most ingenious and satanic piece of work, requiring great skill and adroit ability in its line, but marked by a depth of depravity beyond comprehension. What human being could have such malice toward one so lovely and lovable as Miss Leete?

"Who did this?" I asked in indignation.

"I will tell you the whole story," said Edith, "so far as I know it. I was passing along the street very quietly when a voice called to me:

"'O Miss Leete, please step in; I have something to show you.'

"Not knowing but I could be of service to some one, and never for a moment suspecting harm or wrong, I entered the door, when it was immediately closed and locked behind me. Before I had time to collect my wits, a hand, then a pad, were placed upon my mouth. I was then seated in a large chair with a high back. Three women in masks were present, and one man.

One of the women, who appeared to be the leader, said to me:

"'If you are quiet and do not struggle you will not be hurt. We shall inflict no pain. We simply have a preparation here which we wish to try upon your complexion. If you will be patient and give us no trouble we will soon be through with the experiment.'

"With that they put upon my face, one after another, the horrible things you see, taking pains in transferring them to impress them indelibly upon the skin. When they were done, the speaker said:

"'There, you are a beauty now! Mr. West will be so proud of you you will scarcely be able to bear his admiration. All the young ladies will be envious of the attention you will attract. You can hold your head higher than ever after this, and break all the girls' hearts by stealing their beaux from them. Just look in the glass and see how greatly we have improved your good looks.'

"And she held up a glass before me. I do not know why I did not faint or try to scream. But I did not. I kept perfectly quiet, for which I am now thankful. They evidently expected a scene, and were disappointed. I am glad that this part of their wicked plot failed. They were masked so completely I did not know them, nor did I recognize the voices. Only one spoke. Before releasing me, the woman said:

"'You can rest assured these additions to your beauty will never wear off or wash out. These colors have been discovered by a chemist, who warrants them to be permanent and imperishable.'

"As soon as the door was opened, I drew the veil over my face and came home. In the excitement and hurry of the moment I forgot to notice the house or the number, and am by no means certain I could find the place. That is the story in full. I have tried to wash out the stains, and father has exhausted his skill in efforts to remove them. But the horrible things remain as distinct as ever."

Here the doctor broke in:

"I did not believe that Edith had an enemy in the world. I know she merits the good-will of every person in Boston. She never harmed any one, but has been kind to all. I cannot imagine the wickedness that could perpetrate such an outrage. I never heard or read of such a crime before. It is an unthinkable deed. How could any one be depraved enough to do such a cruel act?"

"And in this age of perfection, too," I said, with a touch of sarcasm, I fear, "when all the wants of men are provided for by a beneficent government!"

"I think you will have to modify your statement by restricting it to the physical wants," said Effie. "Evidently the morals of the people are sadly out of repair."

"When persons are fed, clothed, and housed," said the doctor, "what more can they ask? I have always believed that most crimes in the past arose from either want or greed. This act is a new revelation to me. I am staggered by it. My confidence in humanity has received a severe shock, and my faith is badly shattered."

At this juncture Mr. West came in. He was not at the present time making his home with the doctor, but elsewhere. Further conversation was suspended for the time. Edith gave a sigh, almost a groan, as he entered the door, and immediately covered her face. She was almost overcome with emotion, and struggled hard to master her feelings. Mr. West was amazed at his reception and what he saw. He looked from one to another for an explanation. I came to the relief of the situation, which was becoming painful, and said:

"Miss Leete has met with a misfortune which promises to disfigure her for life. She cannot endure the thought that you shall see her face as it now is."

"Oh, I must," he said with earnestness. "Nothing can be as bad as not to be permitted to see her."

"But if you never can see her again as Edith, and only as a horrible spectacle, what then?"

"She is still Edith to me, and I must see the worst."

"O Mr. West, I cannot bear it!" said Edith in a tone bordering on anguish. "Please do not ask it."

"Under ordinary circumstances your wish is my law; now it is different. Please let me know what it is. Be assured, it will make no difference in my regard for you."

"Oh, but I know it will. It must. I am no longer the woman you loved. I fully and freely release you from all obligation to me."

"And I will not be released for the causes you give. If you dislike me I will be released, not otherwise."

"Oh, nothing of that kind!"

"Please let me know the truth. Suspense is worse than reality."

With an effort almost beyond her strength of will Edith removed the covering from her face, and the frightful pictures in all their ugliness, revealed by the glare of the electric lights, met his gaze. He had braced himself for something terrible, but was not prepared for such a sight. He staggered a moment, as if struck by a blow, but recovered immediately. Edith was quick to notice the shock he experienced, and said:

"Now that you have seen what I am, and can never

know me again as Edith Leete of old, I fully release you from our engagement. I cannot find it in my heart to blight your life by fastening upon it such a monster as I now am."

"I still love you as Edith Leete, and will not forsake you. I did not love you for your face alone, but for yourself, your noble and incomparable self. You are the same, if your face is not."

"But my face is a part of me, and you never could appear in public with me; nor could I go with you and not feel ashamed and humiliated. You must feel the same. I cannot exact such a sacrifice from you. It is too much."

"Not if I choose to regard it as other than a sacrifice, and desire it."

I here suggested that the matter rest as it was for the present and permit time to be a factor in its final disposition. I felt that Mr. West had done all that could be required of an honorable man, and that both he and Edith needed time for calm consideration of the delicate subject. I saw, too, that Edith could not bear the strain much longer. My suggestion was assented to, and we all left for the night, that the family might obtain needed rest.

"Come and see me early in the morning," said Edith to Effie as they parted. And it was so agreed.

The next day Effie spent for the most part with her afflicted friend. Not one of the family had slept a wink during the previous night; they all had a haggard and worn appearance. So had Mr. West, who called to see Edith. I took a walk with him. He was true and manly, but I could see he was passing through a trying ordeal —a fiery furnace of tribulation. It was plain to me that relief must come soon, or all those immediately in-

terested and involved would break down. The tension
upon both mental and physical endurance was too great
to be prolonged many days, or even hours.

Edith was quick to notice Mr. West's haggard appearance, and said to Effie more than once, she could not
endure the thought of marrying him, nor the thought
of giving him up. Death appeared to her to be the
only release from her condition of soul-torture and
heart-anguish. The doctor and Mrs. Leete were well-
nigh distracted. Edith was all the world to them. I
said to them:

"Bear up. Relief may come from some quarter."
I had no idea at the time where any relief was possible,
but desired to comfort if I could. The doctor replied:

"I would freely give my life to restore Edith to her
former self; but I see no prospect, no hope. I have
tried every chemical preparation known; others have
been suggested and tried; but nothing avails. Oh, it
is horrible to think of a life so good as hers to be
wrecked in this manner! Not a ray of light or hope
upon all the dark future! How can she endure it?
How can her mother, or I, or Mr. West bear up under
the infliction?"

As a simple spectator and sympathizing friend it
was more than I could contemplate without a pang.
How must it be to them!

That night I dreamed of the Chemist of long ago.
In the dream I remembered the preparations he had
given me for removing all kinds of stains. I had not
thought of them for over a hundred years. I recalled
the little case in my valise where he had placed them
with such care—an inner pocket or apartment made
on purpose, which I had never opened. I awoke. It
was a dream; but the dream brought to my recollec-

tion the fact so long forgotten. That little arsenal of chemicals might prove to be worth a world to dear friends. I was so exercised over the matter I could not wait for morning, but aroused Effie and imparted to her the possibly good news. She became more interested and excited than I was. With the early light we arose. I went to my valise to examine its long-hidden treasure.

The bottles were there in perfect order, hermetically sealed and labeled. I examined them one after another until I found the one which said: "To remove stains or discolorations from the human skin, from whatever cause produced."

"This is what I want," I said, with something of exultation and excitement, and greatly gratified. Our knowledge of the potency of the Chemist's preparations in the cases where we had tested them gave us great confidence in this one. There was so much at stake, and we were both on such a high key of excitement, that even the possibility of failure made us anxious and nervous.

We went early in the morning to the doctor's. I exacted a promise from Effie to say nothing of our hope until I had interviewed the doctor. I intended to have a pledge from him to prosecute the perpetrators of this fiendish work if detected and arrested. He gave the pledge at first with energy; but when asked whether he would prosecute if Edith should be fully restored, he said yes, but not so earnestly. I knew his goodness of heart and disposition to leniency, and so fastened the obligation strongly, for the public good. This done, I told him I had some hope of removing the stains from his daughter's face, and with his and her consent would try; but that he must be prepared for either success or disappointment. I saw how eagerly he caught at the faintest prospect of relief.

In the meantime Effie and Edith had been conversing. As I approached the door between the two rooms I heard Edith say:

"Yes, it is very noble of Mr. West to remain true to me under this ordeal. But I saw it went to his heart. I saw the involuntary start, the sensitive shrinking as if hurt by a blow, when first he saw my misfortune. That feeling has not left him. I honor him for his manliness; but nothing can induce me to fasten upon him such an object as I am. He might endure it. He may feel that honor binds him to this. But to chain him to one he must ever dread to have his friends behold is more than I can endure, even if he is willing to become a martyr for my sake."

"For his own sake, you may say," said Effie. "I am sure it was not the mere charm of your face that led him to love you, but the far more valuable possession of a loving heart and pure soul. These remain unchanged."

"I know I am unchanged except outwardly. But the casket, in this case, is inseparable from the jewels, if I have any jewels. My mind is made up. It has cost me more, I apprehend, than the pains of a dozen deaths. The bitterness of the agony is past, unless Mr. West should awaken it anew. I have reached a conclusion I believe to be right, and shall abide by it."

"If it blights Mr. West's life?"

"Oh, don't! Don't say that! I can bear any pain but that! If he suffers as I do! How——"

At this moment Mr. West was announced. He still looked haggard and worn. Evidently he had passed a sleepless night; but he was calm, and declared his readiness and full determination to carry out his engagement with Edith. This deeply moved her. Before she told him her own purpose and final determination I said to him:

"You have proved yourself a man of honor, a true nobleman. You have fulfilled our highest expectations. But will you now please retire and return again in two hours? I have the best of reasons for making this request, which you shall know upon your return."

He seemed reluctant to go; yet after loving words to Edith he departed. Edith was visibly affected.

Effie had said nothing to her friend about the main purpose of our visit. I now called the family together, and said:

"I do not wish to awaken any hope that may not be realized; but I think I have a preparation here that will remove this blotch from Edith's face. With the assurance that it will do no harm, with your consent I wish to try it."

As nothing could make matters worse, and as the faintest hope was welcome, an instant and glad consent was given. As the parents were not in a condition to bear the tension of suspense during the test, they were induced to retire and rest in the other room.

With Effie's assistance I immediately proceeded to apply the fluid. A chemically prepared brush of the softest material accompanied the bottle; full directions were plainly given. The first application did not produce discernible effect. I could see, however, that it was doing work. Effie looked disappointed. The tell-tale shadow on her speaking face took some of the faint light of hope from Edith's eyes. I glanced cheerily at Effie and she brightened up.

I made but a few passes with the second application
when success became assured. I signaled to Effie to
keep quiet. As I proceeded silently, taking care to do
thorough work, the stains disappeared. In half an
hour the last trace of the deformity was gone. Edith
was herself, more fresh and beautiful than before. I
took a looking-glass which I had purposely provided,
and holding it before her face asked:

"Can you see any improvement, Miss Leete?"

She looked in the mirror, gave one "Oh!" and sank
back exhausted by the reaction. In a moment she
sprang up, threw her arms around Effie and kissed her
again and again. Then, as Mrs. Leete, attracted by
the slight noise, entered the room, Edith fell upon her
bosom and wept for joy. The doctor threw his arms
around them both. If on earth there was excess of
joy, it was in that room. It was gladness which could
not be expressed. Presently the doctor held Edith at
arm's-length, and gazing in her face with a thrill of
delight and parental pride, said:

"I declare, daughter, you are more beautiful than
ever!"

And now Mr. West returned. I took him by the
hand and led him to Edith, who was then facing her
father, with her back to us. I touched her on the
shoulder. As she turned around I said:

"Miss Leete, Mr. West."

He was fairly startled and stunned for a second.
Then, with an overmastering impulse, he placed his
arms around her and, pressing her to his heart, imprinted a lover's ardent kiss upon her lips. He then
apologized, but was assured no apology was required.
The reader can imagine the gladness of that company—
perhaps. The doctor said he was so thankful and happy

he believed he could forgive the devil for his wickedness. But I held him to his promise to prosecute the miscreants who had been guilty of this satanic crime. They were detected by means of the memorandum I had made on hearing the fragment of conversation between the two women, as previously narrated. With this clue Mr. Hume soon had the guilty parties arrested.

It developed on the trial, as Mr. Hume had suggested, that the crime was instigated by jealousy and malice. A man by the name of Jackson, an unsuccessful aspirant for Miss Leete's hand, had assisted the three women in the infamous scheme. He furnished the designs which were used, and procured the chemical stains from a noted chemist, who was entirely ignorant of the base use to which his skill had been prostituted. It was also shown that no known substance would remove the stains when once made. So the skill of my old friend the Chemist became the wonder and admiration of Boston; for this trial was the most noted that had ever taken place since the inauguration of the paternal government. The crime itself was so revolting, the motive so dastardly, the act itself so inhuman, the whole population was moved. It was something to arouse a community rendered almost lifeless from lack of energy. The culprits were convicted, fined, and imprisoned.

At the expiration of half the term of imprisonment the doctor and Edith Leete with others joined in a petition for the pardon of the culprits. They were released from prison; but the mark of their crime, like that of Cain, could never be effaced.

CHAPTER XXX.

AFTER making further observations, extending through all classes of people and occupations, I was enabled to reach conclusions on a rational basis.

Mr. Acre was sometimes a little radical and severe in his mode of expression; but he was right. He did not exaggerate. The truth fully sustained all his conclusions. The cities served no good purpose in the economy of paternalism except as homes for pensioners. They were not needed as centers of business, manufacture, or commerce. Mr. Acre's view that they should be used for housing the pensioned population was sensible and in the line of true economy. It was clear that the tendency to congregate in the cities on the part of those who owed service must be checked. To attain this end the privilege of choosing an occupation would have to be curtailed or abolished. Compulsory employment where labor was required was the only remedy. This was manifest by the obvious drift of things. As yet I did not know the imminence of the crisis. The surface was still calm and to a large degree unruffled. Men and women went carelessly and indifferently about their avocations, unconcerned whether it was storm or sunshine.

The indulgent and idle life in the cities fostered selfishness and dissipation. Augmentation of population in great centers increased crime. New avenues for open, and especially for illicit, lawlessness were developed. "Secret sins" were rapidly on the increase. The tendencies to fraud multiplied. Stealing both food and clothing from the depositories of the government began about this time to be carried on to an alarming extent. Heretofore thefts had only been of occasional occurrence; now they grew so common that guards had to be employed in large numbers to protect the property in store. This was the legitimate outcome of congregating masses of evil-disposed persons in city limits, where the force of numbers became a fruitful promoter of misdoing. The comparative impunity with which crimes and misdemeanors could be perpetrated stimulated wrong-doers in the way of transgression. As Mr. Acre expressed it, the cities were rapidly becoming Sodomized. Murders and suicides greatly increased. Women were sometimes assailed in the streets. Virtue was no longer its own protector. Vice was aggressive.

The sense of injustice toward the rural population, who performed all the useful and productive labor, while the denizens of the cities enjoyed all the ease and comfort, grew apace. The magnificence and pride of the cities contrasted with their privations, hardships, and obscurity caused a feeling of indignation and discouragement. Such manifest inequality could not long be endured without redress or revolt. Evidently there must be a radical modification of the present order of things, or there would be revolution. I had no means of knowing how the government viewed the situation, nor what measures of relief it proposed, if any. That something must be done, could be felt in the air. I learned more in time, as will be seen further on.

Laborers could be graded as follows:

1. Sailors, miners, and others employed where explosives, chemical products, etc., were handled. Hazardous callings.

2. Farmers exposed to storms and inclement weather.

3. Laborers under shelter, manufacturers, mechanics, artisans.

Mr. Acre's paupers constituted a fourth class, but, being consumers and not producers, could scarcely be dignified as laborers in any legitimate sense. The rest of the population were pensioners.

What could be done to equalize this unequal distribution of the burdens of labor? What compensation could be provided for the extra-hazardous departments of employment? These questions must be met and answered.

In the nineteenth century, and in all ages before paternalism was established, there was perhaps as great diversity of labor, and as much hazard as now. There was, also, as much to complain of in hardships, perhaps more in privations. But action then was the result of individual volition. Men enjoyed the fruits of their own efforts. If exposed, there was with the exposure a constant and cheering hope of gain—of personal benefit. Results commensurate with the exertion and labor were confidently expected. Inequalities then were incidents connected with liberty of action; now they were crystallized into law and custom, iron-bound and arbitrary. Toil and exposure bring with them no hope of personal advantage. Do as he may, the individual cannot better his condition. He can expect nothing in the future. His life stretches away along the dull sands of a desert plain, without even an oasis to cheer the desolate waste.

Formerly thrift, industry, and economy brought their rewards; now there was no real demand for any of these qualities. The indolent, slothful, and careless fared as well as the most punctual and painstaking. This is, practically, offering a premium for laziness. The conscientious toiler gets nothing for his faithfulness; the sloth loses nothing by his delinquencies. Such a system of fossilized injustice and inequality must break down of its own inherent weakness. There can be no lasting cohesion where the moral sense is constantly outraged, where justice is unknown, and where the temptation to be dishonest is ever present. The question will constantly recur, even to an honest man: "Why should I be true when it avails me nothing?" When the wrong-doer shares equally as well as the right-doer, how long will the latter continue faithful? Such a system is sure to develop rogues. It cannot produce men and women of highly developed mental, moral, and spiritual powers. If such are found, it is in spite of their environments.

All the qualities of human nature remain as of old. There is no improvement. Passions are just as strong; ambitions are just as grasping; popularity is craved as greatly as ever; the "master-passion" still rules the human heart. Nothing is changed but law and customs. Idleness and inclination promote vice and crime. People are good now because they resist temptation, as has always been true. My observation leads to the unmistakable conclusion that two persons use their spare time for evil purposes, to where one uses it for self-improvement or the general welfare. Two thirds of each twenty-four hours being at the disposal of all persons up to forty-five years of age, and after that all time, it will be readily seen that the opportunities for mischief are abundant and only the inclination is necessary to constitute of the people so disposed a race of criminals. That the evil tendencies are multiplying is evident. That any check to these tendencies is available does not appear. All the appearances, at first view so attractive, are misleading. Beneath the surface there is no "beauty that men should desire it."

Discontent cropped out everywhere, unless it was among the dissolute and shiftless. These had nothing to gain by change, and were indifferent.

I was amused as well as astonished at one phase of the "woman question." Mr. Hume, as already stated, had secured telephonic communication with every hall or other place of meeting of public or secret societies or assemblies. One of these is termed "The Ladies' Secret Circle." None but the initiated are admitted. Its membership is composed almost exclusively of women who are disaffected, disappointed, or in some manner out of harmony with existing conditions, or sour because of failure in their desires or ambitions —what in the nineteenth century would have secured the appellation of grumblers. One of these meetings was in progress while I was at Mr. Hume's office. He sat me down at the telephone to listen. I should have said that the connection was secured by Mr. Hume to all places of secret resort without the knowledge of the members of the societies or secret conclaves; hence they talked freely among themselves under cover and pledge of secrecy. Almost the first thing I heard was this:

"Every large woman has a right to complain of the action of the government. It requires a larger amount of goods of any kind to suitably clothe a large lady than it does a small one; yet a little woman receives just as much goods or scrip in payment for time as a large one. The small woman can make herself look more becoming than a large one because she can devote more goods to drapery and ornament and yet have plenty for the main portion of her dress. Large women as a rule require more care in dress to make a good and pleasing appearance than small ones. They are more conspicuous because of size, and so defects are more readily observed. The little woman therefore has the advantage to begin with, and can keep and enhance it all the way through; make herself more attractive, and so win greater attention and success. This is all wrong, and it is a wrong that should be speedily righted."

"How can you right it?" inquired another lady, probably a smaller one. "If the little woman does as much work as the large one, and does it as well, she is surely entitled to the same pay. It is the one's misfortune that she is large, the other's good fortune that she is small. I do not see how you can remedy this, or where you will draw the line."

"Line or no line, I am in favor of doing justice to the large woman. Somehow the men nearly always run after the little women, and the large ones do not have a fair show. Then, giving the small ones the advantage in dress is adding insult to injury."

"And what are you going to do about it? What remedy do you propose?"

"We are told the theory of our government is that every man and woman is entitled to a living because they are men and women. Now, I wish to know, on the same principle, why a large woman is not entitled to large pay because she is a large woman? Can you say she is not?"

"If you are going to divide up on any such basis as that, then the person who has a voracious appetite must be paid more than the one who eats less. How will that work?"

"Appetite is a matter of habit and indulgence and may be modified. But one cannot help growing, however she may desire to stop the process. This natural and unavoidable result should be provided for, the same as any other phase of personality requiring special attention. If a person is a cripple, or diseased, or otherwise rendered helpless, such person, male or female, is provided for by the government. So the misfortune of being large should be met by corresponding aid on the part of the government."

"At what point will you draw the line between the large and the small women?"

"It should be fixed at a point midway between the largest and the smallest, and then have a graduated scale for sizes ascending and descending."

"A woman, then, you think should be rated by her avoirdupois?"

"Not exactly; for some women are solider than others and will weigh more to the same bulk. Height and bust measure would probably be the most accurate method of reaching the true standard of measurement."

"What will the little women say to this?"

"Let them say what they please. What is right is right, and should be done."

"But the question of right is the very one involved, and seems to favor the small woman in this matter, according to my ideas of justice and right. And what of the large men?"

"Oh, the government charges so much for a suit of clothes for a gentleman, whether large or small, and there is no difference. It is not so with women. They pay according to the number of yards purchased, and so the large woman is at a disadvantage."

"Suppose we adopt the plan of the gentlemen, and purchase by the suit instead of by the yard."

"That would not work with ladies. They have to suit complexion, figure, shape, and numberless small appendages and peculiarities which could not be met by a general order for a suit. You know how that is."

I was so greatly amused at these, to me new and decidedly novel ideas, that I could not refrain from laughing outright. The telephone carried the laugh into the room where the ladies were, and a sudden stillness followed, after the one exclamation of inquiry:

"Who is that laughing?"

Mr. Hume muffled the instrument quickly, and said:

"I should have cautioned you not to make any noise that the telephone will carry back. I do not wish them to know I have connection with their room and so become advised of all they do. You will readily understand the situation."

"I regret my indiscretion. I ought to have known better. But the affair struck me in such a ridiculous light, the laugh came, like the boy's whistle, of itself," I replied.

"No harm will result. In a few minutes, when they become satisfied no one is listening, they will proceed with the discussion of some fad or hobby, of which they have many. I frequently pass an hour listening to their vaporings. I do this for information, not from curiosity. The discussions in the secret societies give a very good idea of the restlessness, disquietude, and discontent which lie beneath the surface of things. The lady whom you heard just now proposing what appeared to you as a great absurdity is not what the world designates a crank. She moves in good society and is well respected. She would scarcely talk in public as she does in the secret circle. There are those, however, who do openly advocate the views she has set forth, and she probably furnishes them with arguments and suggestions quietly. She is a lady of some ability and intelligence. There are other propositions equally as humorous and absurd as this one, from our standpoint of view, which are advocated by those who favor changes and amendments of our policy. I fancy the turmoil of the nineteenth century is in a fair way to be repeated in the near future. The under-currents are growing stronger and more outspoken. They will soon come to the surface, if I mistake not, and will produce an upheaval."

"Surely there cannot be much like that to which I have been listening," I said with surprise.

"There is any amount of it—some not so much out of the way as we think, while there is plenty of it more foolish and unreasonable than anything you have yet been introduced to or become acquainted with. Men and women with active minds and plenty of unoccupied time conceive wonderful things."

"What shape will change or changes take, think you, if they come?" I asked.

"I am not certain. The number of changes mentioned are numerous, but in some cases are favored by only a small number. Mr. Acre foreshadowed one that is at least probable—a change in the homes of the population, especially of the cities and towns."

CHAPTER XXXI

On the following Sabbath Mr. Hume invited us to his office to hear a discourse by one of the most noted ministers of Boston. The church was filled with people from the country and from distant parts of the city, so we listened in comfort and quiet by telephone. When seated and composed, Mr. Hume said:

"Mr. Barton is an optimist of the advanced type; he is even a zealous enthusiast. You have heard him at the residence of Dr. Leete. He is the doctor's favorite. The two look at things in much the same light. The present to them is all beautiful, the past dark and forbidding. You know in what rainbow colorings Mr. Barton paints the present, and how darkly he contrasts the past with it. With him the past is an abyss of gloom, the present all aglow with the sunlight of hope, joy, and peace. To-day you will listen to a philosopher as well as a preacher—a man who neither longs for the past nor worships the present, but tries to take a candid view of both past and present with the probable results of these upon the future. But as you will hear him for yourselves I need say no more.

"One thing, however, I ought to name. Dr. Butler is thoroughly posted. He will in all probability say or refer to matters which have been discussed between you and Mr. Acre and myself. It may seem to you like repetition; but you must bear in mind that ninety-nine out of every one hundred of his audience are as

217

totally ignorant of many of these things as you were, and that to them it will be a startling surprise. Place yourselves in the position of these ninety-nine, with a realization of how they feel now, and what effect the words of the speaker will have upon them, and you will be prepared as you otherwise could not be to enjoy and appreciate the sermon."

The hour for services to commence had now arrived. With close attention we could hear a whisper in the church or the rustle of a garment, so perfect was the instrument at which we listened. The singing was excellent, unexcelled in sweetness and harmony.

Dr. Butler took his text from Matt. 16:3, latter clause of the verse: "Can ye not discern the signs of the times?" He then proceeded as follows:

"I have been requested to preach by a large number of my congregation and fellow-citizens on a theme which these words will indicate. There appears to be a desire for information on subjects of which our people are largely in ignorance, but upon which they ought to be well instructed.

"Our present civilization has been on trial for a period of nearly two ordinary generations. Its real merits and demerits ought to be manifest. While the place and the occasion demand that the body of this discourse should be principally confined to the social, moral, and religious aspects of the times, yet some facts are necessary to be understood before we can profitably discuss these important features of the theme. All matters calculated to better the condition of men are appropriate to this place and to the sphere of an 'ambassador of Christ.'

"There are two questions fraught with weighty considerations bearing upon the welfare of the race.

" *First,* Was the past a failure?

" *Second,* Is the present a real success?

"Or possibly a more explicit statement of the propositions would be: How far was the past a failure? How much does the present fail of success? As the past is not ours to manipulate or improve, and we can only draw lessons from it, I shall dismiss this branch of the subject with brief remarks.

"No man who reads history aright will claim that the past was a failure. In many respects it was a magnificent success. Confining attention to our own race of people, it brought them from the debasement of idol-worshipers and cannibalism to the highest point of civilization and Christianity, yet attained by men. Indeed, there is nothing we enjoy now worthy of us that we are not indebted to our fathers and mothers for. To call the brilliant achievements of the nineteen hundred years of progress a failure is to trifle with facts. And when nearly all this wonderful development was made in the three centuries preceding our own, including its beginning, the admiration of our predecessors becomes the greater. I am proud of my ancestry. I glory in their matchless conquests in all directions, which lift men up into higher and nobler spheres of thought, action, life, and morals. From serfs and slaves they became men—men, too, crowned as kings and queens who took their destiny into their own hands, bade adieu to old forms and tyrannies, and opened the way for the full and final triumph of that ideal perfection of human desire, 'Liberty, equality, fraternity.' On the side of morality they arose from abject and besotted barbarism to the grandest type of Christian excellence yet developed by mankind.

"These results were not achieved by the present gen-

eration or its immediate predecessor. They came to us
as a heritage. From that past so often derided came
all our best gifts and loftiest aspirations. I proclaim
it here and now, that we do not possess a single blessing
of real value and worthy to be perpetuated for which
we are not indebted to the past. We have originated
nothing new that tends to the elevation of our race.
I am proud of our sires. I thank God it is their blood
that courses in my veins and pulsates my heart. All
honor to the fathers and mothers of the centuries of
progress which illumine the past and gild the future
with the promise of coming grandeur and glory!

"What of the present? 'Watchmen, what of the
night?' Is it still night? Or is this the day, the dawn
of the millennial reign of 'peace on earth, good-will
toward men'? Let us carefully examine the ground
upon which we stand. What is that ground? What
do we really possess? What have we gained? Stripped
of all glamour and tinsel, we have just three things
secured to us as the whole of our political heritage.
They are these: *food, clothing, and houses.* Nothing
else. It is indeed cheering to contemplate the fact that
no one is naked or hungry or shelterless, except by reason of crime. So far as the government is concerned,
these are supplied. It is a pleasing and blessed thought
that actual physical want is banished from the land, so
far as it is possible for a paternal government to do
this. That there is terrible want, suffering, and distress
all over the country, and especially in the cities, is not
the fault of the government but the result of individual
depravity, which has not been cured or even weakened
by our system. No one should lightly esteem these
benefits and privileges. But at what price have we
secured them? Have they cost too much? If we have

paid too much for them, valuable as they are, we lose by the exchange. Let us inquire into the matter. Have we 'paid too dear for our whistle'? We have bartered for these things:

"1. All manly independence.

"2. All real control of ourselves until forty-five years of age.

"3. *We have become slaves.*

"Are you startled? Listen! Can you dispose of yourselves, your time, labor, anything, except as the government directs? Can you secure a morsel of food, a scrap of clothing, or a house to shelter you except as you get them from the government? Not unless you steal them.

"Then you are not your own. What you eat, wear, and use are not yours. Your children are not yours. They with you belong to the government. In a word, our boasted civilization is simply *a vast system of human slavery.* It has been compared to the discipline of an army. The comparison is apt. No bondage is more cruel, no slavery more abject, than that of a soldier in an army. He is bound to obey orders even unto death. And in time of war disobedience is death. He has no choice, there is no escape. He is bound by his oath, and the discipline of the service, to obey and not question. Are we not similarly situated and bound?

"It matters not that the fetters have thus far been silken cords, and so soft we have scarcely felt them. When the iron frets us, as it will, and galls and chafes, we shall realize our condition as we never yet have done.

"What else have we lost? All the advantages of emulation, skill, personal enterprise, incentives to action in all directions, including invention and authorship. Who can estimate this loss? Who can measure the price we have paid for our present position, not of attainment but of sacrifice?

"Our machinery remains unimproved; we have it just as we received it from our predecessors. Not a new idea in manufacture—the same processes as obtained two generations ago. No improvement in agriculture, in mining, in anything. No advance in education. Ambition to excel in virtue or attainments, dead. Incentive to activity, banished. Hope along all lines of achievement, blotted out. Have we not paid a fearful price for our meager possessions?

"But there is another feature of the situation to which I now call attention. I have before me advance proofsheets of the census of the year 2000, furnished by a friend in Washington at my request. They are the very first issued. The facts they reveal are alarming and portentous in the highest degree. I was not prepared for them; neither are you. We have been sitting at our ease, certain that a beneficent government would supply all our needs; that its resources were inexhaustible. No danger of want could ever overtake us; our surplus was supposed to be of such vast magnitude as to place all contingencies out of the question. Like you, I have been congratulating myself that whatever else might happen, our supply of provisions was unfailing as the sunshine and the seasons. This illusion is dispelled by the cold facts. We are here informed that the surplus of all kinds of grain is nearly exhausted. One more year of the same policy will utterly consume all that remains. A radical change is imperatively demanded. These official statements will startle and shock the whole country.

"What is the cause of this state of affairs? We have the answer here. For ten years and more the drift of population has all been to the towns and cities, where the greatest ease and least labor and privation are secured. During the decade the whole population has increased thirty per cent. All this increase has been in the towns and cities. Farmers remain the same in number as in 1990. Then the rural and municipal populations were nearly equal. The thirty-per-cent. increase is therefore all in the latter class, which makes their increase sixty per cent. as against zero for productive farm labor. The outcome of such a policy is plain. It can only be disaster and ruin.

"There is but one remedy—heroic treatment. Government must exercise its reserved authority, and order every man to his field of labor. Choice of occupation on the part of the individual has brought us to the verge of destruction. We ought to have foreseen this, but did not. The number of miners has fallen off one third; of fishermen, more than one half.

"The denizens of the cities and towns must be compelled to go to the mines and on the farms, and pensioners must occupy the places made vacant by their removal. The Executive Council has already prepared the decree, which will be promulgated within the next ten days.

"The supply of coal is exhausted. There is not enough on hand to meet the demands for sixty days. Every miner will be put to work at once in the coal mines. The winter's needs are to be provided. This can only be done by the most active energy. Need I dwell longer on this picture? While we have been sleeping in fancied security, not once dreaming of the possibility of want or disaster, the foundations have been almost removed from under us. We look with trembling dread at the near approach of privation and want. What a narrow escape!

"And yet what else could we expect? Let us look the situation square in the face. With no incentive to produce sufficiency of supplies, how can we expect proper production? With idlers serving only as consumers, swarming to the cities to secure ease and light employment, how could we presume that the exposed toiler on the soil would feel like pushing his work? He gets nothing extra for extra effort. He receives no more for his hard work than the idler in city or country. Why should he expend his energies and endanger his health by exposure to feed the undeserving? How many of you, my hearers, would exercise all the powers of mind and body when no possible personal benefit can be received for twenty-four years of such toil and exposure?—twenty-four years, too, of the very strength of your manhood, the life-period of flower and fruit!

"Suppose I make this matter plain as an object-lesson in few words. The man who does honest and faithful labor gets no more for it than he who shirks and idles away his time.

"The man who invents any improvement in machinery or develops any new processes spends his own time and scrip and gets no benefits for the same not common to all the people.

"The author who writes a book gets nothing for it. He does not even own the book.

"In all these cases, which can be indefinitely multiplied, the government owns the man, his time, and all he produces, invents, or writes.

"It must be so under our system. If government should encourage inventions or authorship, one half the population would prefer these avenues of employment, to those of manual labor.

"Again I ask, have we not paid too costly a price

for what we have received? Who can measure the loss we have sustained by reason of these hindrances to progress, to improvement, and authorship? How much farther advanced would we have been had genius been encouraged and talent repaid? Have we properly estimated these things?

"It is said our system excludes bribery because there is no wealth to offer, and no poverty to tempt or to accept a bribe. But there is strife to secure the same ends as bribery did in other times. Men and women are as anxious to secure places of power or popularity as they ever were, and are as unscrupulous of the means as at any other period of history. Open your eyes and behold, and you will need no further evidence in this direction.

"Our government is coöperative on a large scale. But coöperation came to us. We did not invent or discover it. Free schools and compulsory education are not ours, but the fathers'. Alas, we have nothing new!

"We are told that riches debauched the people of old. As an offset to this, I will say the same of idleness in our day. Nothing is so great a foe to virtue as unoccupied time and talent devoted to wickedness. Then if poverty debased, which is by no means a proved proposition, as many of the greatest and best men of all former times were poor, idleness does so in a much larger degree. Idleness, therefore, does more harm than either poverty or wealth.

"Woman's sphere is greatly lauded in our time. In what manner? I fail to see any marked change. She remains the same as in all ages of high civilization. Her condition was improved a hundredfold more in the ages preceding ours than it has been by us. Her crowning glory has always been motherhood, and always will be. In that glory, and its accompanying responsibilities, she is the world's redeemer and benefactor. I think we have done nothing for woman demanding her thanks. She is the greatest earthly blessing to us of the other sex, and as such we should cherish her as our own life.

"If I have not given our system credit for all it has done, then it is because it has done something which does not appear. It is true a person may use his or her leisure for personal improvement. But how many do so? Not one in ten, for the simple reason that no adequate inducement is held out for such use of time. Lack of food and clothing can no longer be pleaded as motives driving women to ruin. That is included in the benefit. Nevertheless many of them go to destruction.

"I would gladly present any ameliorating features to our civilization other than named if I knew of their existence. I wish to be faithful in both statement and intention. I would rejoice with exceeding joy if we were more rapidly hastening the great jubilee of the race than our ancestors.

"Our system is erected upon a wrong foundation. Its very conception is erroneous. It appeals to man's lower nature as the basis of his elevation in nobler things. How can spiritual life be developed from material soil? How is it possible for the gratification of merely animal desires to feed the soul? How is the divinity within us to be nourished by ministering to nothing but the requirements of the body? There are aspirations in every individual who is not grossly beastly which lift him Godward. How shall these be strengthened? Not by aid of the things that 'perish in the using thereof.' Yet this is the mistake we have made. Our entire energies have been directed to the one end, 'What shall we eat, what shall we drink, and wherewithal shall we be clothed?' How many degrees is this above the brutes? Shall we live on in this lower plane? Shall we bequeath this debasing estate to our children as their heritage?

"Man is a religious being. He worships. If he does not worship God he pays his homage to something less. It may be himself. It may be a golden calf. It may be some other object of his devotion. Have we done anything to aid this part of his nature? Have we provided means for its right development? Neglect, utter neglect, is the verdict written against us. In a large measure we have made provision for the physical man; in no adequate respect for the mental, moral, and spiritual being. All we have in these directions is the legacy handed down to us from our fathers. It came from that dreadful past we are moved to regard as the sum of all villainies.

"If we had succeeded only in destroying selfishness we might boast; but we have not. It is strong and fierce as ever. Its modes of action have been changed in some directions to meet the change of conditions; but it is the same mighty giant who has stalked abroad in all the ages, ruling with a rod of iron. He sways the hearts of men now with the same heartless tyranny that has characterized his action in all the centuries of the past. Hunt Boston from end to end in the broad sunshine of noonday, or with a lighted candle at night, and you will fail to find a human heart where this monster has no habitation.

"It is falsely claimed for our civilization that it makes virtue easy. There is no soft and velvet path along which the untried soul can pick its dainty steps to the high places of virtue and honor. It is the storm-beaten oak that drives its roots deepest in the earth and lifts its branches highest toward heaven. It is not the calm sea but the tempest-tossed ocean that makes a good sailor. It is not removal from the activities of life that builds up a noble character, but the stern battle of life where temptation is resisted and strength of purpose and action developed. He is the accomplished soldier who fights manfully, not he who lounges in camp.

'It is also said that our civilization removes temptation. This is an impossibility. Man is not made for the law, but the law for man. All that we have done is to remove the avenues of temptation in two directions, that of poverty on one side and riches on the other. Temptation is only possible where there is something to respond within the tempted. A tree has life, but it cannot be tempted. A beast or bird cannot be tempted to do wrong, because neither knows what is wrong. As has been said, law has no moral quality and can impart no moral strength. All that makes a man good or bad proceeds from within, not from without. All the avenues of temptation except those named, and these are but partly closed, are still wide open. Satan is not bound for a single year, much less for a thousand years.

"What it has cost us to secure the little we have attained by our boasted civilization, I have tried in a small degree to show you. I may add to what has been said that we have not secured repose by the change. Agitation is rife. We have not secured peace. Discontent is widespread. We are on the verge of revolution. The demand that equality shall be a fact as well as a theory will be pushed until a change is effected. Some go so far as to require that equality shall extend to personal appearance, dress, education, and all else. Wild as this proposition may appear, and visionary and impossible its attainment, it will be presented, get a hearing, and as experiment and speculation are the characteristics of the day and age, who can predict that it will not be tried?

"The evils of our system are growing worse. The benefits cannot be improved. The longer we continue on the present footing the worse we shall become. The shadow has gone back on the dial of Ahaz. It cannot be otherwise when industry is compulsory, enterprise dead, and Progress folds her wings in the shadow of her grief. Worst of all, there is no recuperative power in our methods, no inherent quality of reformation. The outlook is gloomy indeed. If help comes, it must come from without, not from within, our torpid civilization.

"What are our prospects and the possibilities? Where and what shall our children be a century hence under this *régime?* Our predecessors made progress; we are retrograding. Shall we go back into barbarism? Shall we not rather halt and take a new start? Let what little good we have be grafted on to the good of the nineteenth century, removing the defects from both. This will give us the model civilization of the ages. As the chemist of former times excelled the one of our day, as demonstrated in recent well-known cases, so let the best civilization of that century cast out the blots and defects of ours, and gathering all the good and eliminating the evil, let us have that righteousness which exalteth a nation, and once more crown the man and not the means.

"These census sheets report more suicides during the last than in any former decade. At first this surprised me. When the physical wants are all supplied without anxiety, why should people desire death? A little reflection solved the apparent enigma. The needs of the spiritual and mental natures must be provided or the soul becomes a prey upon itself. Our neglect to furnish incentives and outlets for development on these lines explains the mystery.

"No system of government or morals, no social relations, no scheme for bettering the condition of mankind, can prosper which is founded upon the presumption that man is not selfish. It is impossible. The cornerstone is rotten; it will crumble into dust. Selfishness is ingrained in man's nature. In its highest development it is essential to his success in any enterprise. No law or other device of human invention can remove it; it is a part of the constitution of man. What it needs is proper direction. It is a mighty force. Directed aright, it is one of the world's great instrumentalities for good; misdirected, it is evil, only evil, and that continually. Alas, that we do not the best we know! Our consciences continually upbraid us for not doing better. The one ceaseless effort on the part of those who try to do right, to be virtuous and godlike, is *to keep from doing wrong.* From the better part of his nature no one has any regrets for *trying to do right,* nor for any effort *to keep from doing right.* All the battle is in the struggle to overcome the *natural inclination to do evil.* This is the conscious experience of every person. It has nothing to do with dogma. This is the history of each individual and of the race as a whole.

All efforts, whether in the form of instruction or of laws, should be directed in harmony with this underlying principle, if good results are to be secured. The stream cannot rise above the fountain-head. We have failed because our endeavors have been projected on the supposition that these great facts do not exist, or that the law of human conduct could be reversed. The error is vital.

"The highest glory of man is that he was created in the image of God. Out of this sublime truth limitless possibilities grow. Before him extends a boundless future whose crowning glory is immortality. Aspiration has no limit. Onward, upward he may climb, while yet beyond are loftier attainments which lift their high summits in the eternal sunlight of God. The divine method is the only one for bettering the condition of the human family. If there had been a better one, Infinite Wisdom would have provided it. The fountain of man's nature is not material but spiritual. As a son of God the roots of his being center in the Father. All worthy development must be in harmony with these fundamental truths. On this basis alone can the 'Fatherhood of God and the brotherhood of man' be realized. Having disregarded these things, is it any wonder we have failed and now stand on the brink of disaster?

"In the attainment of any real or ideal perfection, personal responsibility cannot be eliminated. Indeed, this is the point on which destiny makes its revolutions in the development of human character. Our economy is defective in so far as it reduces the responsibility of the individual and places it upon the government. The development of the masses along industrial, intellectual, and moral lines, is essential to general prosperity. We have neglected to honor labor, and it has degenerated into drudgery. Compulsory toil is always performed grudgingly. It is felt to be degrading. It appeals to no manly instinct. It is reasonable, therefore, that production should diminish. Threatened destitution is the legitimate harvest of such sowing. Hence it is that we see failure written on the pages of our history. We are not at peace with ourselves. We are battling with our environments. As they struggle beneath their unrequiting burdens, you can hear the great heart-throbs in the bosoms of thinking citizens. Listen! Do you not hear the prophetic mutterings that tell but too plainly that social and political earthquake and upheaval are at hand?

"Let us not be alarmed. Wait calmly. God's hand is on the helm. He directs the mighty and minor changes of time. It seems a part of His infinite plan to permit men to 'hew out cisterns that hold no water,' to devise methods for uplifting the race which have no lifting power. Man must learn the measure of his ability and the limit of his inability before he can become truly wise. As the fullness of time develops, the Hand which alone can lift heavenward will be seen in the hour of need, and will come to the rescue in every crisis. Wait patiently. The day of redemption will come. The divine civilization which ennobles and glorifies men will appear. Wait and work. But work on right lines. I trust we shall become wiser by experience. The errors of the past should be teachers for the future.

"We have learned some things that ought to do us good. Among others we may name these: Paternalism does not promote industry. It does not promote morality. It is no aid to intellectual development. Its influence is paralyzing in all directions. It kills and does not make alive. It blights and never beautifies. It blotches and never adorns. It degrades labor. It debases manhood. It ends progress. It stifles enterprise. It destroys commerce. It estranges our people and makes aliens of brethren. It breeds discontent. It palsies all it touches. It blots out all enthusiasm. It checks right-directed ambition. It develops a race of drones. It crystallizes injustice and inequality. It handicaps genius. It buries talent. It wastes energy. It despoils humanity. It produces no great men. It throttles improvement. Its unemployed time is devoted to evil rather than good. It is the promoter of material death. It is political malaria.

"I pause. The indictment is but half complete, yet is it not enough? Shall we despair? Shall we fold our hands and say, 'It is none of my business; let things drift'? No! Before it is too late, before we have degenerated past recovery and become a nation of imbeciles, let us awake, arouse, and better our condition! We have lost much. We have also learned valuable lessons of truth. Let us name a few things that we have been taught: that feeding the stomach does not feed the mind; clothing the body does not robe the soul; housing the person does not furnish a habitation for the spirit. Man has aspirations which were never born of material things. They are the God part of his nature, not of the earth earthy. Why not provide for these? Why minister only to his lower nature? Why pamper the animal and neglect the angel in him?

"Man is the only being on earth that assimilates thought, intellect, morality, religion. Beasts assimilate food. Are they thereby made wiser or better? Shall man be driven down on the low plain of bestiality? Shall our efforts for his welfare begin and end here? Shall the divine impress which stamps him lord of this lower creation be dimmed or obliterated? It was not the design of paternalism to do this. But has it not tended largely to this end? With all its good intentions, and we concede these, has it not been one of the most signal failures of all time? Failure inheres in it. It touches none of the hidden springs of human action; it kindles no fires of emulation; it holds out no inducements to excel; it lifts no standard of high attainment, offers no adequate reward for endeavor. How could it do otherwise than fail?

"Out of this death there shall come life. Out of this grave there shall be a resurrection. God is not dead. Man still lives. Already the touch of the divine finger has quickened soul-impulses in ten thousand breasts. They have shaken off the lethargy of unnatural ease and are girding on the armor of manhood. They have enlisted in the war for life. The purpose is to raise us all out of this plodding death into the activities of responsible existence; to restore us from servitude to liberty; to make us men and no longer machines. It will take time to complete the revolution, for it must be bloodless. But the first steps are already taken; the rest will follow as quickly as possible. As men see the light they will walk in it. As truth points the way they will follow. The opening of a new and better day shall speedily dawn upon the desolate places of our land. If these facts have alarmed you, look up and fear not. The hour of deliverance draweth near. The wisdom of God and the uplifting power of human effort divinely directed shall glorify our race and nation. Be of good cheer."

This discourse, listened to by so many thousands, made a profound impression upon all who heard it, whether in city or country. That was its design. Its revelations, so utterly at variance with universal belief, fairly took away the breath of the vast audience. People went home silently from the hushed attention given to the preacher. The gravity of the situation precluded all levity. Men wanted to think; women were impressed with a sense of impending evil.

The next day groups of citizens could be seen in all directions discussing the situation. Those who were in the city for ease became alarmed. They dreaded the harder lot which they were so soon to realize. They would have rebelled against the order that would send them to the farms and the mines, but being slaves they had no alternative but obedience or open defiance. They dare not do the latter; the other must be done. But many a dissatisfied head rested upon its pillow that night and for many nights thereafter.

CHAPTER XXXII

THE changes foreshadowed by Dr. Butler came. Farms were divided into parts of ten and twenty acres, and houses were erected on them for the new occupants. The utmost activity prevailed. Every man was busy. It was like a new world. The limit of service was extended from forty-five to fifty years of age. The paupers, as Mr. Acre termed them, were put on the farms and in the mines. Every coal-miner in the land was set to work in the coal mines. The danger here was so imminent that the utmost energy had to be put forth.

Such energetic action on the part of the government had never been known, because no such contingency had arisen. It put new life into affairs. The activity was contagious. After the first sullen and reluctant acquiescence on the part of the discontented, the people responded with alacrity to the demands made upon them. It was indeed their only salvation from impending ruin or suffering. Occupation and motive for action proved a blessing. The erection of so many buildings gave an appearance of thrift which in itself was exhilarating. No such exhibition of activity had been seen by that generation. The change from previous stagnation to quickened life was cheering and inspiring.

By urgent efforts, before winter set in, enough coal was secured and distributed to meet the demands of the country. Comfort and business were thus provided for. Provisions were carefully handled and husbanded so that they held out until the next year's crops renewed the supply. Under the new enthusiasm the crops were the most abundant ever placed at the disposal of the government.

Matters proceeded in this improved manner for a year. The unusual impetus was then over. Gradually things settled down into the old routine. Enforced drudgery moved sluggishly along in its appointed channels. On the surface was the former appearance of quiet and inertia. But the recent revolution had taught the people a lesson. They felt their power. Beneath the languid exterior there was unrest. Groups of men and women could be seen at almost any hour of day or night not occupied by compulsory work, who were usually in earnest conversation, sometimes demonstrative. As there was no immediate danger to be apprehended, this meant discontent. It was the fret under chains; it was the incipient stages of revolt. How long time it would require to obtain sufficient headway and concentrated action depended upon contingencies. The leaven was at work in the measures of meal, and it was only a question of time when the whole lump would be leavened. As the fetters of governmental slavery now began to bind and chafe, the aspiration for personal independence grew stronger day by day.

How to attain this desirable end and yet not surrender the one benefit of general distribution by the government was the vexed question which came up for solution. Various schemes were proposed, some wild, others reasonable, but none that reconciled the two antagonistic principles or policies. How to be freemen and yet receive the sole benefit of slavery could not be adjusted. The great law of compensation intervened, which could not be abolished nor seriously modified. It was but

another attempt of the ages to attain the unattainable
—a feat no genius has ever been able to accomplish.

While this agitation was going on, another feature
of affairs developed to complicate matters. The thieves
who had been in the cities were now on farms. For a
time they conducted themselves properly; but after
the novelty of the new life wore off, they returned to
their old habits. It was comparatively easy to steal
from neighboring farms and live high. Grain, vegeta-
bles, and poultry were taken by stealth, under cover of
darkness. These depredations became so numerous
and the aggregate amounts purloined so great that the
attention of government was called to the subject. A
force of detectives was organized, similar to that of the
Pinkertons in the previous century, to protect the honest
farmers, and through them the government itself, and
to catch and punish the thieves. Hundreds and even
thousands were arrested and proved guilty. Prisons
had to be built to hold the criminals. They were made
to labor, but as their labor competed with no one it
was universally sanctioned. This was an unexpected
development of the new civilization on a large scale.
There could be no excuse for men stealing whose wants
were all supplied; nevertheless thieves abounded.

All these things tended to confirm the discontent and
augment it. There were two classes of agitators: one
desired a return to the old ways of former times with
some amendments, while the other clamored for a more
radical measure of reform than had ever yet been devised by the fertile or fevered brain of mortals. The
dispute became fierce. It had an appearance of the
old contest between capital and labor. Finally a com-
promise was effected. The conservatives would wait
and permit the radicals to try their scheme; if it suc-

ceeded, well; if not, then all were to unite upon the
platform of the moderates.

The scheme of the radicals, to use their own language,
was that men should be equal in fact as well as in name.
The time-honored truths of the old Declaration of Independence were to be made a reality in fact as in
words, and no longer remain "glittering generalities"
without meaning. They would solve for all humanity
and for all time the great problem of the centuries:
liberty, equality, fraternity. How? Reader, do not
smile as their plans unfold. Have not as wild and visionary schemes marked the ages? Do not their wrecks
strew the strands of time on every shore? Is paternalism less ridiculous?

The great end to be achieved was to make all men of
exactly the same size and features, and all women of
exactly another size and features. Each man was to
be an exact likeness of every other man, each woman
of every other woman. To accomplish this, molds
were to be prepared, ranging from infancy to manhood
and womanhood, precisely alike, each to be an exact
fac-simile of all the others. Into these molds all in-
fants were to be placed, and through infancy, childhood, and youth be reared and educated. Fanatical
as such a preposterous measure appears, it was pressed
on the government and finally adopted. But its application was limited to the province of Massachusetts.
Only those who voluntarily chose to adopt the theory
were to be subject to its sway. Those who did not
wish to become parties to the measure were privileged
to remove elsewhere. The exodus was great; but
there remained enough in the province, reinforced by
large numbers from outside, to try the experiment.

Molds were at once prepared and approved. Americans were now to subject their children to the cruel process bodily to which Chinese girls condemn their feet. Men of common sense looked on amazed. The radicals were in high glee. They would teach the world wonderful things.

I was desirous to see the outcome of this freak. The contingencies of life being uncertain, I felt inclined to resort to our former method, and take a nap. I mentioned this to Effie, and she fell in with the suggestion. We mentioned our purpose to our friends. They tried to dissuade us; but the departure of all of these under fifty years of age gave us a good excuse for holding to our plan. Edith then informed Effie that she and Mr. West were to be married in a few weeks, and that at any rate we must remain for the wedding. To this we cheerfully assented.

As an evidence of the change of sentiment which had taken place, not only with himself but in the entire community, Dr. Leete had Dr. Butler, in preference to Mr. Barton, to officiate at the nuptial ceremony. As the parties to this happy event had become famous, the occasion was one of no little importance. It revived the memory of events heretofore recorded. We enjoyed it thoroughly. This over, adieus were spoken and we departed.

CHAPTER XXXIII.

After setting out for home, it was suggested that we take advantage of the opportunity, and by making an extensive personal examination of the various provinces, satisfy ourselves regarding the true situation of affairs as to the people themselves, their opinions, and the condition of the country. We did so. Much was learned. A few incidents only can be given here.

In the south, where the larger part of the colored people still remained, there was more sluggishness than elsewhere. Being again reduced to slavery, though of a different kind from the old, the slave habits returned. There being no motive for improvement as formerly, no aspirations to be gratified which appealed to the senses, the incentive of pecuniary gain or of securing personal liberty being removed, there were not even the few exceptional cases of former times when colored men rose above their surroundings. Men, women, and children would lie around in the sun when it was cool, in the shade when it was hot. They were as indifferent as domestic animals concerning what might befall them on the morrow. To them "sufficient unto the day was the evil thereof." There were some exceptions; but very few of them did laborious or earnest work during the hours of labor, and were idle the rest of the time. The Briggs class was numerous; wasteful and slovenly farming prevailed; cotton was not more than half a crop;

much rice was wasted in gathering. There were rare
evidences of enterprise on the part of white or black.

A few of the more active and intelligent citizens
were posted on national affairs. The vast majority
knew nothing beyond the neighborhood gossip and
the more sensational news from elsewhere published
in the papers. Sensations were rare for the reason
that the general indisposition of the people to exertion, reaching all classes, included the criminals. Railways were so lazily operated that there was no occasion for accidents, and these occurred only through
carelessness. As few people were traveling, accidents
were confined to the destruction of property. It could
be set down to the credit of paternalism that crime
partook largely of the prevailing apathy, and was in-
frequently startling or ingenious, and accidents seldom
destroyed life.

When we reached New Orleans we found the barbarism of old times still perpetuated in prize-fights
and kindred amusements. The fighting, however, was,
like everything else, of poor quality and lacking in
vim. On the whole, the outlook at the South was less
promising than at the North. Large tracts of country, especially along the rivers, once cultivated, were
now permitted to go to waste. The levees along the
Mississippi were in a state of bad repair, and on the
down-grade to demolition. The atmosphere seemed
to be laden with drowsiness and the people afflicted
with lassitude.

In conversation with some gentlemen who appeared
to be above the average in intelligence, the new experiment on trial in Massachusetts was mentioned. They
had not heard of it, and expressed surprise. One of
the number remarked:

"Massachusetts was always a hot-bed of fanaticism and new-fangled hobbies. More humbugs were started there and in the rest of New England, than in all the country besides."

The old Southern prejudice against the Yankees had not died out. Tradition was stronger than knowledge with them.

In the West there was more life than at the South. Some of the olden energy survived. There was also a disposition to be cranky on the part of the descendants of the promoters of the wild schemes of the nineteenth century. Like the Yankees, they were ever on the hunt for some new thing. There being no room or place for the visionary methods, they died in the inception.

Our extensive observations confirmed what we already either knew or believed. There was no life, energy, activity anywhere, to speak of. Improvements of any character were very rare. The general aspect reminded one of the decrepitude of age. Apathy was visible in every department of industry. Enterprise or thrift in any direction was exceptional. Indolence was common—almost universal. There was no comity of feeling between sections of the country. The West was alien to the East, the East to the West, and so of North and South. No commercial or social ties existed worthy of the name. National unity was almost an unknown thing; at best it was but a rope of sand ready to separate at any time.

On the surface all appeared serene and quiet—the quiet of death. Beneath was unrest. Men of culture and thought felt the incubus of paternalism. It was to them a wall of fate shutting out all advancement or hope of bettering the condition of mankind. It

was the octopus whose tentacles grasped and stran-
gled the life out of human endeavor, leaving enterprise and progress dead at its feet. Shackling personal endeavor, it slew ambition and crushed hope.
Ministering to the animal only, it left the higher man
to perish by the wayside.

The men of revolutionary tendencies were resolute.
They met often in consultation. But for the "Massachusetts folly," as they termed it, they would push and
precipitate matters. As it was they must wait. But
they would be ready when the time came. They were
active as well as determined. A peaceful change was
their aim.

We had no desire to be smothered by the miasma
of paternalism nor to be drawn into the conflict for a
new civilization. It was delightful to find ourselves
once more at home in our quiet retreat. We enjoyed
the sweet repose for a few weeks, and then retired for
a prolonged rest.

CHAPTER XXXIV

WE awoke refreshed and invigorated. After a few days of home enjoyment, we again visited the regions we had previously explored. Everything looked old and time-worn; the same general appearance in all respects, except that old age was apparent. Decrepitude was the principal change. This met the gaze at every turn. The scenes, like approaching desolation repeating itself, were too depressing to retain us. We left them all behind and went to Boston.

Many of our former friends were absent. Some had "passed on over the river"; others removed from Massachusetts when the "chimera of equality usurped the place of common sense," as they expressed it. Mr. Hume, full of years and honors, voluntarily remained at his post. Dr. Butler, whose locks bespoke a ripened life, was still the patriarch of his parish, loved of all. Mr. Barton was on a prolonged absence, visiting in New York. Dr. Leete, if still alive, was living in Connecticut with his daughter. Mr. and Mrs. Acre resided in the city, vigorous in old age and alive to every movement on the part of the people looking toward improvement. From all who remained we met a pleasing welcome. They were all astonished to find us no older than when we parted from them a quarter of a century before, while Time had left his touches upon all of them.

Boston was remarkably quiet. What could mean

245

this unusual stillness? I was anxious to learn the outcome of the fad to secure equality. I knew no man who could give me the desired information more readily, intelligently, and fully than Mr. Hume. I could see nothing of the equalized humanity on the streets. I sought Mr. Hume and made known my desire.

"How fares the experiment of making artificial men and women?" I inquired. He replied:

"Outwardly, in the physical aspects, as finally perfected, the experiment has proved successful beyond any belief of its possibility. We have a race of men and women who are exact fac-similes one of another. One gives you a transcript of all. Exactly alike in feature, form, size, contour, expresses the simple truth."

"How can this be? Surely there must be differences in the color of the hair, the eyes, and shades of complexion," I said.

"At first there were differences so decided that the whole scheme was about to break down on incipient trial. But its friends came to the rescue with a zeal, faith, and earnestness worthy of any cause. The system of graduated molds had secured perfect equality in size and shape—a really wonderful and surprising result. How to secure equally satisfactory effects in color then became the problem of difficult solution. Proper rewards brought the chemists to the front. Harmless dyes or coloring fluids were produced, which rendered hair, eyes, and complexion of precisely the same shades of color in each individual. Each person in the experiment was required to use these preparations every day, so as to insure uniformity and success. Then came a difficulty on intellectual lines. Some men and women were endowed with mental fac-

ulties superior to the rest. The variation was extensive and universal. To overcome this inequality orders were issued that only such subjects as should be
selected and assigned each morning by the proper officers should be discussed during the day. The rules
were strict, the lines of discussion closely drawn, and
a fine imposed for the violation of any rule, and fine
and punishment for a second or subsequent violation.
This appeared to work well on the start. The advocates of the measure were in high feather. It was the
first and only experiment in the history of man where
equality for all had been secured fully and fairly.
Envy, jealousy, malice, hatred, partiality, all inequality
and cause for ill-feeling and jars in society, were removed, banished forever from the home, the community, and the world.

"It was amusing at each stage of the advancing experiment to witness the old rivalries creeping out.
Women were jealous of those who had faces more
expressive or of more delicate texture than their own.
Men were envious of those who manifested more intellectual power than themselves. When the dead-level
was reached the enthusiasts cried, 'Eureka!' It had
all the appearance of a complete victory for an abstract
and absurd theory. Those who had been skeptical, or
who had prophesied failure, were silenced for a brief
time. Then came the *dénouement*.

"Wives did not know their husbands. Husbands
could not tell their own wives from those of their
neighbors. Children could not distinguish their parents. As all residences are alike and the street numbers have been obliterated from houses by time, the
confusion was rendered still more confounded. You
can readily conceive what a chaos there was in the

social and domestic world. The only way husband and wife, parents and children, could tell each other in a crowd or company was by holding fast one to the other. If once separated it was impossible to recognize each other from the rest of mankind. I should have told you that in addition to other things the voices were trained to the same tones and modes of expression. The dress of all was precisely alike. Perfect likeness was the supreme aim and end of the experiment, without which it must fail. These outward requisites were attained. Appearance, speech, manners, dress alike. How many exchanges of husbands and wives were made, will probably never be known. If such exchange should be ascertained, shame and self-respect would lead to hiding the fact. Children as well as parents became mixed. They were constantly puzzled to tell their parents when not in their molds. The family entanglements of those days will never be unraveled, I presume.

"The same conditions rendered it impossible to detect thieves or other criminals and bring them to justice. Unless caught in the act and held fast until tried there was no such thing as proving identity. It proved to be the 'rogues' paradise.' All kinds of misdeeds were perpetrated with reckless boldness. The novelist has abundant material here for any kind of probable or improbable story. Property was insecure. Women did not dare walk the streets or the country roads unprotected. In a word, all the evil passions were let loose and had almost unrestrained license to prey upon society. It was astonishing to see how wicked people could be, when shielded from the probable possibility of detection.

"The experiment in the end proved the most dismal

failure ever recorded. The advocates of this phase of the perfection of 'liberty, equality, fraternity,' were the first to demand its abrogation in all that can be changed. The orders for annulling the whole thing arrived from Washington three days ago. You are a little too late to see the thing in its perfection. All who can are remaining concealed until the colors are washed or faded out, so that by shades of skin, hair, and eyes one can be told from another. We did not all see the 'end from the beginning.' There were revelations for all, as the experiment was unfolded before us, measure by measure. We have probably all learned something, and will be 'wiser for our folly.'"

"The one thing that seems most forcible to me," I said, "is the folly of this or any other attempt to improve upon nature's ordinances. The highest achievement possible in this direction is to conform most closely to the irrepealable laws that govern us, which we cannot modify, though we may infringe upon to our hurt."

"That leads me to say," rejoined Mr. Hume, "that our present social and political structure is so entirely artificial and unnatural that it must break down of its own imperfection. Indeed, it is already breaking up and will soon be abandoned. Another generation, if not another decade, would plunge the nation into chaotic ruin."

"Is it as bad as that?" I said.

"Can you not see? Is not decadence written on all you behold? Can you find a man who has any interest or ambition in the work he is doing? I think you used to have a saying like this, 'Uncle Sam is rich enough to give us all a farm.' Well, that is the feeling now. The government is rich enough to keep all the people in idleness, is the feeling of the indolent. Those who would be industrious have no heart to work, because the idlers and vagabonds, who are on the increase, receive as much benefit from their industry as they do themselves. It is the same thing Mr. Acre complained of twenty-five years ago, but growing constantly worse.

"Our alienation has become greater, despite the efforts of patriots and philanthropists to preserve unity and fellowship. We are as much strangers to each other as though living under foreign governments. Indeed, the affinity and intercourse between our fathers and people of Europe were vastly greater than exist now between the inhabitants of the different provinces of this country. The people of Maine have no more interests in common with those of Florida than with those of China. The same is true of New York and California, or any other portion of the nation. People a hundred miles apart know nothing of each other. Marriages are confined to the localities where the parties reside. Intermarriage between persons of different provinces is almost unknown. Ours is a system of isolation. It can be nothing else for the reason that it furnishes no means, provides no facilities, and presents no inducements for intercourse among the people. The motive being absent, the desire vanishes or becomes a mere sentiment without vitality. With nothing to bind us together, disintegration is imminent. All that is needed to separate and distract us is a leader, or a few leaders, to set the machinery in motion. The situation is critical. Prompt action of a very radical character is our only salvation."

"I am fully aware of the truth of much that you

say, but was not prepared for so startling a conclusion. Is the crisis so threatening?" I said.

"It is. I have exaggerated nothing. Indeed, exaggeration is impossible. We are on the brink of ruin or revolution. Fortunately, the government is now composed of able and patriotic men—the best we have had under paternalism. They enjoy the confidence of the people. They understand the situation. They have the nerve and the patriotism to act. Our infant republic had its Washington; later, the nation had its Lincoln: these with their compeers gave us and saved us our country. Our present rulers are men of similar qualities. The eyes of the people are looking to them; the patriots of the land are with them. To-morrow is Sunday. Dr. Butler will give one of his timely and instructive discourses, which will enlighten the populace. Let us adjourn and listen to him."

CHAPTER XXXV

The following day Effie and I and a few other friends were assembled in Mr. Hume's office to listen to Dr. Butler. Expectation was on tiptoe. All the people of Boston and great numbers from the adjacent country were his auditors. The church building was overcrowded. Every telephone in the city was called into use. The doctor had become almost the prophet of the province. His remarkable age and patriarchal appearance gave additional weight to his words. Verging on fourscore years, he yet retained all his mental vigor, simplicity, and lovable characteristics. To men a philosopher, to the truth-seeker a teacher, to childhood a loving and sympathetic friend and counselor, to all as one instructed in the oracles of God and the needs of men, he was reverenced and beloved by the masses, honored and esteemed by the thoughtful, while some regarded him as a "teacher come from God" and endowed with wisdom suited to his high commission. But he was only a wise man, full of love for his kind, gentle, affable, full of simplicity and humility. He was never too heavenly to forget the earthly needs of his hearers or his fellow-men. He did not hide away in abstractions, nor live in fancy-painted Edens, nor deal in high-sounding phrases that neither himself nor his auditors could understand and which have no practical meaning. He kept his heart close by and in unison with the great heart-

252

beats of humanity, so as to know and feel their needs. He prepared himself to "feed the flock" with real food, not with the husks of either men-made creeds or vain philosophy.

As this was one of the rare occasions when he carried secular affairs prominently into his pulpit as an understood part and feature of his theme, and as a means of instruction to those who listened, we will permit him to speak for himself to the people whom he loved, and for whose benefit he had prepared the discourse of the occasion.

DR. BUTLER'S DISCOURSE.

"Twenty-five years ago I stood in this place and proclaimed a coming revolution. That revolution came, as we all know. It was only the prelude to another, more radical and far-reaching. That other is at the door. But for the late experiment to secure absolute equality among men and women, from which so much was expected only to bring disappointment, the change would have occurred ere this. I trust all these experiments make us wiser and better, however unfortunate they may be. This quarter of a century, how swiftly it has sped away! How it has whitened the locks of so many of my hearers! The children of that day the fathers and mothers of this! Have we grown better with age? Have we gathered the honey of knowledge and the honeycomb of wisdom from these fleeting years as they have tripped so lightly past us?

"My text to-day is found in the thirtieth verse of the seventeenth chapter of Acts: 'And the times of this ignorance God winked at; but now commandeth all men everywhere to repent.'

"Paul was talking to the philosophers and wise men of Greece, assembled on Mars Hill at Athens, when he uttered these words. I shall not attempt a theological discussion of their import. The good sense of my auditors will readily perceive their application to the present time.

"I shall not now repeat the sad story of the failure of our civilization. The mistakes we have made are too palpable; our failure is written on every part and parcel of the entire land. If it were inscribed in letters of light and fire on the blue firmament above us, it could not be more distinctly legible. Alas, that it is written upon human hearts as well! Sadder still that human souls have been cramped, mutual sympathies obliterated, unity of interest destroyed, and the ties of brotherly love rent asunder!

"The last experiment was only a logical culmination of what had preceded it. The soil had been prepared for it; only the seed needed to be planted. The antecedent had gone before, not as John the Baptist to prepare a successful way, but as Theudas to lead the people astray. Its confessed failure by its particular friends is significant. It is but the handwriting on the wall which proclaims in trumpet tones the utter collapse of all unnatural and purely artificial expedients for bettering the condition of men. How much better or worse was this last effort to perfect men by molds than its antecedent and contemporary plan of making him noble and good, happy and contented, by material appliances? Why does not the shape of his body have as much influence on his mind and soul, as the shape and measure of the food he eats and the clothes he wears? If fitting him to the grooves of a mechanical mode of living can produce magnificent results, why not fitting

him to artificial molds have the same effect? We des-
ignate one of these experiments as chimerical and visionary beyond reason. Why not the other also? If
equality of occupation will improve and elevate us,
why not equality of person? If no virtue, no reward
attaches to ability of mind or skill in labor; if we run
all men in one set of common grooves, so much to do
and so much to receive, whether they are capable of
greater or less achievements; in a word, if labor and
recompense are dealt out to all in one measure, and all
qualifications to do better or worse are either ignored
or cramped down into this one common adjustment,
why not make men alike in physical appearance, mental pursuits, and all that pertains to them? Where is
the folly if the artificial in one case does not apply
with equal force in the other? I leave these pertinent
questions for philosophers to dispose of and proceed
to discuss matters practically before us.

"Our system of distribution is not equal. It requires that the man of great mental and physical
powers shall be required to do no more than he of limited ability. If in any case the strong person does
more than the weak one, it is because he is better than
the system. He is under no obligation to do more,
and receives no additional compensation if he actually
does more. On the theory that remuneration and labor
should be equal this is correct. No less, no more to each
individual. How unreasonable is this on the broad
basis of endowment and responsibility being coexten-
sive! Our standard of equivalents is just on the basis
of our unnatural adjustment, for if I only do so much
I should only receive so much, and *vice versâ*. But to
ignore the natural capabilities of men in these as in all
other particulars is radically wrong in itself.

"The wisest of all teachers knew better than this. He understood the true relationship existing between endowment and responsibility. No two men are exactly alike. To lengthen one by violence and shorten the other by amputation to fit the one Procrustean bed is the policy we have been pursuing, while that of the Master was to give and require five, two, and one talents of His stewards, to each man and from each man according to his several ability. But we say to the man with five talents, 'One talent is all that is required of you,' and the same demand is made upon the man with one talent! Is it any wonder we have failed, and that the failure is unto death?

"Personal responsibility to the full measure of each individual's abilities and opportunities is essential to the welfare of any people; without it there can be no robust manhood. Our fatal mistake has been that this great law of development has been ignored. Government has usurped and exercised the prerogatives of the man. It cannot perform his duties. It deprives him of the privilege of performing them, and so they are unperformed, and the loss is personal and national. Look at results.

"A quarter of a century ago Boston was beautiful. Her buildings were painted, decorated, embellished; to-day they are dingy, dust-covered, time-worn, and unattractive. Then her streets were covered with awnings from end to end, to shield from rain, snow, and heat; now these awnings are either gone entirely or are hanging in tatters. This city is a typical emblem of the country from center to periphery. It is in a condition of decay and decrepitude morally and financially. Could we reasonably expect any other result? Is it possible for such causes to produce a different effect?

"As has been already said, no sturdy morality can exist where personal responsibility is eliminated. As a necessary correlative, the less responsibility the less moral stamina. We have removed or greatly lessened responsibility by making servants of the people. They are not required to do anything but work. They have only to perform their allotted tasks. With that, accountability commences and ends. Even the sick have nurses provided to care for them. The helpful tonic of fraternal sympathy is not provided for. If the afflicted receive it, they get that much more than our system provides for them. Like machines, we move as we are directed. Development into stalwart manhood and womanhood under such conditions is a manifest impossibility. A few individuals may rise above these disabilities; the masses, a whole people, never.

"While the moral and intellectual powers are dwarfed by our methods, the passions, the merely animal nature, develop by the simple process of growth. They require no stimulants. They need checks. With enervated morals and strongly developed passions, what but misfortune can be our deplorable condition? No object-lesson is required to tell the sad story. But for the almost universal lack of energy, which embraces all the faculties of mind and body, the situation would be desperate.

"As it is, these insidious evils have been undermining the home life and the social fabric. While we have slept, an enemy hath sown tares among our wheat. Boston would be startled if her people but realized their danger. Thousands are only asleep as yet, but they sleep on the brink of a precipice. In the language of the prophet, I would call upon all to 'Awake, awake! Put on thy strength, O Zion! Put on thy beautiful garments, O Jerusalem! No more let the uncircumcised and the unclean come unto thee! Loose thyself from the bands of thy neck, O captive daughter of Zion! Ye have sold yourselves for naught, and ye shall be redeemed without money.' Yea, friends, it is high time to awake out of sleep. Sleep is not rest. It is death! The enemy is at the door. Bolt and bar against his entrance. If already within the sacred precincts, expel him promptly.

"And what of the religious aspects of the times? If possible, worse than the others. The fact that each person receives only enough from the government for a comfortable support leaves nothing that is not taken from such support for benevolent or religious purposes. No one can now 'lay by as the Lord prospers him' for His treasury. The government prospers the people, not the Lord. And that accounts for the kind of prosperity—or lack of it—we have. Persons can only lay by from the government's stipend. The minister receives his support from the government the same as other citizens, not because he is a minister, but because he is a man. This may be all right. I do not complain of it. But I do complain of that paternalism which places all men on the same level, whether they have one talent or five talents. Such a system ignores ability, intelligence, integrity. Skill counts for nothing. Honesty, talent, genius, manhood, count for nothing. Ignorance, laziness, indolence, slothfulness, are equally paid and honored with industry, energy, thrift, and economy. Under such a *régime* righteousness drops out.

"The churches are all crippled in their work at home. Missionary work is practically abandoned in foreign fields. All new church edifices are built by the government, which is not interested in this work. Then it is next to impossible for the government to act in this field without causing jealousy between denominations. Each sect fears some other will get an advantage. This is all wrong, but it is an infirmity of human nature that needs to be eradicated. It requires but a glance at the situation to perceive that it is unfortunate indeed. The dead blight of paternalism rests upon everything we touch..

"As of old, church and state are separate. Government dare not act with energy in anything pertaining to church work without exciting general distrust. Under such conditions progress is impossible. The churches are handicapped and so is the government. The kingdom of Christ does not advance. The wheels of Zion stand still.

"Shall we be discouraged? No! As far as possible let us shake ourselves from the body of this death. Let us lay hold of the Infinite resources, which are able to lift us out of and above these dismal, discouraging, and disastrous surroundings and hopefully place us on the highway of prosperity with all our powers reinvigorated, all our hopes rekindled, all our purposes to be stronger and better awakened into new life. Up! and shake the dust of listlessness from our feet.

"'As a man thinketh in his heart so is he.' This being true, it becomes an important question, What shall we think? As our characters will be modeled after our thoughts, they will be noble or ignoble according to the mold in which they are formed, or the plan after which they are constructed. The building first exists in the thought of the architect or designer; then it takes form, and the visible structure is exactly the reproduction of the invisible one previously constructed in the mind. So character is the counterpart or visible manifestation of what previously existed and took form in thought. What is the character of your thoughts, my hearers? Are they like the dead sea about us?

"Next to right thinking is right believing. If a man does not believe in the existence of virtue, he will not be virtuous. If he does not believe in the possibility of a virtuous life, he will not try to live such a life. If a man believes he cannot live a better life, he will not try to better his condition. If a man does not believe in the existence of God, he will not try to become like God. If he says there may be a God, but he don't know anything about it, he will not seek to be in the image of God. To him there is no original and hence no image. If a person believes there is a God but He neither hears nor answers prayers, he will never pray to Him for any aid or favor. These are plain, primary principles. How are we squaring our lives? By these negations, or by a positive faith and pure and elevating thoughts? Are we dead in unbelief or alive in a faith that lifts us up into the Infinite Life? Are we trying to become godlike? Or are we drifting on the tide of indifference on this sea of stagnation? All our environments invite to indolence in morals as in other things. We must arouse and shake all lethargy from the soul. The night about us is dark truly, but only the more need to be active.

"As paternalism's failure is a failure unto death; as fanatical equality has failed, a sad failure unto anarchy in social and domestic life; as the outlook from all human and artificial methods is dark as Egypt— where is help to arise? Is hope dead? Are we abandoned to impending destruction without help or possibility of deliverance? No! A thousand times no! Our failures should be lessons of instruction. Out of this valley of death we should hasten into the light of a new life. The bow of promise shall yet span this cloud of night and darkness. Only be men—men to dare and do.

"When the words of the great Teacher cease to be mere platitudes, lifeless as paternalism, and glow with divine beauty and energy; when they move men's hearts and lives with heavenly impulses and inspired action; when men shall really love their neighbors as themselves, which is the sum of all duty of man to man; when men shall 'do unto others as they would that others should do unto them'; when men 'shall bear one another's burdens and so fulfill the law of Christ'; when they shall 'look not every man on his own things, but every man also on the things of others'; when these living principles shall permeate the hearts of men and become to them the moving motives to action—then truly will ripened experience end in sublime reality. Then will millennial glory, so long prayed for, yet delayed through selfishness and unbelief, shed its hallowed and divine radiance over the world, crowning men with the halo which dawned upon the cross of the Crucified. Then shall men be fused into one great brotherhood of fellowship, the culmination of the angelic announcement to the shepherds of Bethlehem, 'On earth peace, good-will to man'—the reign of purified and perfect love.

"Let us not be deceived. Because we have trusted in human efforts alone and been disappointed, we should not despair. If these cisterns hewn out by men are empty; if the body of human laws have no life in them; if the genius of men has made fountains that have no water in them; if all the expectations of men in man's wisdom have perished—yet we should lift up our heads into the light which shines from the eternal Sun and never grows dim. The reign of peace and love will only be achieved by the coöperation of human and divine agency. We have tried the human alone, and where are we? On the outer brink of the desolation of ruin! Man is selfish. God is love. Selfishness must be conquered. It need not be killed; but, like love, be directed to the highest ends of life here and hereafter. An enlightened and sanctified selfishness is pure and angelic. Let us attain it. How? By becoming godlike.

"That love which makes of mankind a brotherhood is not born of time, of earth, of human device. It has its root in that inexpressible tenderness which dwells in the bosom of Eternal Love. It is this that shall bless, crown, and glorify humanity. The rest we should seek is not that which comes from legal enactments, but the ineffable repose that the weary soul shall find when it folds its tired pinions on the loving breast of Him who says, 'Come unto me, all ye that labor and are heavy laden, and I will give you rest.' It is not the light of man's reason that shall illuminate the world, but the 'light that shines in our hearts to give the knowledge of the glory of God in the face of Jesus Christ.' It is His 'glory that shall cover the earth as the waters cover the sea.'

"As we stand amid the wreck of worldly hopes, as we gaze on the failure of human devices, as we find the staff of paternalism upon which we leaned for support a broken reed in our hand whose sharp and jagged points pierce us, as man's wisdom has proved such a dismal failure, let us cease to trust in those 'things that perish in the using thereof,' as we see all about us, and turn to Him whose infinite wisdom is always helpful.

"We are entering upon a new era. Old things are passing away. As the rickety foundation of our civilization is removed from under our feet, let us be careful that we stumble not on the slippery places where its deceptive structure has left the slime of its presence. As I said to some of you that day a quarter of a century ago, so I repeat now, change is at the threshold. This time it will be radical. Men will be restored to themselves. Mastership of the government will end. The palsied hand of disease will be lifted from the body politic. Responsibility will be removed from the central power to individuals. Out of the artificial groove we will return to nature's channel. From machines we will be restored to men. Out of bondage we will emerge into liberty, out of slavery into freedom. The taskmaster's work will soon be ended, the degradation of servitude pass away. Are we ready for the change? Are we prepared to be men? Shall we meet our new responsibilities in the strength and pride and glory of our ancestors? Again I inquire, 'Watchman, what of the night?' And I hear the response, 'The morning cometh.' Glad morning for us! Glad morning for America! Glad morning for the world! Farewell, O night of darkness and death, farewell! And not a tear to shed over the grave of thy buried dead! Depart ye! depart ye! Go ye out hence and return no more to blight and curse our once happy land.

"How shall we welcome the new life? Shall it be with a song of joy upon our lips? Will any of us murmur after the flesh-pots of Egypt? Will any linger in the doleful shadows of paternalism?

"What a multitude of questions rise before us! What a new world of activity opens to view! How the manhood within us begins to stir, as a chained giant in its prison cell! How the shackles fall at our feet with a dull thud of welcome to the aspiring soul! The breath of the new life already invigorates in anticipation. It is like a draught from the fountain of life —like odors from sweet Ambrosia. Wait just a little!

"A word, dearly beloved, for you and me. Let us not enter rashly or thoughtlessly upon the arena of this new life. We must avoid past errors. We must cultivate fellowship. Brotherhood in fact as in name should be our aim. Be true to the human and also to the God side of your nature. It is the coöperation of the human and the divine which alone can bring the perfection we desire and should earnestly seek. 'What our hands find to do, let us do it with our might.' The waste places are to be reclaimed, the deserts made to bud and blossom. We are to form a heritage of civil and religious liberty. Let it be worthy of us and of the children to whom we shall bequeath it. In this new world we are about to construct and enter, let love reign as queen in kingly power—love that shall crown us all with its deathless halo of glory; love born in the bosom of God, whence it sheds its radiance upon the hearts of men. Let this love make of earth a paradise regained, and then lift us up into the dwelling-place of the tabernacle of the Most High, where the light of eternity's morning shall shed its ineffable sweetness upon the resplendent habitations of immortality."

This discourse, like its predecessor, stirred the people of Boston and vicinity as they had never been moved before. They were thoughtful. They went to their homes in silence. It also awakened expectancy, and in many bosoms kindled hope. It also prepared the population, in a measure at least, for what was to come.

CHAPTER XXXVI.

As intimated by Dr. Butler, the government issued its manifesto to the people of the nation, setting forth the present condition of affairs, and the necessity of a radical change. Only a few of the salient portions of the document will here be transcribed. The Executive Council, which is the mouthpiece of the government, said to the people:

"It is no longer wise or safe to hide the true situation of public affairs from the people at large. If we would avert impending disaster, prompt action must be taken. We have waited for the collapse of the experiment in Massachusetts to artificially make all men equal, for we did not wish to interfere with the trial of any theory whose promise of good, however visionary, might break the force of what we have to say.

"We have known for years that the present system of government is a failure. Any system which removes personal interest in what one does, or personal responsibility for the manner of doing it, and for actions in general, from the individual to a central power, must fail. What a man has no personal interest in, he cannot love. What he cannot claim as his own, he ceases to cherish. The governmental care of all things removes all incentive to activity or desire to excel. Ambition has no place in our economy, if we except the few who reach places of command or authority. The honorable mention for superior work with the medals

bestowed, which in the beginning of our present form
of government caused some men to exert themselves,
has lost all its significance and all power to influence
citizens to put forth any effort to secure so evanescent
an honor. Apathy is the word which most nearly
expresses the feeling of men, and the spirit which per-
vades all the avenues of activity—or what should be
activity—in the land. It is an apathy which is the
precursor of dissolution or the harbinger of speedy
decay. We will briefly summarize the situation.

"1. There is a falling off of production in all departments of industry, whether of skilled or unskilled work,
including agriculture and horticulture.

"2. The supply of provisions now on hand is short.
A poor crop next year, or partial failure, would bring
actual want to the people. With a full crop there will
be no surplus.

"3. It is impossible to awaken interest, enthusiasm,
or activity in any of the departments of industrial labor.
The tasks assigned are grudgingly, often imperfectly,
performed. Negligence is quite common. In some
cases there is entire avoidance of work on one pretense
or another. It being impracticable, if not impossible,
to provide overseers for each individual, a remedy for
these evils has not been devised, if indeed one can be
found.

"4. There is no homogeneity of interest or feeling
over the nation. Our people are strangers to each
other. There is no more fellowship or intercourse
between the people of the far west and the far east or
the extremes of north and south than between the
inhabitants of this country and foreign lands. Indeed,
this lack of communication extends to the interior, and
people who live a hundred miles from each other are

perfect strangers. As the government does all the business of the nation and is the medium and active operator in all exchanges, there is no occasion or necessity for intercourse on the part of the people; and as the means of travel are not possessed by any class of the population, almost no travel is indulged in. Where there is nothing to bind together so vast a territory as ours, it is almost certain to be divided. Lack of cohesion with so extended a domain is sure to terminate in the separation of the parts—a breaking down of its own weight.

"5. There is no real improvement in any direction. There is no adequate incentive to induce improvement, and none can be offered by the government without a departure from the central idea of our present system of operations, namely, that the person is to be cared for because he or she is a human being, and not for the possession of any gifts or endowments. A premium upon the latter would produce discord at once.

"6. Having no personal interest in and no acquaintance with each other, our people are fast losing the sense of nationality and the patriotic love of country as a whole so essential to stability and prosperity. The national feeling is simply a tradition, not a heart-felt possession. The people of each locality have the natural attachment for their native place, but care little or nothing for the next province or State, or its citizens. Hence there is no broad sense or feeling of national pride and patriotism such as glowed in the bosoms of our fathers. Lack of personal interest in the homes they occupy, the land they till, or the occupation they follow, adds to this weakening of loyalty and love of country.

"7. There is no remedy, no recuperative power in

our system by which new life can be infused into it.
It is radically and inherently defective. It is out of
harmony with those principles and interests which must
be a personal possession and inheritance in order to
the production of the highest development of humanity,
or that unity of sentiment, feeling, and purpose essential to good government and stable institutions.

"8. After careful observation and every effort possible to improve affairs, without success, we are fully
persuaded there can be no bettering of our condition
under the present order of things, and that a change is
imperatively demanded, and should be made with the
least possible delay. Time is valuable at this juncture
in our history.

"The disease is inherent and incurable. The remedy
must be radical. We therefore propose to the people
of the nation, a return to the government of the nineteenth century under the old constitution of the United
States, with such modifications as may be deemed wise
and expedient."

Then follow a number of suggestions and recom-
mendations, the most important of which are here
summarized in brief:

Ownership of land to be restricted at the start to one
hundred acres for each family, then reduced gradually
in quantity as population increases, until finally it
should rest at twenty-five acres. At each reduction the
owner was to be permitted to sell the overplus of land
held at such price as he or she could secure, and the
proceeds of the sale to be his or hers.

Income taxes were to be collected on all annual
incomes of over one thousand dollars, the rate of taxation to be graduated. One thousand dollars income
to each head of a family was to be exempt from this

species of tax. The second thousand of income was to pay two per cent. per annum, with an increase on each additional thousand until fifty thousand was reached, on which the tax was to be fifty per cent. of the income. This rate included all above fifty thousand dollars.

The funds thus secured were to be expended in public improvements of a national character, upon which labor was to be given to such as were out of employment. No idlers were to be tolerated.

No person whose annual income should be one hundred thousand dollars or more should be eligible to the offices of President or Vice-President of the United States, governor of any State, or judge of any court of record, either national or State. This was recommended to discourage the accumulation of vast wealth in few hands.

The people of the several provinces were earnestly advised to select their best and ablest men to represent them in the national convention called and provided for. Voting places and rules and regulations for the conduct of elections were announced. Every detail was provided for, and such regulations adopted as should secure order at the polls, and uniformity in the conduct of elections throughout the realm.

The propositions were promulgated so that the proposed changes might be thoroughly discussed by all the people.

Having exhausted all their resources to better the affairs of the country unavailingly, they express a feeling of great relief at the prospect of laying down the burden of care and responsibility at the feet of the people. Presuming that the convention soon to assemble would find it necessary to assume some legislative

functions, the following suggestions were put forth for
the consideration of voters:

"1. That all lands be leased to the tillers of the soil,
and, as far as practicable for the general welfare, to
the present occupants, at a low rate of rental, with the
privilege of purchase by making annual payments at
a low rate of interest, on such terms and under such
conditions as Congress may adopt.

"2. That farming implements be left on each farm as
they are to be used, their use free the first year, under
suitable guarantees for proper care and preservation,
and charges for loss or abuse. If Congress approves
the proposition, to be afterward sold to the persons
using them at cash value, on terms similar to land
sales.

"3. Provision should be made for operating the railroads, telegraphs, and postal system, until Congress can
provide for the permanent disposition of the same. At
present, for reasons well known and apparent, none
of these institutions pay running expenses. They
have been a burden and heavy tax upon the government for many years. The roads have carried the
freights, but for which they would have been abandoned. The telegraph has been used instead of the
mails for communication between the government and
the provinces, or it would have fallen into disuse.
The mail routes do not pay a tithe of their expenses;
they have been kept up because the railways had to be
used, and these having to be operated for other purposes, lessened thereby the expense to the mail service.
All these will doubtless become useful and remunera-
tive under the new order of things.

"4. The present clumsy currency should be super-
seded by one of greater convenience and better adapted

to the needs of a commercial and self-supporting population.

"5. Temporary markets and methods of exchange or for the sale of produce will be required.

"6. Provision must be made for the continued care and support of pensioners above the age of fifty years, as these cannot be relegated to the producing classes.

"Permanent regulations for most of these matters belong to Congress; but seasonable temporary provisions may be properly made by the convention, if so instructed by the people.

"Other measures of present utility or necessity may come before that body. As there are practically no individual rights of property to conflict with the formation of the new government, there will be a comparatively smooth sea into which the new ship of state may be launched. The existing government will do all in its power to promote the general welfare until the new machinery is put in motion, when all its burden of care and responsibility will be laid down with rejoicing."

This document, properly authenticated, was sent to all parts of the country to be read and pondered by the inhabitants, and to prepare them to act their part in the momentous events about to transpire. It contained facts already known to the reader, but of which the body of the people were in ignorance. It was necessary to place these facts in an official form, that they might go forth clothed with authority as reliable data for popular action.

CHAPTER XXXVII.

This action of the government, expected only by the comparatively few who were advised of the situation and posted on passing events, caused great excitement everywhere. The people were aroused from a state of indifference and sloth to one of inquiry, intensity, and ferment. Heretofore the election of the few rulers had been a matter of trifling interest to the mass of voters. Now, for the first time in fifty years, and during the lifetime of a majority of the electors, large assemblies were convened in all the provinces, where measures of public policy were discussed. The people were deplorably ignorant and needed instruction on even the rudimentary elements of self-government, and of a "government of the people, by the people, and for the people." Public meetings became public schools for the dissemination of political information and education. By these means the voters became acquainted with the men best qualified to intrust with the duty of forming a constitution and founding a government. They were uncorrupted by political demagogues and entirely ignorant of the machine-methods of political parties of the nineteenth century, and so selected as their representatives the men who proved themselves to be the most worthy and the best equipped for the great work they were called upon to perform.

The convention met. It was composed of the best men of the nation. It did its work wisely and well.

With some modifications, the features proposed by the old government were adopted. Some new ones were added. One provision reënforced the right of the States in local, municipal, and police regulations. The national character of the new government was amply secured. The best of the ancient constitution was adopted; those parts not desirable, or no longer applicable, were rejected. The paternalism of the expiring *régime* was utterly and entirely eliminated. The instrument, when completed, was a masterpiece of political workmanship.

The people ratified it with great unanimity and rejoicing. State governments were simultaneously instituted and set in motion, with new and excellent features. Marriage and divorce laws were made uniform throughout the land under constitutional provisions, national and State. Old defects were avoided and valuable new provisions adopted.

Congress and the legislatures of the several States met and enacted plain, simple, and forcible codes of laws, free from ambiguities and unfettered by customs and precedents, or any other entangling complications. These were easily understood. The wheels of government were set running smoothly, without jar or friction. All that remained was for the people to adjust themselves and become adjusted to the new order of things. This they did with as much readiness as could be expected.

The change which followed was marvelous. Torpor was turned into activity, indifference into energy. New life was infused into every department of industry. Business proper was born again. It had been dead and buried so long, as far as individual effort and control were concerned, that its new existence was like that of one raised from the grave. The whole aspect of affairs was so changed that the transformation was scarcely short of a transfiguration. So manifest was this that the people inquired of each other :

" How did we manage to live before we knew how?"

And the reply was sometimes made :

" I guess we did not live at all in the true sense of the word. We simply vegetated."

*　　*　　*　　*　　*　　*

Effie and I returned to our native place. We had no difficulty in establishing the title to both our estates, and took possession of them with joyful hearts. I was restricted to one hundred acres of land, but cared for no more.

In time Effie had her home restored to its original design, beauty, and adornments. Here we were to reside, and no pains or expense was spared to make it pleasant and desirable. The structure was solid throughout, and had weathered the storms and neglect of a hundred years with remarkable success.

When we passed through the house we found still remaining many of the permanent features as of old, with their dear and sacred associations. They lingered as cherished pictures in the halls of memory. There was Effie's own room, with a thousand sweet recollections flooding through it. As all this past came back to her heart, Effie's eyes filled with tears of sweet joy and her spirit bounded with gladness. I had not seen her so radiant with soulful delight since the day of our nuptials. It was *home*, with all that precious word means. No one can enter into our feelings who, like us, has not been banished from home, wanderers in a barren land, with no spot to place a foot upon and call it ours. It was like awaking from a troubled dream into the sweetest and dearest realities of real life. My wife went singing from room to room with new-born melody in her heart, the brightest, best, and most royal woman in the wide world. I fully shared her happiness, and felt how blessed it was to have such a companion and such a home.

After putting our house in order, I proposed to Effie that we take some excursions into the country and visit the places we had seen before, that we might ascertain from personal observation what changes had been wrought. Many wonderful stories had come to us of transformations and improvements; but to see for ourselves would be much more satisfactory. At first she was a little reluctant to leave the cherished home, but assented cheerfully after a little reflection.

We passed over the same regions a quarter of a century before. Then the entire aspect of the country was dreary as desolation; a palsied torpidity was visible on every side. Now the desert had been made to "bud and blossom as the rose." It was a fruitful domain. Far as the eye could reach the waving fields of grain gave promise of the coming harvest of abundance. Thrift and industry were visible everywhere. Men were active; women were cheerful; children were happy.

It was a new life with new experiences. Its very novelty was a charm. The gloom of the previous period of night had taken the wings of the morning and flown away. Activity quickened the pulses of the people. They were delighted by the new ownership of themselves. They were inspired by the right to dispose of their time, labor, and persons. Their earnings were their own. There was ambition to be something and to do something. To excel was a new incentive. Emulation was kindled in every breast. Hope flung out her banner. The bow of promise gilded the mist cloud of the future. The world was an arena of light and gladness. Sloth was ignored. Idleness was banished. Energy was at a premium. A listless person was a curiosity. The evidences of universal occupation were in advance of anything we had seen even in the olden time. Interest taken in business was universal. Snatches of song and whole melodies of rejoicing told more plainly than words the bubbling joy in the people's hearts.

The changes were as radical as those described in stories of fairy-land. Beauty, taste, adornment—these were seen on every side. They added a charm to the more prosy labor necessary for the wants of life. Smiling faces, happy children, cheerful homes—these were the evidences of a new order of existence. At first we were absorbed in almost silent admiration; then came exclamations of delight. We were more than gratified; we were exhilarated. The blood tingled in our veins to the tips of our fingers. My wife exclaimed:

"This is coming out of darkness into light, out of death into life."

And so it was. It was the dawning glory of the morning of a new era of progress, whose meridian splendor no one could foretell. It was burying the remains of the dead past and covering the world with the brightness of a living future. I said to Effie:

"You do not wish to return to the system of governmental control, be relieved of the burden and care of providing for yourself, and have no anxiety for the morrow or the future?"

"Not for the world! Care and toil are sweet when glorified by love. All my experiences and recollections of paternalism are sad and gloomy. Not a truly bright spot appears as an oasis in all the bleak desert of death. It is more like a horrible nightmare than anything else. As I personally knew so little about it, what must it have been to sensitive souls who felt all the weight of the burden! How the fetters of the government must have chafed! How the degradation of humanity must have humbled! How the aspiring mind must have writhed in the iron grasp that held it down! I shudder at the very thought of that period of desolation."

We went among the people, to learn by personal intercourse how they felt. Expressions like these came to us from every quarter:

"We have something to live for now, we never had before. We know what life really is; before this, we only existed. The sense of ownership is sweet. Until now we did not own ourselves, and knew nothing of the delight of self-possession. To go as we please, where we please, and when we please is a luxury—a new and cheering experience. To be men, and not machines or slaves, lifts one out of degradation into manhood. To have something we can call our own is a new and invigorating experience. To reap the fruit of our own endeavors, to dispose of ourselves and our earnings, is a precious privilege, the value of which we were strangers to until now. You see the result: the old dead-appearing houses burnished; vines and flowers adding beauty and fragrance; dreariness made inviting. We go to our homes now with a sense of pride. They are retreats made attractive by love, hope, and ownership. In fact, we are in a new world. 'Old things have passed away, all things have become new,' and we are new men and women."

As we moved from place to place beholding the de-

velopments of the new life in city and country, there
were numberless incidents witnessed which made glad
the heart. The stretch of mind and body for something better was itself an inspiration. The onward
look of a soul that had a future to construct for itself;
the sparkling eye; the radiant countenance; the ex-
pectant gaze; the awakened ambition; the keen incentive to excel; the dread of being left behind; the up
and at work everywhere—these were the ever-visible
evidences of a people just aroused to a sense of their
own capabilities. It was better than the nineteenth
century in that its novelty left no room for torpor, its
equality no ground for envy. It was the best of the
former times, as to persons and actions, made almost
universal. This applies, of course, to outward activity;
the inner life could not be seen.

There was another feature which affected us differently. As we were moving very slowly past a residence in the country, the notes of an instrument and
a sweet voice sang out clearly and tenderly, "Home,
sweet home."

We paused to listen. As the dear words and music
of other days came home to our hearts in the gathering twilight, Effie said softly:

"Oh, how precious! I have not heard that dear
song, so full of sacred associations, for a hundred
years. It has been one of our banished treasures."

While she spoke the dew of tears was in her eyes.
When the song ceased, and a hush fell upon us and
the scene, she said:

"Let us hasten home. I wish to feel this joy in our
own dear bower."

It was but a few miles to the city. We were returning from a distant excursion when the incident arrested

attention. In a few minutes we reached our destination. Effie scarcely waited to remove her wraps before she sat down at the piano, and while the spell was upon her sang those words as I had never heard them sung before. Her soul was in them; the flush of inspiration was on her face, the light of love and pathos in her eye. Holy memories came trooping home as from her dear lips, moved by a divine impulse, the words came like a benediction, so full of all that was tender, touching, and endearing.

The home of my childhood and youth! Mother! Father! How they stood before me! Oh, the dear recollections! Then our own beloved abode, so full of all that can make life blessed! As Effie finished I caught her to my breast with impassioned impulse and imprinted a long, lingering kiss of love upon her lips, while the words were still ringing in my ears as melody from the skies:

"HOME, SWEET HOME!"

No more should the song, the sentiment, the possession, be driven from our happy land. PATERNALISM WAS DEAD!

THE END.

www.ingramcontent.com/pod-product-compliance
Lightning Source LLC
Chambersburg PA
CBHW021049030726
47496CB00006B/1748